"**An alien movi**
Those things are creepy.

"Oh, poor Jacob is afraid of a few little fictional creatures." Leah pouted, clearly mocking him, and why that made him smile was completely beyond him.

"You better be careful. I'll wrangle you into a chick flick."

"Oh, please. Aliens over chick flick any day of the week." But she stood from the table and went to the mudroom, where her coat was hanging. "What about the one with the race car driver? The main guy is hot, and I hear he gets naked."

Jacob shrugged into his coat. "Why do you have to say things like that?"

She laughed, an uninhibited rumble, and something cross-wired in his brain, suddenly making him think about *her* naked. Nope. Nope. Nope. Not allowed.

He glanced at her as they stepped outside. It was *not* a date. It was a distraction.

Dear Reader,

By the time this book hits shelves, it will be literally years since Jacob and Leah, the hero and heroine, started hanging out in my head. Jacob came first because he was the brother of the heroine in *Too Close to Resist,* my first Harlequin Superromance (June 2014). I knew Jacob was an affable, somewhat clueless guy who cared very deeply about his tight-knit family. And not very far into writing that story, I also knew he'd need a happily ever after of his own.

As I worked on the first of my Bluff City books, I wanted to create a family of sorts in the people who worked with Jacob. He's the kind of man who would naturally befriend the people he works with on a daily basis. And, since I like putting women in somewhat atypical professions, I immediately knew the electrician working for MC Restorations would be a woman.

So, Leah was born, and the minute she was, I knew she was the perfect fit for Jacob. Friends who argue, banter, but share a passion for their jobs...and possibly for each other—on the down-low, of course.

I was so excited to write their story. Leah and Jacob's personalities and secrets surprised me, even for as long as I had thought about their story before writing it. And in the end, they became one of my favorite couples to write. (It's entirely possible I say that at the end of every book, though.)

I was sad to be done with them, but so excited to share them with you! I hope you enjoy their journey as much as I enjoyed writing it.

If you're on Twitter, so am I (probably more than I should be). I love to talk to readers, @NicoleTHelm.

Happy reading!

Nicole Helm

www.NicoleHelm.wordpress.com

P.S. Keep an eye out for my upcoming titles from Harlequin E, out later this year!

NICOLE
HELM

—

Too Friendly to Date

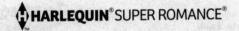

HARLEQUIN® SUPER ROMANCE®

Recycling programs
for this product may
not exist in your area.

ISBN-13: 978-0-373-60879-9

Too Friendly to Date

Printed in U.S.A.

HARLEQUIN®
www.Harlequin.com

ABOUT THE AUTHOR

Nicole grew up with her nose in a book and a dream of becoming a writer. Luckily, after a few failed career choices, a husband and two kids, she gets to pursue that writing dream. She lives in Missouri with her husband and two young sons, and wishes she knew anything about restoration so she could fix up the old Iowa farmhouse her grandfather grew up in.

Books by Nicole Helm

HARLEQUIN SUPERROMANCE
1927—TOO CLOSE TO RESIST

HARLEQUIN E
ALL I HAVE
ALL I AM

Other titles by this author availabe in ebook format.

To Piya. Thank you for helping me make each book stronger than I ever could. Harlequin was my dream, and I will be forever grateful for your part in making that dream come true.

CHAPTER ONE

LEAH SANTINO HATED the little red dress she was wearing. It was uncomfortable, way too bright and made men she had no interest in approach her. Since she was at a work party and couldn't tell them to take a long walk off a short pier, but instead had to smile and politely decline their advances, she was on considerable edge.

Of course, the dress also made Jacob McKnight stare. Which she shouldn't like but totally did. Just because it was inappropriate to have a crush on her boss and friend didn't mean she was immune to his staring.

"See! I told you you'd wear it more than once." Grace McKnight greeted her with a big grin. "Perfect color for a holiday party."

"I'm burning it the second I get home," Leah muttered. The last thing she needed was Jacob's sister, who just happened to be her best friend, reading into any…staring. It would do Leah good to burn the dress.

Of course, she wouldn't actually do that. This holiday party for MC Restorations' clients wasn't the last time she'd be forced to dress up this year. Jacob had a smaller New Year's Eve gathering prepared, and she was darn well going to get her money's worth out of this dress. "Lighter fluid, matches, the whole bit."

Grace rolled her eyes. Grace was one of the few people who really knew her. Could read the dry humor and didn't find it offensive or annoying. Basically, Grace and her MC coworkers. Her family? Not so much.

Leah shifted uncomfortably. Speaking of her family. She was running out of time. She scanned the room for Jacob.

For the millionth time she tried to talk herself out of asking for this favor. There was no way he'd go for lying, not to mention having Jacob, of all people, pretend to be her boyfriend was dangerous business.

Then Leah thought of Mom and Dad and Marc finally coming to visit for Christmas. Of her whole family being with her over the holiday. It would be the first time in a long time, but only if she made her little white lie a truth.

Leah pressed a hand to her nauseated stomach. She had screwed things up royally. Again. Jacob was her only hope.

Grace nudged her. "Are you okay? You look a little pale. You didn't eat the mushroom appetizer, did you? It had walnuts on it."

Leah shook her head. "No. I won't be going into anaphylactic shock." At least not from walnuts.

"So, what gives?"

Leah's eyes finally landed on Jacob. He was

wearing a black suit and smiling with perfect white teeth. His dark brown hair was that casual mussed look, which she was 90 percent sure he worked very hard to achieve. He was currently sporting about a week's worth of facial hair, which she sadly and pathetically kept track of.

She hated herself for the little inward sigh. Hated that she thought he was perfect.

Because Jacob McKnight was so not perfect.

"Earth to Leah?"

Leah forced a smile and looked at Grace. "Sorry. I've got a lot on my mind. Uh, my parents are coming to visit for Christmas. My brother, too."

"That's great. You don't talk about them much, but I can't wait to meet them."

Leah's smile faded. "Yeah. Sure." She didn't mention that not talking about them was on purpose. Didn't mention that for years she hadn't even spoken to them, let alone invited them for visits. This new relationship was tenuous.

Tenuous enough she was going to have to ask Jacob for something totally insane. And it meant enough to check some of her pride at the door.

In other words, it meant everything.

"I need a drink. You want one?"

"Kyle's getting me one." Grace touched her arm. "You sure you're okay?"

Leah waved her off. "Fantastic." She moved toward the bar and away from Grace, smiling at clients along the way.

For five years she'd poured her life into MC Restorations as their electrician. For just as long she had ignored any and all attraction to Jacob. He was her boss, kind of, but he'd also become her friend and then his sister had become her best friend this year and…nothing about being attracted to him or halfway in love with him was acceptable, sensible or smart.

For the past ten years, Leah's life had been all about being sensible and smart. Some sad attempt to make up for all the ways she'd been anything but as a teenager.

The bartender handed her the glass of wine she'd ordered and, after making sure no one was looking, she downed it all in one gulp. She wished she could drink the whole damn bottle, but that wasn't an option.

Leah touched the scar over her heart through the fabric of her high-collared dress. Not one person in this room knew about it, and she wanted to keep it that way. It would be hard with her parents around, but she would try.

There were a lot of secrets to juggle. Too many, really, but it was the only way to get what she wanted. Keeping her scar and where it came from under wraps meant Leah could live her life how she chose, without anyone hovering or worrying. Letting her parents believe Jacob was her boyfriend was going to give her the same thing and get her her family back.

A few little secrets. A few little lies. What could be the harm?

JACOB HAD SEEN Leah wear that red dress only twice now, but he hated it. Hated every last inch of the bright, clingy fabric that was bound and determined to scream at him that Leah was a woman. A hot woman.

It was so much easier to ignore in her usual getup. Flannel shirts or ratty T-shirts, baggy jeans, work boots. Not that he didn't notice her then, too. It was just way easier to pretend he didn't when she wasn't a bright red dot of fantasy right before his eyes.

She was coming his way, so Jacob looked for an escape route while reminding himself of all the ways Leah was off-limits.

She was his employee, his friend, and she could be downright mean. She was as tall as him in heels, which meant she was too tall. And her swearing was way more creative than his.

She hated the Cubs. Which was, by far, the worst strike against her.

He was only thinking about her *that* way because he still had four weeks left of his self-imposed six-month women sabbatical, and just about anything had him dreaming about the next time he'd have sex.

Not that he was ever going to think about *Leah* and *sex* in the same sentence.

Okay, it was too late for that. But a guy could pretend, couldn't he?

"Hey, can I talk to you?"

Jacob offered his best version of a smile under the circumstances. "Sure. What's up?" He wasn't going to look her in the eye for fear she might see something unacceptable there, but then he found himself glancing at her breasts.

Yeah, eyes. Way better choice.

"Um, can we do it in private?"

Not a good idea. Not when he'd apparently regressed to being a teenager and "do it" made him think of sex.

It was just the sabbatical. The get-yourself-together sabbatical. No women. No relationships. No sex. He was figuring himself out.

Five months in, and he still had no idea what was wrong with him. Why he was attracted to women who inevitably broke up with him for a wide variety of reasons he couldn't make any sense of.

"Jacob?"

"Right. Private. Uh, now?"

She nodded and for the first time he realized she looked nervous. She was chewing on her bottom lip and kept clasping and unclasping her hands. Which was so unlike Leah he actually got worried enough to forget about the other stuff.

"My office?"

She nodded, heading for the stairs. Jacob followed, keeping his eyes on the oak of the staircase. The planks of wood he'd refurbished himself, this house being MC's first restoration project.

He smiled. It had been his dream to bring new life to old homes since he'd had to watch his grandparents' falling-apart house be demolished, and now he got to do that every day. Bring life to old. Save memories. Thinking about that never failed to bring him satisfaction.

Then he stepped into his office, Leah in that stupid short dress showing off long, toned legs, standing in the center of his room. All satisfaction faded into discomfort.

"So, what's so important?" Jacob focused on the ornate wood trim in the room. Trim it had taken him months to bring back to its former glory. If he focused on that, he wouldn't have to think about how the makeup Leah was wearing made her blue-green eyes even more noticeable than usual.

"My, um, family. They're coming to visit for a week over Christmas."

Jacob let out a breath of relief. He didn't know why he was relieved, but whatever this was was about her family. So innocuous. No big deal. "That's great. I know you've had your problems. That's really great. You need time off? You didn't need the buildup and the nerves. Of course you can—"

"That's not why I wanted to talk to you."

"Oh." The relief disappeared. He leaned against his desk, tapping his fingers on the smooth, glossy wood.

"Um, so, this is going to sound crazy, but hear me out. Actually, it doesn't just sound crazy. It *is* crazy. Nuts. Totally cuckoo."

She paced the bright patterned rug in front of his desk, in front of him. Jacob focused on the pattern of black and gray. Anything was better than red.

"But…I have to ask. Only choice." Her voice was low enough he wondered if she was talking to herself more than to him.

She stopped pacing, took a deep breath, which caused his eyes to wander to her chest until he mentally reprimanded himself.

"My parents are old-fashioned. Really old-fashioned. You know, think a woman needs a man to be safe and happy and all that."

Jacob snorted. No wonder she didn't get along with her family. That was about the opposite of everything essentially Leah. She was fiercely independent and took shit from no one.

She was not someone he worried about being safe. Or at all in need of a man.

"So, you know, I haven't always been on speaking terms with them, but we've been trying. Trying to get back to being a family and the past year has been good. Really good."

She started pacing again, her heels faint thuds against the rug. "So, to keep that going, to keep them from annoying the hell out of me by insinuating I can't take care of myself, I…told them I had a boyfriend."

Jacob was trying hard to follow what this had to do with him. Maybe she wanted him to corroborate her story if she brought her parents around. But why the secrecy and the uncharacteristic nerves?

"The thing is… Okay." She stopped pacing, took a

deep breath and let it out. "I kind of told them you…
were my boyfriend."

"Uh, say what?" He'd heard wrong. Or something.

"I know. I know. It's totally insane, and please
don't read anything into it. It's just…I'm around you
every day. I know everything about you. I couldn't
get caught up in a lie because it'd all be the truth.
Except for the us-being-together part."

"You don't know everything about me."

She waved the sentence away as if it was an in-
consequential bug. "Please. You're an open book."

He frowned, not at all liking the assessment. Besides, if she knew everything about him she'd know
he was attracted to her. She obviously didn't or she
wouldn't be walking around his office in a short
dress and heels. So, there.

"The thing is, I can't tell them it was a lie, because then things will go to shit again. They'll be
mad about the lying and I'll lose it with my mom
about the man thing and…" She shook her head,
looked at the ceiling as if she couldn't believe what
was happening.

He couldn't believe what was happening, either, but
he wasn't the one pretending she was his girlfriend.

"I know it probably doesn't make sense to you,
but if you, as my friend, could do me this one favor
and pretend, just for a few meals, that we're more
than friends…I would owe you so big. So big. Anything. Anything."

He couldn't think of a time when Leah had ever seemed this vulnerable. Usually she was guns blazing, no one was getting in her way. She was tough as nails and didn't ask for help unless it was absolutely necessary.

He'd always admired that about her.

The fact that she was asking, almost pleading, must mean it was absolutely necessary. "Okay."

"I— Okay? Just like that? Okay?" Her voice was all baffled edginess.

Jacob shrugged. When it came to favors for friends, he'd never been any good at saying no. Besides, he excelled at charming parents. What was a few dinners with Leah and her family? She'd had plenty of dinners with his. All he had to do was pretend to be a boyfriend.

How hard could it be? Long as he kept his hands to himself, easy.

"Not up to anything kinky, are you?"

She scowled, all hints of vulnerability disappearing into that I'm-gonna-kick-your-ass glint in her eye. "No."

"Then sure. Why not?"

"What are you going to make me do to make it up to you?" she asked skeptically.

He grinned and rubbed his hands together. "Hmm. I will have to think about that one. So many options."

The scowl deepened until her eyebrows all but touched each other. "Damn it, Jacob."

"Hey, now, I'm doing you a big favor. So, there are going to be a few rules."

"Yeah, like what?" She crossed her arms over her chest. Jacob found himself wishing her dress had a lower neckline.

He shook that thought away. "Like, for starters, you can't be all prickly and pissed off with me. If I'm your boyfriend, you're in love with me, right? Women in love aren't prickly."

"I'm *always* prickly. And you like to bring it out in me." She dropped her arms at her sides. "You're really going to do this?"

"Why wouldn't I?"

He couldn't read her expression. Not even a little bit.

"Thank you." The words were heartfelt and it knocked some of the teasing out of him. The Leah he knew didn't do heartfelt.

"You're welcome. Just let me know when. Don't have to kiss you, do I?"

She screwed up her face. "God, I hope not."

He didn't care for her answer, but kept the easy smile on his face. "Good. Probably be like kissing my sister." Yeah, not by a long shot.

LEAH KICKED HER heels off the second her door was open. They landed with a thud in a pile of other shoes and clothes in her entryway. Some magazines and junk mail littered the floor, too. She was really going to need to clean up before her family arrived.

She could have had them stay in a hotel, but she knew how much Mom and Dad hated hotels. Or, more accurately, the expense of them.

The fact they had to pinch their pennies was one in a long list of things that were Leah's fault, so she owed them.

Maybe Grace could help clean up. Maybe Kelly and Susan, too, if they were surviving their first month as new parents. MC's interior designer and administrative assistant hadn't been around much since they'd adopted their baby, taking maternity leave and switching off days when they did work. Leah had missed having them around as she was almost as close to them as Grace.

But Leah's place was definitely not suited for a baby, so they'd probably have to pass. At least for a little while longer.

Leah dropped her keys on the cluttered kitchen table, then remembered how she'd been late to a job last week because she hadn't been able to find them. She retraced her steps, found the bag she took to work every day and tossed them in there.

The house itself was a work in progress. A falling-down English cottage–style one-story built in the '20s, it had been abandoned for ten years before she'd bought it, and the price had been right for a handy woman making a modest living. The past five years she'd put a lot of work into it, but she cringed at the thought of Mom and Dad seeing it. Her salary and Jacob's help only went so far.

Maybe if she showed her family "before" pictures, they'd be impressed with how far she'd come.

On a sigh, Leah stepped into her room. Yeah, she was definitely going to need some help in the cleanup department. She smiled a little. It was nice knowing she'd have friends who'd chip in without a second thought.

MC and its employees had become her second family. For a while, she thought it'd be enough. She could do without her parents, and the brother she'd never been all that close to, because she had friends who cared about her. She didn't know when that suddenly hadn't been enough. But it wasn't anymore.

She slipped out of the dress and examined the long white scar down the center of her chest. Mostly she tried to pretend it wasn't there. A reminder of too many things she wanted to forget.

Fifteen years. For fifteen years someone else's heart had beat in there. The five years directly following the transplant, she hadn't treated it or herself or her family well. In fact, her careless, selfish, destructive behavior had almost broken them all apart as much as it had almost killed her.

So, she'd left Minnesota and moved in with the black-sheep aunt no one in her family talked to. She'd gotten her life and health together, put herself through electrician training. And without her and her health issues in the way, Mom and Dad had gotten back together after the stress of her health and hospital bills had caused them to separate.

Now she had this life. And it was good and enough time had passed that she wanted to heal. Wanted to have a family to spend holidays with. Wanted her brother to forgive her for wrecking their family. She wanted to make up everything she'd ruined.

So, if she had to lie, cheat or steal to accomplish it, she would. Hopefully it ended with the lying. Even more hopefully, it ended without her even more screwed up about Jacob than she already was.

CHAPTER TWO

JACOB STOOD IN front of the dilapidated old Victorian on Jasmine Street in the heart of Bluff City, Iowa. It was surrounded by renovated or completely rebuilt houses and small businesses. It was an eyesore and for sale.

Perfect.

Leah stepped out of the house followed by Henry, MC's plumber. They were both covered in dust and wore hard hats. Jacob had already toured the place twice before he'd brought out Leah and Henry, so today he'd stayed outside, not wanting to hover over them while they checked it out.

"Have to rewire everything, and I mean everything. There's not crap for restoring, electrically speaking." Leah stood next to him, squinting at the old house.

"Plumbing, too. Have to redo everything. Shit hole." Henry's plumbing estimation.

"Pipe dream, boss." Leah clapped him on the shoulder, but he barely felt it.

Yeah, pipe dream, but he could see it. He could see it fully restored and absolutely perfect. With Grace and Kyle—his business partner and now also his sister's boyfriend—moving out of the main house once their house was finished being built back in their hometown of Carvelle, Jacob was thinking about selling that first project. Without people sharing the same roof, the big house on the bluff was too much for him. MC had a strong enough reputation he didn't need the grand showpiece as an office anymore, and he really didn't want to think about living in that monster by himself.

This house would be a better size. He could work and live there like he did at the main house. It could still be a bit of a showcase of what he could do. Right in the heart of town. And if he bought it, it wouldn't be demolished and turned into a strip mall.

"Jacob."

"Hmm?"

"It's a money pit."

Jacob spared Leah a glance. "My favorite kind."

She shook her head. "One of these days it's going to blow up in your face. You can't keep taking risks like this."

"What's life without a little risk?" Jacob turned his attention back to the house. Especially when the risk was this perfect. "I'll put a lowball offer in. See what happens."

"What about the Perkins house?"

"I can do both."

Leah shook her head again. She did that a lot when he got on one of his extracurricular projects, but she also always pitched in. She'd complain and poke fun until she was blue in the face, but she'd be the first one there with him and the last one to leave. He supposed that was how she'd somehow suckered him and Grace and Kyle into helping her clean up her house before her family's arrival.

Speaking of that. "You gonna have food tonight?"

Leah slid the hard hat off her head, began tapping it against her thigh. "I'll order some pizza. Buy some beer and sodas."

"Dessert?" He grinned over at her when she scowled. She had a big, dirty coat on over her sweatshirt. Her hair was a static mess from the hard hat. Her cheeks were pink from the cold.

Jacob looked back at the house. This sex drought was really, *really* getting to him.

"I'll get some snickerdoodles."

"If it doesn't contain chocolate, it is not a dessert."

"I'm not buying a bunch of chocolate and watching you guys scarf it down when I can't have any. Cruel and unusual."

"Not our fault you're allergic to everything."

"One pan of brownies. Store-bought. And you're taking all the leftovers home with you."

Jacob grinned, slung his arm over her shoulders. "You drive a hard bargain. Guess I can live with that while I'm slaving away cleaning your pigsty."

She wiggled out from under his arm. "Think of it this way. You get a front-row seat to the look on Kyle's face when he sees how messy I really am."

Yeah, seeing his anal-retentive partner's face when he got a load of Leah's place was going to be fun. "Fair enough."

"You two gonna blab all afternoon? Freezing my balls off." Henry marched over to the truck.

Leah rolled her eyes and followed suit. Jacob took a few extra seconds to give the house one last look. It was going to be his, money pit or no money pit.

"LEAH, MY GOD, how do you live like this?"

Leah had to bite back a smile. She was messy. Definitely. She knew it wasn't an attractive quality and it embarrassed her...sometimes.

But Kyle's complete and utter horror was too funny.

"Thanks for coming, guys. Food and drinks are in the kitchen. Grab what you want. I did actually clean that room."

It had taken all weekend and then another hour this afternoon when she'd gotten home from work, but it was one room down and she was determined to keep it clean until Friday, when her parents and Marc arrived.

"As far as cleaning goes, trash anything you want. Everything with any sentimental value is in my room, which I don't need help with." It needed help, no doubt, but she didn't like the idea of Jacob poking around in there. Not when he was likely to find all sorts of things she didn't want him seeing. Pill bottles, inhalers, old pictures. No, she didn't want him, or any of her friends, seeing any of that.

"Leah, this isn't going to take an evening. This is going to take a decade."

Leah patted Kyle's shoulder. "Don't worry. You'll survive. I promise. If you start having chest pains or a numb feeling in your arm, you just tell Grace and she'll rush you to the hospital."

"Ha-ha." But he smiled, which was becoming more and more normal. Man, that was nice. Leah liked seeing Grace and Kyle together. The easy way they balanced each other out, made each other happy.

Anytime she thought of that and felt a little bit jealous, she immediately blocked the feeling out. She refused to be jealous of anyone anymore. That was part of what had caused her so many problems after her surgery.

Jealous everyone else got to do what they wanted, whenever they wanted. She'd been less and less inclined to take care of the second chance someone else's life had given her.

Jeez. What was wrong with her, thinking about that right now?

She handed out paper plates and let everyone grab what they wanted. Her cheese-free pizza was a sad commentary on the state of her life, but what could she do? The body she was born with was a mess of allergies and malfunctioning parts.

For the next four hours she, Jacob, Grace and Kyle worked through the scattered piles of debris.

Organizing, putting things away, sweeping, mopping and dusting.

Damn, what would she do without these people?

After emptying the vacuum canister for at least the fifth time, Leah stood in the kitchen and took a deep breath. Her lungs were a little tight from the dust and exertion, so she slipped away to her bedroom for a sneak hit on her inhaler. She needed to grab a mask, too, but when she stepped back out, she heard a noise down the hallway.

It sounded like it came from the worst room in the house. The room she wasn't going to bother cleaning because she hadn't even begun renovations on it. She was going to block it off. There was no way she'd get it viewable by next week.

Mask forgotten, she walked to the open doorway. When she looked in, expecting and dreading to find evidence of mice, she found Jacob instead. He was standing in the middle of the room, little work notebook in hand, jotting notes.

It wasn't fair he could look so damn good in jeans and a flannel shirt and a beard. Minus the beard, it was what she was wearing, and she knew very well she didn't look like someone anyone wanted to jump.

Ugh. Why did she have to want to jump him? Since that thought was so frustrating, she put extra accusation into her voice. "What do you think you're doing?"

"Making a list." He didn't even glance at her.

Instead, he kept writing in his little notebook just like he did at work.

She took a step inside. "A list of what?"

"Things that need to be done before your parents come stay with you."

"What?"

He finally looked up, tucked the pen behind his ear. Why the hell was that sexy? Oh, right, because she was dumb, dumb, dumb, dumb, dumb.

"Look, if I'm your boyfriend and I'm a contractor, they'd expect these things to be taken care of."

Defensiveness settled through her and she crossed her arms over her chest. "It's a work in progress."

"You've lived here five years. How long have we been together?"

She didn't understand how he could be so casual about it. But it was Jacob. Jacob was casual about everything.

Except his work. MC was the one place his laser focus and intense dedication went. Well, that and his family.

"Leah? Hello? You want this lie to fly you're going to have to think about these things. Details and—"

"I know. I know. They think we've been dating a year," she muttered, kicking at the warped floorboard.

He let out a low whistle. "Damn. You ever been in a real relationship for a whole year?"

"No." She didn't need to ask him if *he* had. She knew the answer to that since she paid way too close attention to his dating life. Jacob could barely manage a six-week relationship.

Though it might have something to do with the way he went about dating. Like a mission. A to-do list to get to his wanted destination. Family.

Which was *none* of her business. Fake relationship or no. Especially since "family" wasn't something she'd ever be able to offer anyone.

"You know, if we've been dating a year they're going to expect us to actually, oh, I don't know, touch each other. Possibly even sleep together."

Her face burned. So embarrassing. "I don't think my devoutly Catholic mother is going to be concerning herself with our sex life."

He walked toward her, tucking the notebook in his front pocket. "'Our sex life.' Weirder words I'm not sure have ever been spoken."

"No shit." Leah tucked her hands into her armpits, hugging herself close. They were alone and this was weird with a capital *W.*

"So, you know, speaking of our sex life, how do you see that going?"

He was joking and grinning, but the proximity meant she was having a hard time getting that through to her brain. Actually, not so much her brain as her sorely neglected libido.

Leah took a breath and summoned all the unaffectedness she could muster. "Why are guys so gross?"

"After cleaning up your house, you do not get to talk to me about gross."

Fair enough. "You're not doing anything to this room, Jacob. I'm blocking it off. We've been too busy building MC to work on my place. Got it?"

He made a considering sound in his throat and then left the room. Damn it, she hated when he did that. The no-answer thing meant he was going to do something stupid.

Well, it couldn't be any stupider than her asking him to be her fake boyfriend.

JACOB KNEW HE should leave with everyone else, talk to Leah about this situation somewhere…safe. But there really was no time like the present.

He plopped himself onto her newly-cleaned-up couch. "So, we ever going to talk details about this whole fake-relationship thing?"

Her whole body visibly stiffened, and then she rolled her shoulders. "Yeah. Sure. I just…"

"You remember this being *your* idea? You begged me to agree to it."

Some of her tension morphed into irritation, which was exactly what he'd been going for. "I did not beg."

"Pretty sure the word *please* was used."

"Begging and being polite are two different things. Can we talk about this some other time? When I'm not exhausted and covered in dirt."

She did look tired. Pale, and there was a weird

rasp to her voice. He noticed she got that whenever she'd been working particularly hard.

But he also knew if he left, she'd keep working. There was no quit in Leah. "You know me. I like a plan. Blueprint. Details. Fill me in."

"Right. Right." She pulled the cuffs of her shirt down, then pushed them back up to her elbows. And then repeated the process two more times.

He wasn't used to nervous, unsure Leah. It was fascinating. Something he wanted to poke at. "Where was our first date?"

She glowered at him. "What?"

"How did I ask you out? What do you love about me?" He grinned, knowing it would irritate and fluster her more.

"What does that matter?"

"You don't think your mom might be curious as to how we started dating? What you see in me, besides my good looks, that is."

She opened her mouth, then closed it and rubbed a hand to her chest.

"You okay?"

"Yeah. Look, my family won't care about that, and if they do I'll make something up."

"You've obviously never pulled off an elaborate hoax before. Or seen a romantic comedy." She made a face and didn't stop rubbing her chest. "Leah, what is up with you?"

"Nothing," she snapped. "Can't you just go away? We can talk about this some other time."

"No time like the present." He certainly wasn't going to leave when it looked as though something was wrong with her. Maybe she was coming down with a cold. He was about to offer to run and get her some soup or something when she abruptly turned away.

"Give me a second." She disappeared down the hallway, so pale and strange-sounding he couldn't fight the impulse to follow where she went.

The door to her room was cracked open and he looked in as she took a deep breath with an inhaler to her mouth. He'd seen her use it once or twice, but had never given it much thought.

He nudged the door open wider. "You okay?"

"Does privacy mean nothing to you?" She took a deep breath, then another puff of the inhaler, all the while glowering at him.

But she was so damn pale and he'd never seen her so shaky. So, instead of backing off like she obviously wanted him to do, he plopped on the bed next to her. "So, the answer to my question would be no."

"I'm fine." She inched away from him. "Please, don't push." Then she coughed, and it came out all wheezy and awful-sounding. He thumped her back and took her hand, about five seconds from calling an ambulance.

She gulped air and he rubbed her back. Obviously something was really wrong if she wasn't pushing him away. "I'm going to call 9-1-1."

She grabbed his arm before he could stand up.

"No way in hell." With her free hand she took another puff of the inhaler. "Don't you dare move."

"Hey, look at me because you're starting to freak me out."

She looked him square in the eye, those pretty green-blue eyes fierce and determined. "I'm fine," she said firmly, but she was trembling. "It's asthma, Jacob. Had it all my life."

"I'm getting you some water." She released his arm and he hurried out to the kitchen and returned with a glass of water. She was still pale, but her breathing had eased.

"Do not look at me like that." She snatched the glass of water out of his hand, and when he sat next to her again, she inched away.

But she drank the water and slowly stopped looking so gray. She wasn't trembling anymore and her breathing seemed easier. "Don't look at you like what?"

"Like I'm dying. I'm not. Go home. Please."

She was squeezing the glass so tight it was a wonder it didn't break, but there was no way he was going home. He covered her hand with his, but before he could say something, she gave him that direct look again.

Yeah, not much about Leah's kick-ass, tomboy, tough-girl self was *pretty,* but those eyes were.

"I am okay. I promise. I'll admit I made a mistake tonight, and you know I don't admit mistakes easily. I pushed myself too hard, but it was just a…blip.

I'll get a good night's sleep, and I won't go mucking around in dust without a mask again."

She was right—admitting mistakes wasn't in her M.O. So it was hard to doubt the rest. Besides, Leah knew her body better than he did. Way better than he did. So he should back off like she asked.

She pointedly looked down, presumably because his hands were covering hers. On her bed. Yeah, okay, things had gotten a little weird.

"I'll get out of your hair." He stood, shoved his hands in his pockets. "If you're sure you're okay?"

"I swear to God you ask me that again I'll kill you and show you just how okay I am."

She wasn't a hugger, but despite the insult, he had the urge to do just that before he left. She looked so…weak, the opposite of the Leah he routinely saw.

Instead, he kept his hands in his pockets and managed a smile. "See you tomorrow." Leaving seemed so damn wrong, but she wanted him to. She wanted him to and him staying was only going to aggravate her, so he should definitely go.

"Yup." She nodded toward the door.

He took a few steps toward the door, then sighed. "You call if you need anything."

"It's asthma, not paralysis."

"Asthma isn't exactly a cold."

She swore under her breath. "Don't do this, okay? Do not start treating me like I'll break. I can't take it. I cannot take it."

He wondered at the fury in her voice. He was just

trying to be nice. Leave it to Leah to be pissy about it. "Fine. Pardon me for caring."

She just kept staring at her floor, so he rolled his eyes and finished the walk out. He made sure to lock the door behind him, hoped she remembered to flip the dead bolt. He'd text a reminder to her, except knowing Leah, she'd leave it unlocked just to piss him off.

Jacob climbed into his truck, then sat in the driver's seat, shivering in the below-freezing temperatures. He jammed his key into the ignition and then laughed when the engine wouldn't turn over.

Yeah, that seemed about right.

CHAPTER THREE

WHEN A KNOCK sounded on her door, Leah wanted to punch something. Scratch that. Someone. Lungs aching, head pounding, she trudged to the door ready to give Jacob a piece of her mind.

She didn't have the energy for this. She was too busy beating herself up for being careless and letting Jacob catch her in her carelessness. He was such a worrier, and she hated the thought of him worrying over her.

She'd been through the smothering thing. She didn't handle it well. Or at all. The last thing she needed was to screw up her life all over again because the people around her wouldn't let her breathe, make her own decisions, be in charge.

MC, her friends, everything about the person she was now was what she wanted. Desperately. She was happy, for the first time in too long to remember. Life was good, and she was steps away from getting her family back.

If Jacob ruined that by hovering, by maneuvering, by being everything she couldn't stand, it would end it all.

Jesus, could she get any more overdramatic? She'd handled a hell of a lot worse than an overworried friend/boss. She wasn't going to let him be the end of anything. No way. Which meant she had to put on the tough-girl shell and prove once and for all there was nothing to worry over.

The tough-girl shell was a little exhausting after a long day of hard work and setbacks. On a deep breath, Leah wrenched open the door and fixed Jacob with her most furious glare. "Go. Away."

"Truck won't start." His shoulders were hunched, the collar of his coat almost reaching his ears. Cold air whipped in through the open door. "Going to make me freeze?"

"No," Leah mumbled. She moved out of the way so Jacob could step inside.

"I'll call a tow truck, have Kyle come pick me up. Just need some warmth for a bit." His voice was gruff, his posture stiff. Jacob was angry and, well, that didn't happen very often.

Crap.

"I can take a look."

"Don't bother."

Yeah, double crap. "Just let me—"

"Don't worry about it." He was typing something into his phone, expressly not moving any farther into her house or taking off his coat. His ears and nose were bright red.

"You want something hot to drink?"

He glanced up from his phone. "*Now* you're offering me hot drinks? Because about fifteen minutes ago you were all but kicking me out."

A mix of guilt and irritation and shame propelled her toward the kitchen. Oh, she hated that even temper of his. Because she never could be angry in the face of his anger. It was so hard to piss off Jacob and she got irritated at the drop of a hat.

Which meant, if Jacob was mad and snotty, she'd stepped over a line and the tough-girl shell wasn't the answer. Unfortunately, reason and apologizing were the answer. She hated apologizing and, damn it, she hated being wrong enough to have to.

"I don't have coffee or hot chocolate. Just tea."

"I'll survive. Here. Found a tow number."

"Don't call a tow truck. Let me look at it first." When she turned to face Jacob, he was standing in the entry to her kitchen, frowning.

"It's freezing out there." He didn't mention earlier, though God knew that was what this was about. Even pissed, he was worried about her.

For a second, just a sliver of a second, there was some stupid, girlie part of her that thought it was kind of sweet. Until she remembered how fast worrying could snowball to babying, controlling.

"I have a jacket. A hat. Gloves. All these magical things to keep me warm."

"And just how many brain cells do you think you lost when you practically couldn't breathe for a few minutes? Not sure I can trust your judgment."

She gritted her teeth, did everything to keep the snap out of her tone. "I'm fine."

"Oh, are you? You hadn't mentioned that eight million times. Just shut up for a few minutes so I can call the tow."

She grabbed the phone out of his hand as he held it to his ear. "Don't be stubborn and stupid."

He snorted. "You oughta talk."

"I'm…" Oh, God, she hated this part. "Sorry. I'm sorry I was kind of an ass before. I just can't stand being hovered over."

His eyebrows lifted. "I was hovering?"

Okay, not really. Not suffocating, anyway. She'd been pretty bad off and he'd been worried. It was just, she couldn't tell him why that scared her or put her back up. She couldn't explain it was the thing she most feared.

Because she wouldn't admit to anyone she feared anything. "I said I'm sorry. What more do you want?"

He rolled his eyes. "Not a damn thing, Leah. Just give me my phone." He held out his hand and she stared at it.

They came to impasses like this from time to time. Both so certain they were right. Both irritated and defensive. She hated the way it tied her up in knots. She hated feeling guilty and stupid, but most of all she hated the thought of him being angry with her.

Which was so pathetic it was laughable.

"My family thinks you asked me out at New Year's last year." It was the only thing that would distract him no matter how much she dreaded discussing it, and it was better than arguing. "Besides that, I haven't talked much about it. If Mom asks I say we went to a movie or dinner and I change the subject. It's not like I've created some elaborate fantasy. You're a prop. I don't enjoy lying to them. It's just necessary."

He studied her with an unreadable expression. So rarely did he have a poker face, it made her nervous and uncomfortable. She went back to focusing on making the tea he probably wouldn't drink. Then she remembered she still had his phone, and she stopped abruptly halfway between him and the stove.

"Why is it necessary to lie?"

The heart that wasn't hers ached in a place that was. "I told you why. The whole thinking-I-need-a-man thing."

"Okay, I get why that bugs you, but why lie to them about it? You're not exactly the pretend-to-be-something-you're-not type."

Leah frowned. It was true, but this was different. So much more important. "They're my family."

"They should love you for who you are."

"I owe them too much for that." Disgusted with herself for saying it, she handed him his phone. "I'm going to go put my coat on, find a flashlight and take a look at your car. Might be able to jury-rig something."

"Leah—"

She didn't stick around to find out what he wanted to say. She'd revealed too much already.

"THERE. START IT."

Jacob looked down at the engine Leah had been fooling around with. Between the streetlight and her flashlight, he could see well enough. Unfortunately, he knew jack about cars, so seeing it didn't help the situation. "You really think you fixed it?"

"It's below freezing. Start the damn car and we'll find out."

Since her teeth were chattering and he wasn't exactly warm and cozy, either, he hurried to the driver's side and turned the key in the ignition. When the engine started, he stared, a little dumbfounded and possibly a little emasculated. "You did it."

Her mouth quirked into a grin. It was dark, but her face was illuminated by streetlights and headlights. He stood with his hand on the keys, wondering at how he'd let a girl fix his car.

"Aw, come on. Don't be one of those guys."

"One of what guys?"

"The guy who gets his panties in a twist because a woman knows more about cars than he does."

"My panties aren't in a twist," Jacob grumbled. He wasn't one of those guys. More power to her. Really. He'd work on that feeling, anyway.

Leah laughed. "Your car works. Go home, huh?"

Jacob scowled at her. She was all bundled up in her heavy jacket and bulky stocking cap, but she was smiling and even in the dim light he could see she wasn't as gray and pale as she'd been.

"Your color's back." He didn't realize it was a mistake until his fingertips grazed the skin of her cheek and something electric and upending met with the touch.

She didn't back away, didn't looked shocked or disgusted or angry or amused. For a second, just a nanosecond, it was almost as if she leaned into it.

That…couldn't be. Jacob pulled his hand away, trying to make sense of it. That she might *want* him to touch her. That was crazy, though. They were friends, and she'd always gone out of her way to make sure he knew he was not her type.

"Good night, Jacob." Quickly, she walked away. The weird moment was gone, but he couldn't stop turning it over in his mind.

He watched her go, a big, shapeless figure in the frigid dark. She disappeared inside, her door closing with a distinct thud.

Leah. Wanting him to touch her. Liking him touching her.

You touched her cheek, you whack job.

Yes. Yes, that. It had been an innocent touch in the cold and there was nothing to sit here and think over. He jammed his hand back into his glove.

But even as he got in his car and drove back home, the moment stuck in his mind. And he wondered something he'd never allowed himself to wonder before.

What if this little attraction he'd always shoved to the back of his brain wasn't so lopsided?

He didn't have an answer for that, but he knew one thing. The question was going to haunt him for a very long time.

"SO, WHAT'S UP with you?" Grace plopped in the seat next to Leah. The kitchen at MC was always a revolving door around lunchtime, everyone eating on varying schedules. Ever since Grace had moved into MC earlier this year when the ex-boyfriend who'd beaten her up had gotten out of jail, it wasn't unusual that Grace and Leah would eat together, but Leah had to admit she'd been hoping to eat alone today.

So, she almost said she was fine. Almost smiled and shoved the offensive sandwich in front of her down her throat, but that wouldn't solve her dilemma. "I need to tell you something, and, for the sake of my sanity, I need you not to tell me I'm nuts."

"Even if you are?"

"Especially if I am."

"Gotcha. Shoot."

"So, you know how my family is coming on Friday and we haven't always been the kind of close-knit family you have and all that?"

Grace nodded, cracking open a can of pop and thankfully giving Leah time to spit it all out.

Leah pushed the plate away. She couldn't beat the nausea that all these nerves and stress were causing. "Well, they have this thing about being really overprotective, and in an effort to downplay some of that overprotectiveness, I kind of lied about a few things to them."

"You want us to corroborate?"

Leah nodded. If she was a hugger, she'd have her arms around Grace right now for understanding so well. But then, she hadn't told what they needed to corroborate yet, either.

Leah swallowed. "I made up a boyfriend."

Grace laughed. "Wait. Seriously?"

"Yup."

"Okay, so…if they bring up a boyfriend we just smile and nod and pretend like we know about him. We can do that." Grace squeezed her arm. "Hardly a favor worth getting nervous about asking."

"I'm not totally done."

"Oh. Okay. So, what's the rest?"

"I didn't make up a boyfriend, exactly. I used someone real as my fake boyfriend."

"Really? Who? If it was Ryan Gosling I don't think you're fooling anybody."

Leah wished she could laugh, but the nerves and fear over Grace's reaction closed her throat, making it impossible.

"Leah? Who is it?"

"Jacob."

Grace laughed. "Am I supposed to understand whispered mumbling? Come on. Who is it?"

Leah stared hard at her hands, and this time when she spoke she made sure to enunciate. "Jacob."

"Jacob," Grace repeated.

Leah could only nod.

"My brother, Jacob. That Jacob?"

Again Leah nodded. Preparing herself for a lecture on being crazy or explaining how it would never work or anything besides understanding.

"Makes sense."

Man, the McKnights sure didn't make it easy on her to beat herself up. Both Jacob and Grace acted as if it was the most normal thing in the world for her to pretend Jacob was her boyfriend.

"Have you told Jacob?"

"Yeah."

When Grace didn't say anything else, Leah thunked her forehead against the table. "And this is where you're dying to tell me I've gone batshit crazy."

"No." But a weighty silence followed and Leah braced herself for something. "And Jacob agreed to pretend, I'm assuming."

"Yeah." Leah shook her head, gave her forehead another thunk. "Say it. Just, whatever it is, tell me. I can handle it." Maybe.

"Don't you think it might be a little awkward pretending to be with Jacob considering…"

Leah straightened in her chair, the heat of embarrassment climbing her cheeks and forehead. "Considering what?"

"Well, you guys just have…a thing."

"A thing?"

"Yeah. Like a weird energy. Like maybe there's a little interest or attraction there. Kyle and I have both definitely noticed a thing."

"There is no thing. We're thingless! Well, he's not. I mean, I assume he's not. It's not like I actually know. Oh, my God. Shut me up. Please."

Grace was doubled over laughing and Leah wanted to disappear into the floor, but it was all so ridiculous she found herself laughing, too.

When was she going to accept this plan was stupid? Crazy? When would she accept lying probably wasn't the best way to reunite with her family?

Probably never. Because she'd thought about this problem for months. Going over every detail in her mind. Every possible scenario, but none of them worked. None of them allowed her what she wanted. Nothing except this crazy scheme.

"Leah, be straight with me."

Leah met Grace's steady gaze and sighed. "Okay, maybe there's a little thing. But it's…nothing. It won't be awkward. It's a favor. We're just friends, and I can't imagine anything that would change that."

Grace looked less than convinced, but she didn't say anything more and that was why she was Leah's best friend. "It's just pretend. For a week. What could possibly happen?"

Grace shook her head, but before she could offer

any worst-case scenarios, Jacob and Kyle walked into the kitchen.

In the end, Leah didn't know if the interruption was a good thing or not.

CHAPTER FOUR

WHEN JACOB WALKED into the kitchen of MC, he wasn't surprised to see Leah and Grace eating lunch together. The two had become close since Grace had moved in. But the pink tinge to Leah's cheeks was weird, even weirder when it deepened to a full-blown red as she glanced at him.

What had they been talking about that would make Leah, of all people, blush?

"Are we interrupting?" Kyle asked.

Grace glanced at Leah. "You want to tell Kyle, or do you want me to?"

Leah made a go-ahead gesture with her hand, eyes never leaving her sandwich. Funny, Jacob couldn't seem to take his eyes off the stain of color on her cheeks.

"Or should Jacob be the one to spill the beans?" Grace said in a syrupy sweet voice.

"What are you yapping about?" Jacob muttered, finally tearing his gaze away from Leah. "The favor I'm doing Leah?"

"Mmm-hmm."

"If someone would care to clue me in, I'd be

appreciative," Kyle said, sliding into the seat next to Grace. Grace leaned over and gave him a brief kiss on the cheek.

It was still a little weird seeing his best friend with his older sister even after months of getting used to it, but it was hard not to admit it worked for the guy. Kyle hadn't changed into a different person overnight, but his tightly wound self had loosened a little.

And Grace loved him and was going to move back to Carvelle with him, the town they'd all grown up in. It was only fifteen minutes away from Bluff City, but it would be strange. Kyle had been his roommate since college and, until his relationship with Grace, hadn't gone back to Carvelle since they'd left for school.

Still not something Jacob could wrap his head around.

"It's no big deal. Jacob's just going to pretend to be my…boyfriend while my family visits." Leah pushed her plate around, never once touching the food on it. "It's hard to explain, but it'll help me out. And it's not a big deal and we should all just agree not to talk about it as much as possible."

"Your…" Kyle blinked a few times. Then he coughed. "Oh, I see."

Awkward silence descended, and when Jacob caught Grace studying him, he crossed to the fridge. Anything to avoid his sister's scrutinizing stare.

He didn't need Grace reading anything more into this whole favor than just a friendly gesture. Or, worst-case scenario, telling Mom. That was another ground rule he needed to set with Leah. No telling *his* parents while they were trying to fool hers. God only knew what his guidance-counselor mother would read into the situation.

"I put an offer in on the house on Jasmine Street." Way better to discuss business than anything remotely related to relationship stuff. Of the real or fake variety.

"Jacob." The disapproval in Kyle's tone was enough to loosen any awkwardness. Kyle's conservative business nature, Jacob knew what to do with. How to circumnavigate it when he'd rather take a risk.

"Personal project." Which Kyle very rarely approved of. Probably because they never stayed personal.

"You have a plethora of personal projects. What you don't have are unlimited funds. Leah, tell him." Her body kind of jerked in response. "Why me?"

"He listens to you."

She snorted, glanced his way and quickly looked back at her plate. Abruptly, she shoved her chair away from the table. "You know what? I gotta go." She disappeared before anyone could argue.

Jacob ignored Grace's frown and Kyle's considering gaze and focused on making his sandwich. Even though he'd agreed to Leah's plan, he hadn't thought about the reaction from people they knew. What those people might think.

"Look, you two can get the pinched, worried looks

off your faces. The thing with Leah is not a big deal." And it wasn't. A favor. A gesture. That was what friends did for each other. Why everyone was being *weird* about it was baffling.

"No big deal to you," Grace said.

"What does that mean?"

Kyle and Grace exchanged a look. It was one that conveyed some shared idea, only Jacob didn't know what it was. He hated that.

"Be careful with her," Grace finally said.

It was the kind of admonition that irritated him. As if he was somehow careless with people. Just because he dated. A lot. "I don't know where everyone got this idea I'm an ass to women. They do the breaking up—"

"You know Leah has a thing for you. You have to know that. And I think you've got a weird if not fully realized thing for her, and this pretending? It's going to be messy. Leah's been a really good friend to me. I don't want to see her get hurt."

Jacob frowned. What a…weird idea. He just couldn't imagine. Even for those seconds he'd imagined maybe, just maybe, Leah felt that weird attraction, too, he couldn't imagine hurting her. Attraction or no, she'd never hesitated to kick his ass before. "Leah is tough as nails. How is she going to get hurt?"

"My point exactly." Grace glanced at the clock. "I have to go to the gallery. Just… We can talk about this later."

"There's nothing to talk about," Jacob called after her. "There's nothing to talk about," Jacob repeated before taking a bite of his sandwich.

"Ah."

"What's that 'ah' about?" Jacob demanded with a mouthful.

"Nothing. Nothing at all. I'm sure it will be totally fine. And nothing will go wrong. And you two won't…"

The way Kyle trailed off was meant to insinuate something, but Jacob wasn't biting. "Mind your own business, Kyle."

"It affects our business. The one we own together. And Leah is a marginal owner as well, if you recall. And then there's the little fact that you weren't exactly silent when Grace and I started…seeing each other. Maybe I am minding my business by speaking up."

"So you guys don't want me to do the favor she asked me to do because you think we're going to—what? Fall in bed together and end up hating each other?" Which was really weird to think about. Both sides of that hypothetical equation.

Falling in bed together, well, it may have crossed his mind once or twice, but hating each other? They'd been friends for a long time. Friends who disagreed and argued and still remained friends. How would they end up hating each other?

"I don't know the circumstances behind it, so I can't say you shouldn't do it. But I don't think Grace cautioning you to be careful is unreasonable. There are some things at stake. Even more than Leah's feelings, whatever they may be."

"Because I'm such an asshole? We can't even trust me to be around people?"

"Because…relationships are tricky. Especially when people are in business together. Because, though you are not an asshole, your track record with women is…less than desirable."

"Everyone seems to be forgetting the fake part of this whole deal. It's pretend. I've been around Leah for years without hurting these precious feelings she suddenly has. We aren't really going to be dating. You guys understand that, right? It's *pretend.*"

"But whatever…undercurrent runs between you and Leah isn't."

Grace said Leah had a thing for him. A thing. Whatever that meant. What could it mean? He was actually afraid to find out, because when it came to Leah, he wouldn't be in control. So, he'd forget Grace had said anything. He'd ignore the things he randomly felt from time to time. They'd pretend for a week, then go back to normal.

"You guys are overreacting." And they were. They had to be. Whatever "undercurrents" that were there had been ignored for this long. What would change just because they were going to have a few meals pretending to be a little more than friends?

Nothing. And that wouldn't be hard. Not with a

game plan. With a game plan, anything could be accomplished. So, that was where he'd start.

LEAH ATTACHED ELECTRICAL tape to the base of the light fixture she was rewiring to be put in the Council Bluffs house. The smaller work had always been her favorite part of being an electrician, even more so since she was working in restoration. Most of what she had to do was throwing away the old and putting in something new, but these smaller light-fixture projects meant making something old and past its prime useful again. It was all good work, fulfilling work, and it never failed to remind her how lucky she was.

These small projects also gave her the opportunity to work in her little shed office in the back of MC's big house. She could blare her heavy metal and not listen to Jacob or Kyle whine about their ears or her mess. This was her domain.

She set the finished piece into some bubble wrap, then a box. The next few weeks would be slow until the planned trip to Council Bluffs at the end of January. She'd finished almost all her work on the Bellamy project and Jacob's little side project downtown. She wasn't needed on anything in the big house for a while. So, it was just light fixtures until mid-January.

The slowdown was purposeful for the holidays. Time to visit families, and most people didn't want work done on their homes then, so it all made sense.

In years past, she'd thrown herself into her own house, but this year she would actually have family around.

The thought filled her with equal measure hope and dread. Hope she could repair the lingering rifts with her family; dread this whole Jacob thing was going to blow up in her face in more ways than one.

She didn't want Grace blabbing to Jacob she thought they had a thing or that Leah had admitted as much. Leah hadn't been lying when she'd said she saw no scenario that would change her current relationship with Jacob. They might be friends and she might have a small investor's hold in MC, but he was still her boss.

And she had a lot more secrets than being all but in love with him. Secrets that would change the way he acted toward her, that would kill any idiotic feelings she harbored. Jacob would hover. He would micromanage. He would ruin the life she'd built, simply by knowing and being himself.

Which was what she had to remember. Always. With her parents around, that shouldn't be hard. In fact, worrying about this was silly. Everything would be—

A knock interrupted her pathetic attempts to convince herself she wasn't an idiot.

When Jacob stepped in, she pointed a screwdriver at him. Antagonism was always the best shield against weakness. "You are not allowed in here, and you know it. Not after last time."

"I was trying to organize—"

"And I couldn't find my ammeter for a week." She waved the screwdriver at him. "What do you want?"

"Can you turn that crap down so I don't have to yell?"

Her music was not that loud, but she grumbled a complaint and walked over to push the off button. When she turned to him again, he was bending over to pick something up off the ground.

"You touch that I will kick your ass."

He scowled at her, still bent over. "Because you're leaving that screw on the floor for safekeeping?"

She merely raised a brow, and after a few seconds he grunted and stood up, leaving the screw right there. Oh, she so did enjoy winning. Especially against Jacob.

"At least take down the Joe Mauer poster. It's not professional."

"So? Clients don't come back here. Besides, he's dreamy. Don't be jealous because the Cubs don't have a decent-looking guy on their team."

Jacob grimaced. "Girls are so weird."

"Like you wouldn't have swimsuit models plastered all over if you had a workshop."

"I most certainly would not."

"Lies."

"Well, not *all* over."

"Ha!"

"Listen, we need to talk."

Leah's stomach sank. Nothing good ever came

from a sentence that started with *listen,* especially if it ended with needing to talk. "Um, okay."

"We need a schedule."

Leah furrowed her brow. "For what? The Jasmine Street project? You haven't even bought—"

"For your parents."

So, it was about that. Hello, awkward city. "Oh. Oh. Well."

"We need a blueprint. We need to plan. We can't go into this willy-nilly or we're going to get burned." He stood by the screw on the floor, businessman face on. *This is what we're going to do.* It served him well as a business owner and contractor. She didn't like it being transferred to real life, though.

"God, you and your blueprints."

"You know I'm right."

Ugh. He probably was. She'd been so worked up about asking him for the favor, she hadn't fully planned out the *how* part. How was this going to work? What did she expect him to do?

She had to look away from him or that idiotic heat that had been stealing over her face a ridiculous amount lately would be blatantly obvious.

Yes, maybe a blueprint was the way to go. If they had a set way to deal with it, nothing could go… awry. "Okay, so, what do you suggest?"

"Well, we need to think about how this is effective. I come to dinner with you guys once or twice? They come see MC? And how do we handle Christmas? I don't think getting my parents tangled in this is a good idea, so we need to make sure there's no overlap there. Mainly, we need to start thinking like a couple."

Leah snorted. She might have the hots for the guy, but them seeing eye to eye had never been a strong suit.

"Hey, you're the one who told your parents you were in a yearlong relationship with me."

"Yeah. Probably because I wanted to strangle you that day, so you were the first name that popped out of my mouth."

He shook his head. "Anyway, stay for dinner. We'll get Grace's help. No reason not to get extra help to think through everything."

Leah couldn't decide if Grace's help would be good or bad. But what other choice did she have? "Thanks. You're…going above and beyond here. Thank you. Really."

"I like you grateful. It's a nice change of pace."

Leah rolled her eyes, but because she was an idiot, him liking anything about her made her feel weird and jittery.

"What were you talking about today?"

"Huh?"

"You and Grace, when Kyle and I came in… What were you talking about that had you blushing?" He leaned against the door, studying her face intently as if looking for said blush.

"I don't blush." But the heat was stealing over her

cheeks and with skin as fair as hers there was no hiding embarrassment.

"You're doing it right now."

"It was nothing."

"I'm finding that harder and harder to believe."

"She just thought we had a thing and I told her we didn't." Before she told her they did. "And I told her nothing would ever change that."

"Nothing?"

"Nothing." In a fantasy world? Sure. But she didn't live in a fantasy world. She lived in a sickly, shorter-life-expectancy, didn't-handle-smothering kind of world. Jacob could only exist in that world as he was. No amount of pretend could allow her to forget that.

"So, I'll stay for dinner. Can I get back to work now?"

He stood there staring at her for another minute and she purposely avoided his gaze. Whatever he was looking for, she wouldn't let him find it.

"Yeah, sure," he finally said and left her little work shed.

Leah let out a long breath and sat down on her bench. She'd known this wasn't going to be easy, but she'd thought the hard stuff would start with her parents' arrival, not before.

Well, she didn't have a choice, did she? Time to gird her loins, or something less…loin-related, and handle the hard stuff. Because the result was going to be a relationship with her parents and brother, whom she'd missed. And that was worth a little hard and a little embarrassment.

She'd do good to remember that.

...armed... both the... organ...
and calling chicken chicken soon.
She'd thought to say otherwise.

CHAPTER FIVE

JACOB SAT AT the kitchen table armed with a note-book, a calendar, a pen and a pencil. He wasn't Kyle's level of anal rigidness, but he liked to be organized. He loved a good plan. How could you ever get what you wanted if you didn't have a plan?

Leah, though, looked at everything as if it might bite and poison her. She was a great electrician. He'd never had one complaint about her work or her work ethic, but he had no idea how she did it all in the constant state of disarray everything in her orbit seemed to be in.

"Isn't this all a little much for one week of…whatever?"

"Consider it a business plan."

"If you say so," she muttered. "Where's Grace with the chicken?"

"She should be back soon. Now, let's start with arrival. Flying or driving? And when do they get here?"

Leah let out a gusty sigh. "Driving. Friday. Get here around three o'clock."

"Should I be there?"

"Hell no."

"Is that a Leah 'hell no' or a girlfriend 'hell no'?"

She worked her fingers through her messy braid, making it even messier, so the light brown strands framed her face.

Not that he was noticing that. Nope.

"I don't think they'd expect you to be with me. I haven't seen them in years."

"And why is that?"

When she only pursed her lips, he leaned forward on the table, trying to catch her eye. "Don't you think they'd expect me to know what the source of the problems you guys had is?"

"I…" She shook her head and swallowed. "It's really complicated and I don't think it'll come up. I… Jacob, we just don't get along. And part of that is because I was a shit teenager, and I…I wasn't a good person to them. Okay, so let's just go with it's my fault and that's all you need to know."

"I can't see you being shit to anyone who didn't deserve it."

"They didn't." She was so emphatic. "I was… Things were different. I'm a different person and I owe them…so much. Probably the truth, but I'm not sure I can keep being this person if I give them that. So here we are."

The whole conversation was so vague, but the obvious anguish and guilt in her words kept him from pressing further. After all, she was right. It wasn't as if her family was going to sit around rehashing all the bad stuff between them with him around.

Of course, that didn't stop him from being curious. Or concerned. Well, that wasn't his place, either. He scrubbed his hands over his face, then focused on his calendar. "Okay, so you don't need me Friday. What about Saturday? Sunday and Monday are Christmas Eve and Christmas Day, so I'll want to spend the majority of those with my family. We should definitely do something Saturday. Dinner?"

Leah nodded. "Yeah. Mom will want to cook for you."

"See? This isn't so hard. Now, we need to cover some basics of our relationship."

"Our fake relationship."

"The key to fooling anyone is believing it. Trust me."

"Why? You've pretended to be something you're not so often in your life?"

He shrugged. Maybe he hadn't pretended to be someone else, but he'd done plenty of pretending. Plenty of fooling people he loved. "I know a thing or two."

"Please."

Thankfully Grace chose that moment to walk in with the food. "All right. Sustenance. I see you've started without me." She plopped the bags on the table and went to collect plates and silverware. "How's it going so far?"

"Jacob is telling me all the tips and tricks of fooling people. Because apparently he's an expert."

"Jacob? Pretend?" Grace glanced at him, a screwed-up expression on her face. "What are you even talking about? I hate to give him a big head, but one of Jacob's greatest assets is his honesty."

"See? You're no great pretender." Leah helped herself to a drumstick and some green beans, apparently quite pleased with herself.

"Caught me." He managed a laid-back grin, one he didn't feel at all. "But I still think we need to cover all our bases."

"Can't hurt," Grace agreed, biting into a biscuit as she looked at the calendar. "You sure your family won't expect to see even a little of Jacob on Christmas? My parents expect to see Kyle."

"But Kyle doesn't have a family of his own or anywhere else to be."

"Well, yeah, but if you had a boyfriend, wouldn't you want to spend part of the day with him? I mean, especially if you've been dating an entire year."

"I haven't seen my family in many years. As far as they know, I've spent every Christmas with Jacob. Trust me, they won't question it. And if they do, I'll tell them I wanted to focus on them."

"It makes sense," Jacob said, even though Grace was frowning.

They ate their chicken and discussed the day after Christmas. Planned out a time for her family to come see MC with Jacob around but not too many other people. The fewer people they involved, the better. At least on that they agreed.

The back door opened and after a few seconds Kyle stepped into the kitchen.

"Hey, you're back early," Grace greeted, all way-too-wide smiles.

Kyle nodded, and Grace grinned at him and then he grinned back. Jacob grimaced, glanced at Leah, who had her nose wrinkled and mouth all screwed up.

"You guys need me for anything else?"

"I think we'll manage without all your genius contributions," Jacob muttered.

Grace grinned, popping out of her seat. "Great." Her and Kyle exited, Grace's laugh echoing down the staircase.

"How do you live with that lovey-dovey crap?"

"It's a very big house and I hide a lot."

She kind of half laughed, but her expression as she looked at where Kyle and Grace had disappeared wasn't so much amused or disgusted. No, it looked a lot wistful. And it echoed his own feeling on the matter.

It'd been almost six months since he'd been in a relationship, and he missed that ease with someone. Sure, he'd never been in a relationship as long as Kyle and Grace, but it was nice to always have someone to call up and spend time with instead of hiding from his sister and best friend feeling each other up all the time.

"You want to go to a movie?"

"Huh?"

"It's early. They're…" He grimaced. "Doing whatever. Unless you have plans. Let's go do something. That way if your mom asks what we did on our last date we can say, 'Oh, we went and saw *Boneheads*.'"

"I am not going to see *Boneheads*."

"It's supposed to be funny."

"It looks idiotic." She pushed some hair out of her eyes. "What about *Incoming*?"

"An alien movie? Are you crazy? Those things are creepy."

"Oh, poor Jacob is afraid of a few little fictional creatures." Leah pouted, clearly mocking him, and why that made him smile was completely beyond him.

"You better be careful. I'll wrangle you into a chick flick."

"Oh, please. Aliens over chick flick any day of the week." But she stood from the table and went over to the mudroom, where her coat was hanging. "What about the one with the race-car driver? The main guy is hot and I hear he gets naked."

Jacob shrugged into his coat. "Why do you have to say things like that?"

She laughed, an uninhibited rumble, and something cross wired in his brain, suddenly making him think about *her* naked. Nope. Nope. Nope. Not allowed.

He glanced at her as they stepped outside. It was

not a date. It was a distraction. A precursor to their ruse at best. Definitely not a date.

But it kind of felt like one.

WHAT THE HELL was happening?

It seemed innocuous enough, and it *was*. A movie. Friends went to movies all the time. Even friends who were going to pretend to be a little more than friends for a few days. This was normal.

Leah stared at the seat in front of her while sex noises filled the movie theater. Friends might do this all the time, but it was so not normal.

Planning their fake relationship out over dinner had actually helped alleviate some of the weird. It seemed way more doable to say they'd pretend for two dinners and one afternoon at MC rather than pretend for a whole week. So, he'd been right and things had started to feel more manageable and less…freaky.

And then they'd sat down in a dark movie theater next to each other and watched a movie that seemed to have a whole hell of a lot of sex in it.

Luckily no one could see in the dark that her face was bright, bright red. It wasn't as though she'd never seen a movie with sex in it; it was just…watching it with Jacob. Occasionally accidentally bumping arms. Oh, God, it was so weird.

When Jacob leaned over and whispered in her ear, she nearly jumped out of her chair.

"I have to go to the bathroom."

"Oh. Right." She awkwardly twisted sideways so he could get by. She glanced at the movie screen where the main couple was really going at it. Oh, *Jesus.* She couldn't do another second of this. She really couldn't.

She scurried out of the seat and down the aisle. The lobby was bright but lacking the grunting and "oh, baby" chorus, and she felt as if she could breathe again.

She situated herself near the exit of the men's bathroom. When Jacob *finally* appeared after what felt like hours, he gave her a quizzical frown.

"I'm sorry. I can't sit through any more of that movie with you."

Relief washed over his features. "Oh, thank God. Let's go home."

"Yes. Please."

The entire drive home was awkwardly silent. The stupid movie just kept playing over and over in Leah's head. Boobs and groans and butts. She couldn't erase it. It would be etched there for the remainder of time.

"Just FYI, we cannot tell my parents we saw that movie."

Jacob's laugh was a little rusty. "Noted."

"And we should probably never go to a movie we don't know much about without doing some research first."

"Agreed."

He pulled his truck into the back lot of MC. She

didn't dare look at him. Didn't dare say anything else except a goodbye.

"I...should head home."

"Right."

"Right." She pushed out of the truck, hopped onto the concrete. Her truck was parked up front, so she started along the walk in that direction.

"Leah?"

Oh, God. She didn't know why him calling her name filled her with dread; she only knew the last thing she wanted to do was turn around and answer him. Face him. But what choice did she have?

"This is going to come out all wrong," he said, walking toward her. He cleared his throat, stopping a couple feet away. In the dark, it was hard to see him, but the streetlamp gave her a general idea. "But that did get me thinking your parents are going to expect a certain level of...intimacy between us."

What? What? "But—"

"I'm not talking about sex," he was quick to say. Really quick. "I just mean, you're not very demonstrative as a rule. You don't even hug Grace, but they're going to expect you to hug your boyfriend. Hold hands. Kiss on the cheek at the very least."

Which was all true, but she didn't know what that had to do with...intimacy. Between them. Ahh. "Okay, so what's your point?"

He cleared his throat, took another step toward her. Made the throat-clearing sound again. "We need to be able to do that without you blushing and me clearing my throat like an eighty-year-old with a cold."

"And how do we do that?" she squeaked.

"You also can't squeak."

"Jacob."

"Maybe we should give it a go a few times with no one else looking or paying attention. Just so we can get those nerves and weirdness out of the way." Again he took a step toward her. She wanted to bolt. Run for the safety of her truck.

"I don't think that's possible." But it was sensible, and that was the only thing that kept her rooted to her spot as he advanced. Maybe she could at least get over the squeaking or the blushing. Or the insane urge to run in the opposite direction for fear of making a fool out of herself.

But once he was close. Really close. Like she could reach out and touch him and vice versa close, giving it a go seemed like the worst possible idea ever thought up.

His hand rested on her shoulder and she jumped.

"Oh, come on. It's not like I've never touched your shoulder."

"Well, not with, like…intimacy intentions!"

He chuckled at that. "Fake intimacy intentions."

"Right. Well, they may be fake, but it's still weird."

"Suck it up because it's about to get weirder."

And it did, but probably not in the way he thought she meant. He merely brushed a kiss across her cheek. His arm never strayed from her shoulder; he didn't linger. It was nothing, really, but her body did not seem to understand that *at all*. It heated from the inside out. It wanted to lean in. It wanted to press her mouth to his to see what that would be like.

Luckily she'd spent a lot of time making sure her mind ruled her body and not the other way around.

"Maybe we should try that again and this time you don't act like I gave you an electric shock."

Oh, God, again? She might spontaneously combust. "Maybe it'd be easier if *I* did it." She'd be in control, of the cheek kiss and herself, so it wouldn't be so…stupidly amazing.

"Okay."

Jacob wasn't that much taller than her, but she still had to kind of go on her toes to lean in while keeping herself far enough away so that their bodies weren't touching. Because that might kill her.

He smelled like sawdust and popcorn, which shouldn't be appealing but somehow was. How was this happening?

"I can't."

"Oh, just do it. I did it. You can do it."

Well, true enough. If she thought about it like a competition. If he could do it, so could she. She certainly wouldn't give Jacob any kind of upper hand.

No matter what kind of warped upper hand this was.

She leaned forward, balancing her hand on his shoulder as lightly as she could possibly manage, and quickly brushed her lips across his cheek. Enough to feel the stubble. Enough to *feel* and that was so bad. So very, very bad.

She swallowed, still kind of half standing on her tiptoes. Too close. Her mind told her she was way too close and it was time to step away, but for the first time in years, her body simply wasn't listening.

Even in the dark she could make out his eyes on her face. Maybe even her mouth. No, he would not be looking there because—

With no warning, no preamble, he dipped his head and pressed his mouth to hers. A kiss. A real on-the-mouth kiss. Brief. Brief enough she couldn't even react or reciprocate, and, oh, thank God for that.

He pulled away. "There. Now that's out of the way. Good night." And he stalked to the back door of the house.

And she…she was pretty sure she died.

JACOB STOOD IN the mudroom and scrubbed a hand over his face. He kept thinking if he scrubbed hard enough he could make some sense out of what had happened.

But he couldn't. He rubbed a little harder, then gave his hair a quick tug. Nope. He'd still kissed Leah. On the mouth. He'd done that.

And he could pretend it had been to get over the jumpy nerves between them. He could maybe even, after a few hours, convince himself it was completely platonic. It was all about the fake relationship.

And nothing about the way her lips had felt on his

skin, the gentle pressure of her hand on his shoulder, the smell of old house that lingered in her coat.

But he'd need a few hours to get there and to get the images from that damn movie out of his mind. Out of his imagination somehow tied up with Leah.

"Are you okay?"

Jacob laughed. He couldn't help it. Just the weirdest damn night of his life. He looked up at Grace standing at the top of the stairs and knew he had to manage a way to not seem guilty. She might think he couldn't lie, but she really didn't have a clue.

"What were you two doing?"

"What?"

"I heard your truck pull up at least fifteen minutes ago. What were you doing?"

If she was teasing him, maybe it wouldn't bother him, but she had that concerned big-sister look on her face and it blanketed all the uncertainty and weirdness and even the kind of giddy confusion.

"Don't."

"Don't what? I'm worried."

"We were talking. That's it. Don't make this into something I'm doing to hurt Leah. Because I'm helping her."

Right. Because kissing her was a real big help.

"Jacob, I don't know why you think I'm trying to hurt your feelings by being worried about you and Leah. I'm not saying you're a jerk. I'm only saying Leah looks at you a certain wa—"

"Just don't." And he walked away. Because if he

didn't, he'd get angry, or worse, he'd want to know *all* the ways Leah looked at him. He'd had enough angry this year, and he had no business thinking about his friend that way.

Not when Grace was right. For whatever reason, despite his best efforts, he couldn't make relationships work. And having something not work with Leah was never going to be an option.

CHAPTER SIX

LEAH DECIDED TO skip working on rewiring for the morning and focus on errands. Errands that could plausibly wait until, oh, say, next year, but she wasn't going to let herself dwell on that.

Because, yes, of course she was avoiding Jacob after last night. What the hell else would she be doing?

Leah sighed heavily and glanced at the stoplight. It was getting close to lunchtime. Usually when she was doing errands downtown around lunch and Grace was working, she'd text her and see if she could take a lunch break.

Leah didn't feel much like seeing Grace right now, either. Or Kelly or Susan, the rest of her MC family who would be back at the big house with Jacob, Susan doing her administrative duties or Kelly working on the interior design of the Council Bluffs project.

If she went back to MC and talked to them, she'd be tempted to tell them about Jacob kissing her and hell to the no.

She didn't know why she kept saying it like that.

He hadn't really kissed her. Okay, he had, but it was his let's-get-the-weirdness-out-of-our-system plan. Because if it was a real kiss you didn't say, "Now that's out of the way" directly after as if it was some dreaded chore you'd finally crossed off your list.

But damn. Damn. Damn. Damn. Quick. Surprising. Completely out of left field, and she still couldn't stop playing it over and over in her head. She hadn't even reacted in the moment. She could not read anything into it.

But that was exactly what her idiotic mind was doing.

The play of shadows. The contrast of cold air around her, except where he'd touched his mouth to hers.

Aw, crap, this was trouble.

Maybe what she really needed to do was plan a breakup. It was still a lie, but she wouldn't have to do this *stuff.*

Of course, then her mother would hover. Ask if she was okay. Start hinting Leah should move back to Minnesota so someone could watch after her. Just in case.

Just in case.

As an adult she could find more understanding in her mother's smothering. As a teenager it just felt like an affront, but now she could see it through the lens of a mother desperately worried about her daughter's health. A legitimate worry considering.

Leah wanted to be able to let that understanding

make her easy with it. Accept it without having to make up a boyfriend. Maybe even accept it enough that the thought of moving back to Minnesota didn't make her throat close up with anxiety.

But she lacked whatever decency would allow that.

She needed her space, her autonomy. She'd never be considered 100 percent healthy, but she was the healthiest she'd ever been. She managed her allergies and her asthma, except for when she was cleaning the other night. She took her medication, only occasionally indulged in alcohol. Ate rightish. Exercised more often than not.

It had to mean something. Not just that she could take care of herself, but that she wanted to. Needed to in order to be happy.

Leah drove back to MC with a heavy weight in her chest. It was strange that this impending visit from her family could twist her up in knots, push all those old insecurities and suffocating feelings to the forefront when all she wanted was the family that had caused those feelings.

She wanted Mom to send her care packages with homemade nut-free cookies. She wanted to talk with Dad over a car engine. She wanted to tease her big brother about being as straight as an arrow stick in the mud.

She'd lost all that in the self-destructive years. The support, the comfort, the *family*. She didn't want their suffocating ways of showing they loved her, but she did want their love.

Maybe it was too much to ask for. Maybe she simply wasn't cut out for it.

She groaned into the silence of her truck cab. Once she pushed it into Park, she rested her head on the steering wheel.

She was not going down the self-pity hole. If the past seven years had shown her anything, it was that she was capable of building the life she wanted. So, all she had to do was keep working at it.

And if that meant things getting momentarily weird with Jacob, well, she'd survive it. She'd survived a lot more than some weird inappropriate crush and a fake relationship.

On a deep breath and determined shoulder straightening, she stepped out of her truck and walked into the back entrance of MC.

Voices drifted through the mudroom from the kitchen.

"You're so good with babies, Jacob."

Leah stepped into the kitchen and immediately wished she'd gone to her work shed instead. Because Jacob standing in the middle of the kitchen holding Kelly and Susan's one-month-old girl was just... Was this some kind of karmic punishment for lying to her parents?

But of course, there he was, holding a freaking adorable baby on his hip. Might as well have a puppy lying at his feet and dinner he made on the stove. While doing the ironing.

Well, not with the baby nearby.

Get a grip, you lunatic.

"Hey, you didn't tell me it was a baby day. I would have put off errands." Probably not, but she was happy for her friends. Adopting little Presleigh had been something the pair had been working toward for a long time.

And here they were, a pretty little family. She'd focus on that instead of Jacob cooing at a baby. Because, really, karma *was* a bitch.

"You want a turn to hold her?" Kelly asked.

"Oh, she's going to need to firm up a bit before you let me near her."

Susan rolled her eyes, but smiled.

God, babies made her uncomfortable. All that love and need and…expectation. She'd done a pretty good job of hiding that fact from Kelly and Susan, using humor to mask her discomfort. Lack of experience to excuse holding or interacting too much with the gorgeous bundle of blankets.

"How can you be afraid of babies?" Jacob demanded, smiling broadly at Presleigh.

Leah was pretty sure this was killing her. "I'm not afraid. They're just all soft and…bobbly. I don't know what I'm doing."

"It's easy."

"Oh, don't push her. It is something to get used to if you haven't been around babies much. I think it took me a week to stop shaking every time I picked her up." Kelly gave Leah a reassuring smile.

Presleigh fussed and Jacob easily maneuvered her onto his shoulder, crooning soothing words and patting her back.

Leah was pretty sure her ovaries exploded.

And then the baby spit up a bunch of white curdly goo down Jacob's shoulder and back. Ick. Ovaries back in place.

"Well, that is unpleasant," Jacob said, though his tone was amused rather than upset. He handed the baby off to Susan, grabbed a rag out of a drawer and tried to wipe off the offensive fluids.

"Give me a hand here, huh?"

Aw, crap, he meant her. Leah crossed to him and took the rag and gingerly wiped at the spot on Jacob's back. He glanced over his shoulder at her, and for the love of God, why was she blushing at that? *Because you are loony tunes, Santino.*

"There," she muttered, handing the rag back to him, avoiding all eye contact.

Jacob's phone dinged. "Conference call," he said, and since she refused to look at him she had no idea if he was looking at her or what. And then he left, thank God. Her whole body relaxed, until she turned to face Kelly and Susan.

Susan stood next to a sitting Kelly, who was now bouncing the baby on her lap, but all three of them were staring at her, heads cocked in identical scrutiny. Okay, not the baby, but Leah wouldn't put it past the itty-bitty creature with big blue eyes to be scrutinizing, too.

"So…" Kelly offered.

"So what?" Leah crossed her arms defensively.

"Did you guys sleep together or something?"

"What?" Leah screeched.

"That was weird. Like…sex weird."

"No, it wasn't. We did not have sex, and we're not going to have sex, you nut jobs. I just…asked him a kind of weird favor and we're still working everything out."

"Was the favor sex?"

"Good Lord. Do you have sex on the brain? And should you even be talking about sex around your baby? Isn't that kind of wrong?"

Kelly shrugged. "Maybe."

"He's…just going to pretend to be my boyfriend while my family is here. It's nothing. Except a little weird. But definitely not *sex* weird."

Kelly and Susan exchanged a look and Leah groaned. "Save me your married looks and your disbelief. It's just…it's just…"

Kelly and Susan waited expectantly, but Leah didn't even know what she was arguing at this point. She was flustered and embarrassed and about two seconds away from confessing the weird pseudokiss last night. Because these were her friends and usually she confided in them about all manner of man stuff, but this was all wrapped up in stuff she told nobody.

Besides, if she confessed the fake kiss, then they'd

really think this was about sex. "It's nothing. I have work to do." She stomped off and repeated those seven words over and over in her head, hoping desperately that they were true.

LEAH WASN'T GOING to like it, but Jacob was used to doing things Leah didn't like. And, okay, maybe he got a little thrill out of riling her up. Maybe.

He stood on her porch trying to ignore the prick of conscience. This was a little bit of a line cross, especially considering he'd kissed her last night. And she had acted incredibly uncomfortable around him all day.

He supposed that should bother him. But it didn't. Not in the way it should. He didn't feel bad or want to get rid of it.

He wanted to explore it. He wondered, way too much in the span of twenty-four hours, What exactly might be the harm? *Aside from screwing everything up, remember?*

He was having a hell of a time remembering.

He knocked on Leah's door. Kyle's and Grace's disapproving faces annoyingly popped into his mind, but he pushed them away. He wasn't a complete and utter moron. He could keep his hands to himself.

He could also not keep his hands to himself without ruining everything.

Okay, if history served, that wasn't true at all, but he'd never exactly gotten handsy with someone he'd been friends with first before.

And when you were a twenty-eight-year-old man using the word *handsy* in your internal monologue, you really, really needed to get a grip.

"What are you doing here?" Leah demanded, not even opening the door the entire way. In fact, she seemed to be using it as somewhat of a shield.

Jacob held up his toolbox. "We have work to do."

"I told you—"

"And you really thought I'd let that stand in my way?" He shifted from foot to foot. "I'm freezing very important bits off here. Please let me in."

She cursed and grumbled, but the door swung open and he stepped into the warmth of her cluttered entryway. She was wearing an oversize sweatshirt, baggy sweatpants and her hair was a haphazard mess on her head.

He made himself look at her face instead of the freckled shoulder exposed by the too-big neckline of her sweatshirt.

"You know Friday is only three days away, right?"

She glared at him. "Cleanliness isn't my strong suit. I get it. I'm trying to work on it, but—"

"But it's impossible to put your shoes where they belong?"

"But I like doing things *my* way. Which is why I don't want you butting in on that third room."

"I can't take it. It's eating me alive. Just sitting there in disrepair. Let me. Please." He grinned at her because he knew at least this was their common ground. House stuff. Restoration. They could disagree about everything but this passion they shared.

Do not think about the word passion.

She pressed her lips together in the way she did when she was trying not to smile. Some days he tried to poke out the smile as much as he tried to get under her skin.

"It is hard to say no when you say please."

"I'll keep that in mind." He didn't exactly mean for that to sound suggestive; it just came out that way. She turned away and he wondered if she was blushing. Like this afternoon when she'd wiped baby spit-up off his back. That was a weird moment. Weird in its domesticity and proximity and everything.

Christ, what are you doing?

He was going to do a little restoration work, that was what he was doing. He nodded, following Leah to her extra room. He'd lose himself in measuring and planning and he wouldn't think about Leah that way and if he did...

Grace's words niggled at him. *Be careful with her. I don't want to see her get hurt.*

Aaaand now he felt vaguely sleazy even if he did consider Grace's admonitions ridiculous.

He needed to start dating again. All this alone time really screwed with his mind.

"Ah, my precious." He set his toolbox down, immediately going for the measuring tape and notebook he'd jotted notes down in the other day. "How can you stand it?"

"The same way I stand a lot of things. Willful ignorance," she muttered. Then she glanced around the room. "We have four days. What can we do?"

"I don't have any pressing business this week. I can get the floor done tomorrow."

"Too much damage to get it done in one day even if I help you. Besides, I don't have the money for this."

"Well…"

"No."

He hated the way she shut him down before he even suggested anything. She was always doing that. As if she could read his mind. Except, obviously she couldn't or they would be doing a lot more interesting things than talking about money and floors.

Or maybe she was just being sensible. Which was also quintessentially Leah.

"A loan."

"You already sign off on my paycheck, asshole. You're not giving me money."

"Asshole? Seriously? Calling the man who signs your checks 'asshole' seems like a bad move."

She pinched the bridge of her nose. "Oh, you are giving me a headache."

"You invested in MC. We can cash you out."

She dropped her arm, blinked incredulously. "So then I'm *not* invested in MC?"

Okay, he hadn't thought that through. "Just take a damn loan, Leah."

"Take a damn step back, Jacob." She glared, so he glared back. This was often where they ended up. And yet, at the end of the day, they still walked away friends.

It was one of the few things in his life he couldn't work out.

"Why are you really here?" she asked, sounding far more exhausted than she looked.

She looked rumpled and pretty. Usually she had that tough-girl exterior, all put together like armor. But in her slouchy clothes and with her messy hair, obviously tired and fed up with him, she looked infinitely touchable. "Do you really want to know?"

She looked away. "No," she grumbled. "You're right. I don't."

"Well, then let's talk about drywall."

"No. I'm closing the door. They're not going to see it, and on the off chance they ask why my contractor boyfriend hasn't had his grubby paws all over it, I'll tell them the truth. I can't afford it. I have one guest room suitable for my parents, and Marc can crash comfortably on the pullout couch. It's *fine*."

Another thing he couldn't work out was how easily she irritated the crap out of him just by being so damn reasonable. Because she wasn't wrong, and he wasn't right and he hated that.

"Fine. You're right."

"I'm sorry—can you repeat that?"

He scowled. "Bite me."

She smiled and it didn't take that clingy red dress from the party for him to think about the fact her bedroom was right across the hall.

Yeah, seriously, why had he come here? Did he really think he was just going to walk in and redo this room? No, he'd been thinking...well, not thinking. Feeling. Restless.

Maybe he needed to tell Grace to be his babysitter because he couldn't trust himself with the idea of a "thing" hanging between them.

"Why don't we talk about why you really came here?"

"I thought you didn't want to."

"Well, maybe we need to." She looked up at him, brow furrowed, blue-green eyes shading toward blue in the darker light. "Why did you kiss me?"

Full truth or half-truth? In this case, as much as he *wanted* to let the full truth go, the half-truth was the right way to go. Knowing Leah had some kind of low-level interest in him didn't change a thing because she hadn't acted on it. Not once in five years.

And he hadn't, either. The red dress certainly wasn't the first time he'd thought of Leah inappropriately. This whole pretending-to-be-involved thing was bringing it to the forefront, but he'd been reasonable for five years, too.

Maybe if he wrote it on his palms he'd remember that before barreling over here whole hog again.

Yeah, half-truth was the way to go. "We're going to have to."

"Why on earth would we have to?" Throwing her hands in the air, she stalked away from him, then back. "People don't make out in front of their parents."

"It was a peck on the lips. Your parents are going to expect that. If there aren't at least some teeny tiny gestures of affection, they're going to think we're not happy, and if your mom really is so desperate for you to have a significant other, she's not going to want to see you unhappy."

"But…"

"You know I'm right. I'm sorry kissing me was such a terrible hardship for you, but this was your idea."

She didn't say anything about it being a hardship or not, and maybe it was idiotic of him to hope she would. Maybe actually kissing her had killed whatever "thing" Grace thought Leah had for him, because it had been the lamest kiss of all time. And maybe that was a good thing. Too bad it hadn't done the same for him.

"Who knew you could think like this?" she finally said.

"Like what?"

"Like…all devious and good at lying. I just… It's not something I would've given you credit for."

"Leave it to you, Leah, to give someone credit

for being devious and good at lying. I told you I've had practice."

"But you won't tell me what. Is MC some kind of drug front?"

He spared her a withering look. "Really?"

She crossed her arms over her chest, stubborn glare fixed on her face. "Tell me."

He could argue. He could walk away. He could do a lot of things, but, eh, why not tell her? Maybe she'd trust some of his suggestions if he did. "Okay, you asked for it. When I was in high school, my mom was diagnosed with breast cancer."

Her expression, her stance, it all softened. "I... didn't know that."

"Neither do I, technically."

"Huh?"

"Mom didn't want to tell anyone. Not wanting people to worry and all that bullshit. Grace found out somehow, but they decided to keep it from me."

"But you knew."

"Of course I knew. But they didn't want me to, so I pretended like I didn't. I figured I could give them that. But, let me tell you, it wasn't easy to do. It is not easy to watch your mom lose a ton of weight, not easy to pretend the wig she was wearing was real. And it's really not easy to watch her pretend everything is fine when all the while she's practically dying. It takes real skill to pretend that doesn't exist."

The silence between them filled him with an unfamiliar panic. He'd never told anyone that before.

Mom and Dad and Grace still thought he was clueless. He'd never confided in Kyle or anyone else at the time, and it had never seemed pertinent after.

"Jacob."

"It's not a big deal." He suddenly felt very uncomfortable. Uncomfortable enough that he had to move. And not look at her. And move. He walked around the room, poking at peeling plaster and warped floorboards.

But eventually the silence was too much, and when he looked up, she was still standing in the same place, watching him with a kind of pained look.

"What?"

"It's…" She swallowed, and if it was anyone besides Leah he might think the bright sheen to her eyes meant she was about to cry. But Leah… He could not picture Leah crying.

"I think the fact that at sixteen or whatever you… carried that burden and didn't tell anyone. I think that is really…amazing. I was not that together as a teenager. Not even a little."

He shrugged because it hadn't been about being together. It hadn't been about anything except doing what they wanted. Sure, he'd been scared and it hadn't been easy not to hug Mom a little more tightly, stay home instead of hanging out with his friends. It wasn't easy, but it was just…what had to be done.

She touched his elbow, her fingers curling around his arm. She swallowed again. "I really do think that's amazing."

The compliment made his chest ache in a way that was entirely new to him. It wasn't exactly a pain, just a kind of weird…pressure. The fact that she thought this was such a big thing made it feel bigger even though it was twelve years ago.

"Well, you know, you do what you have to do for family."

She nodded. Obviously she agreed. They were doing this ridiculous pretending thing. But she wasn't letting go of his arm. Her hand held him there in a tight grip.

And that meant he couldn't step away, and it meant stepping closer was too tempting to resist.

Her eyes didn't leave his, and she didn't move away. They just…stood there, and all he could think about was last night when he'd kissed her. A nothing kiss. Seconds at most, born of some weird frustration and none of the heat or sparks he felt standing right here, right now.

He could kiss her this time and it wouldn't be veiled in pretend, and it would be a hell of a lot better than a peck in the dark.

But in the heaviness of the moment, he couldn't force himself to act, thinking or not. It felt too important. Everything between them felt too important to complicate with a kiss.

This was getting…out of hand. He wasn't thinking, and that was just not something that usually happened. He was almost always thinking and planning and anticipating, but this was…

He cleared his throat. "Why don't we talk about your family? They're going to expect me to know some things, and I know nothing. Except you've had some problems."

She took a step back. "Yeah." She shoved fingers through her hair, loosening the tenuous pile even more. "And a drink. I need a drink."

Yeah, he could definitely use a drink. Or ten.

CHAPTER SEVEN

LEAH LEANED HER head into the fridge and prayed for divine intervention. Like maybe a lightning bolt to strike her dead. Well, maybe not dead. But it would ideally cause enough of a distraction.

Sadly, no lightning bolts descended, no roofs collapsed. Nope, she had to sit down with Jacob and talk about her family after…that.

"Can't find anything?"

Right. She was supposed to be finding beer. She made a big production out of moving things around, then pulled out two bottles.

Jacob wrinkled his nose. "You seriously drink that stuff?"

"Sorry I'm not a hipster into autumnal blends."

"It's not being a hipster. It's having taste buds." But he took the offered bottle and slid into the seat at her little kitchen table. The table itself was cluttered with mail and various winter garments like hats and scarves, but she'd kept stuff off the chairs and the counters all weekend, so she was getting better in the tidying department. Betterish.

She slid into the seat across from him, pulling

her sleeve over her hand and screwing the cap of the bottle off. Jacob did the same, glancing around her kitchen. She imagined he found it lacking. Or cluttered. Or both. But he didn't say anything. His gaze turned to her in that considering, heart-jitter-inducing way he had.

"Your family."

Yes. That was the topic they were discussing. "Right. Well, Dad's a mechanic, Mom's a lunch lady and my brother, Marc… He's a cop."

"And they live in Minnesota?"

"Yeah." It was weird talking about them, even these minor, glossed-over details. It was weird thinking about them and thinking about Jacob. It was still so much like two different lives. Two different Leahs.

"Come on, Leah. You've met my parents. Eaten with them. Listened to my dad's jokes. My mom has forcibly hugged you. Think about the things you know about them and tell me the same stuff about yours."

How could he be so rational? How could he be so smart about this while she was just a floundering idiot? She thought about his story and pretending he didn't know his mom was sick and her heart ached for him.

Because even with Jacob's secret, he was close with his family. The McKnights weren't perfect, exactly, but they had the kind of family togetherness

Leah had envied in her lesser moments. They talked; they hugged; they loved.

God, what a story. At the age she'd started drinking and sneaking out because she was tired of being confined to hospital beds and being admonished to take it easy, he'd carried the burden and fear of knowing his mother was fighting a possibly life-ending illness. All because he knew that was what she wanted.

If she thought too hard about that…about what it might mean if extended to her, she'd make a grave mistake. So she focused on what she knew about the McKnights.

"My mom makes the best cannoli." She shook her head. "That's dumb."

"No. It's perfect. Then I can say, 'Mrs. Santino, I hear you make the most amazing cannoli.' And then I can quote *The Godfather*. Perfect."

Leah sighed, resting her chin on her hand. "She's going to love you." And Mom would, because on the surface, Jacob was perfect. Handsome and successful and good with people. He would schmooze Mom, win over Dad, buddy up to Marc.

Jacob grinned. "You say that like it's a bad thing."

"It's going to make it a little harder when I have to tell them we broke up." She fiddled with the label on the bottle she'd yet to take a sip from. She could tell them that now, avoid this whole pretending thing. Self-preservation.

But the only self it would preserve was the one

idiotically wrapped up in her kind of boss/friend. In a man she knew couldn't make a relationship work, especially with her and all her baggage. And she'd be sacrificing the girl who desperately wanted her family back.

So here it was, and here they were.

"A year is a long time to date someone, then break up. What's the plan there?"

"I guess I'd kind of hoped I'd find someone real eventually. But, yeah, I'm not sure how much longer I can hold out hope for that." Hard to build a lasting relationship when you had a huge lie about yourself written all over the scar on your chest.

"I guess I hope they'll see the life I've built here and maybe see…I'm not the idiot screwup they need to smother anymore."

"What did you do that was so bad?"

"Oh, you know." She shrugged and shifted in her seat. "Teenage crap." Not really a lie. Wasn't teenagehood the time for self-destruction and nearly killing yourself with bad choices?

"Like what?"

"Trust me when I say my parents aren't going to talk about that."

He frowned. "Maybe I'm not asking as part of the pretend thing."

"I thought that's what this was supposed to be. Preparation for the big masquerade."

"We're friends. I've known you for over five years. We spend a ridiculous amount of time together, and even knowing you didn't have a close family, I never would have pegged you as a teenage rebel. Unless by rebellious you mean having a mouth like a sailor and the cleaning habits of a prepubescent boy."

"No."

"So tell me."

Ten years she'd spent working out lies to answer these kinds of questions. She kept her scar hidden, downplayed the trajectory of her adolescence. It was like second nature to diminish, to lie, to put it all away.

It was frightening how much she didn't want to do that with Jacob. The truth was a million words in her head, dying to get out. Dying to see if he'd do what he'd done as a teenager for his mom, pretend it didn't exist.

Damn.

"I had a lot of health problems, and I didn't always deal with them very well. And sometimes I made decisions I knew would put me in danger."

"Well, that's the vaguest story I've ever heard."

Leah shoved away from the table. She couldn't do this. And it wasn't just because it was Jacob and that moment in the spare room still had her all warm and gooey and tied up in a million indescribable knots. It was because she really hated remembering, reliving, rehashing those years.

It made everything feel small again. The embarrassment, disgust with herself, just…ugh. No.

"I don't like to talk about it or think about it or

anything. I left home when I was eighteen and I didn't talk to them for five years. And for the next four it was all sporadic and weird and only this year have we finally started to find a way to make it work, and I want to focus on that. On the future."

She knew he was watching her, but she leaned against the sink and refused to turn around. "I sucked. Then I left and I got my life together and things got better for them and The End."

When his hand touched her shoulder, she tensed. Partially because a little piece of her sighed dreamily and dreamed about leaning into him. How about hell no?

"Leah." He squeezed. It was all friendly. Nothing he hadn't done before. Nothing she hadn't pretended didn't affect her. "You don't have to get upset. I won't press."

"Well, good."

But he didn't move and his warm hand was on her shoulder and what was this? All of this? Because she'd caught his meaning earlier. He wasn't here to fix the room. Not really. And he wasn't here to learn how to play her parents.

He'd come for other reasons. Reasons she'd told him she didn't want to hear. Because she didn't. Couldn't. She'd learned a lot of lessons from her dark days, but coming out of them had taught her that ignoring and pretending solved a lot of problems.

But when she looked up at Jacob, he was studying

her. Particularly her mouth, oh, Jesus. The part of her brain that knew better kind of stuttered to a stop.

She could kiss him, and he'd probably even kiss her back. She knew he'd been on his stupid no-dating thing for months. She could probably even convince him to have sex with her.

And then what? What the hell good would come out of that except a few minutes of probably awesome? All that would be left after was awkwardness, embarrassment and the crumbling of this new life she'd built.

"Maybe you should go," she said, a little disgusted with herself when her voice wasn't steady.

He released her shoulder, but he didn't walk away. Instead, he slid right back into the chair he'd vacated, took a sip of his beer. "You still have a father and brother to tell me about."

Leah slumped against the counter. What was she doing? What was *he* doing? She didn't have a clue. All she knew was she didn't have a choice.

JACOB WONDERED IF she had any idea the way her expressions changed as she worked through a problem. Bafflement. Irritation. Gritty-eyed determination.

It wasn't the first time he'd noticed it, but he'd worked on ignoring it over the years. Because otherwise it became a fascination. Reading Leah. Odd, it had become such normal practice *to* ignore Leah that paying attention to her was like discovering her all over again.

Yeah, he was really losing it.

"What else do you think you need to know?" She eyed him warily as she took the seat across from him. She still had yet to touch her beer.

"Tell me about your dad."

"I told you. He's a mechanic."

"Oh, yes. 'Hello, Mr. Santino. Leah tells me you're a mechanic. That's it, really. Now, me? I know nothing about cars. So we should have lots to talk about.'"

Leah glared, but he countered it with a grin. "Give me something I can work with, baby."

"Baby? Baby? Are you serious?"

"Okay, *baby*'s out. How about Honeysuckle?"

"How about that beer must have been infected with a hallucinogenic?"

Jacob laughed. "I really pegged you for the endearment type."

"Here's an endearment for you, asshole." But she was smiling, and the comforting banter they were so used to defused some of that…weirdness. Touching weirdness. Moment weirdness. As much as he kind of wanted to explore that, he didn't like the way she got all tense. Making her uncomfortable was never his intention. Irritated, sure, but not uncomfortable.

"Dad loves Robert Frost."

"Robert Frost?"

"Yeah, the poet? He always talked about how much he hated poetry, which my mother loves. And the only poet he ever liked was Robert Frost. So he used to recite 'A Line-storm Song.'" She smiled, picking at the label of her bottle. "'The line-storm clouds fly tattered and swift, The road is forlorn all day.'"

"Leah Santino reciting poetry. Well. You never cease to amaze me."

She leveled him with a steely glare, but her mouth curved into a smile. "I said *he* recited it. Whenever he was in trouble with Mom. Which was frequently. Thus, I remember."

"Tell me the rest."

"Ha. No."

"Come on."

"You're that interested, look it up."

"Just one more line. Please. You said you couldn't resist my 'please.'" He flashed his most charming grin and she took her first sip of beer. *Sip* was really too dainty of a word. It was more like a gulp.

He should *not* like that.

"He'd never get much farther than the first verse-thingy. He'd say 'Come over the hills and far with me, And be my love in the rain.' And have Mom in the palm of his hand."

"That's nice."

"Yeah. Well." But she was smiling, obviously remembering something good. What could have gone so wrong to have her not speaking to them for *years*? He barely went *days* without at least texting one of his parents.

"So, is that what I need in my romantic life? Some

poetry. Then I won't get unceremoniously dumped after a few weeks."

She shook her head. "You seriously don't know why you get unceremoniously dumped all the time?"

"Apparently I have terrible taste in women." Although, Leah wasn't his usual type. But she was off-limits. Which he seemed to be doing an okay job of remembering when push came to shove.

"You know that's not the problem, right? Please tell me you've figured that out."

"What do you mean?"

"It's not them, Jacob. It is so you. Don't get me wrong—some of them sucked. But most of them were just women. And them breaking up with you… That was all you."

He straightened in his chair. "How can that even mathematically be possible?" He was a little tired of everyone believing *he* was the problem. Okay, maybe sometimes he was, but surely not all the time.

"You know how you get when you've got your eye on a new project? You start taking notes and making up plans before you even have the property or the measurements. You probably already have a list of the things you want to do to the Jasmine Street house, in the order you're going to do them, with pricing all figured out."

He shifted in his seat, scowling at his beer. *Well, so what?*

"You get this idea and run with it, planning every inch before you even know what you've got."

"Now you're insulting my business practices?"

"No, it's not an insult. You're passionate. But that doesn't work with people. Houses you can change. You can knock out a wall and put a cabinet over that pipe. People are people. You see a woman you think is attractive and you think, *What do I have to do to get her to be the one?* You don't ask if she *is* the one. You go about trying to manipulate the relationship into where you want it to go. They're a project, not a partner."

"That's not… That's…"

"It's right-on. And a woman doesn't want to be a project, even for as wonderful as you can be. If you don't see them, what's the point?"

"You believe there's some magical one for everyone?"

"No, but you have your eyes set on finding a wife."

"I…do…not…"

"Please. I've watched… I mean, I've known you for five years. It doesn't take a brain surgeon to notice you get the same master-planner light in your eye when you see a dilapidated house *and* an attractive woman."

"You've been paying attention."

She looked down, and just the faintest tinge of pink spread across the fair skin of her cheeks. "Hard not to when they're a revolving door. And that's another thing—you're never alone. At least not before your embargo. Half those women you dated were probably just because you were bored or lonely."

"I am not lonely and I don't manipulate people." Okay, so maybe he got a little antsy when he was by himself and didn't have work to do. Still. Lonely and antsy were two very different things.

She shook her head, her eyes meeting his again as the embarrassment seemed to fade away. "No. You're sweet and kind—don't get me wrong. You just get this preconceived notion of how a relationship should go before you even start it. Then you try to control everything to make it so. And I think your intentions are honest and good, but that tactic doesn't work."

"So, how's it supposed to work, Ms. Expert?"

She shook her head, looking a little sad. "I'm not saying I'm an expert. I'm just saying people don't want to be controlled. They don't want to be maneuvered. People just want to be able to be themselves."

"Did some asshole break your heart?"

She laughed, but when her eyes met his, something squeezed painfully in his chest. And since he wasn't a big fan of pain, he pushed it away. He'd ignore whatever that was. Whatever it meant.

"I think I've broken my own heart plenty, without the help of anyone else." She pressed a palm over her heart, a faraway look on her face as if she was thinking about something else. Maybe even someone else and that also gave him a little stab of pain. "But you can't keep bashing against the same wall hoping it will break. You have to change."

"Or maybe I just need to find the right person."

She shook her head. "You're not getting it."

"Maybe you're wrong." He really wanted her to be wrong. She had to be. He'd been alone for months now, which sucked, but he'd done it. And he didn't treat people like houses. Man, if he could do that, things would be a hell of a lot easier.

Leah didn't say anything else, and since he'd finished his beer, he pushed away from the table. "I should probably head out. It's getting late."

She nodded wordlessly and followed him toward the door. He reached to pull it open, but her next words completely stopped him.

"So, I'm sorry."

"You're...sorry?" He turned around slowly. "Are you...having a stroke?"

She sighed. "You're doing this big crazy favor and maybe I shouldn't have said the stuff about...relationships." She looked at her feet, then muttered a quick "Even if I'm right" at the end.

"That is possibly the worst apology I have ever received."

"I'll try to find worse for next time."

He couldn't help grinning, and she grinned back, and they were back on even ground. No weird moments. No wondering what it might be like... Nope.

She shrugged and looked away. "Anyway."

"Listen, it's going to be okay. In fact, everything is going to work out just fine." And he really did believe that. Leah wouldn't have asked him for this if it wasn't necessary, and he was very good at making necessary things happen.

"How can you be so sure?"

"Because I have a blueprint. And I will manipulate the situation to go exactly as I want," he said in a robot voice.

She shook her head in disgust. "Good night, Jacob. Work on letting that one go in the next ten years."

"Hmm. We'll see. Now, before I go, I'm going to kiss you on the cheek and you're not going to jump like I've zapped you with a cattle prod."

She rolled her eyes, but he saw the nervous swallow before she turned her cheek toward him.

It was a mistake, but as far as he was concerned, it was a harmless one. He rested his palm against the cheek she offered, let his fingers glance across her hair. He leaned forward, then gently turned her face the other way.

"I prefer this cheek," he said softly, mouth way too close to hers. Briefly he thought about kissing her again there. Lingering. A real kiss, not some crazed outburst. But that would be a mistake that wasn't harmless, so he brushed his lips against the soft skin of her not-offered cheek and then stepped back.

"Night," she said, her voice firm and sure. Her expression looking anything but those two things.

He nodded, though, because lingering was unacceptable, and turned to walk to his truck. Something heavy weighed on his chest, so he couldn't resist a joke. "Make sure to ogle my ass as I walk away.

Then your parents will really believe you can't keep your hands off me."

"Your ego is astounding."

Jacob laughed, offering a wave as he glanced back. Maybe it was a trick of the light, a figment of his imagination, really ill-advised wishful thinking, but he could swear she *was* staring at his ass.

It was definitely going to be a long week of pretend. Lots of different kinds of pretending.

CHAPTER EIGHT

LEAH WATCHED OUT her front window with her heart in her throat. She wiped sweaty palms against the thighs of her jeans. Ten years since she'd seen her parents and brother face-to-face, and they should be arriving any minute.

Why did she think she needed to do this? Was it really necessary to go through all this pain? She liked her life, had a support group of friends she cared deeply for. Did she really need her family back?

She glanced at the clock. They were pretty close, according to her brother's text. Everything in her chest jittered and ached. Another glance out the window and she saw the familiar blue minivan.

How the thing was still running fifteen years later was something of a miracle. The engine was probably held together by duct tape at this point, but Dad had a way with eking every last ounce of goody out of an engine.

The nerves weighing down her stomach made her sick, but she still hurried to the door and slipped her feet into boots and her arms into her coat. As she stepped outside into the frigid afternoon, she wondered how she was going to navigate all this heavy awkwardness.

And then Mom stepped out of the passenger side, and tears sprang unbidden to Leah's eyes.

Ten years had changed her, changed them all, and yet the recognition was immediate. Leah had been afraid there would be awkwardness. A kind of stilted not knowing how to be around each other, but the moment her eyes locked with her mother's, nothing else mattered.

She crossed to her mom and they had their arms around each other almost immediately. Leah had never been much of a crier; she'd built an intolerance to it over the years of being poked and prodded and sliced open. But today, standing in the middle of her driveway, hugging her mom for the first time in ten years, she sobbed like a baby.

She wasn't sure how long they held on to each other. Her tears or her mother's or both all but freezing to her face and neck. Finally Mom pulled away, grasping Leah's face between her palms.

"My beautiful girl."

Leah didn't even try to get herself together. It was no use. This was…big and messy and emotional, and no amount of toughness or pretending it wasn't would change that.

"Hi, Mom." Time had added wrinkles and gray. Where Leah's memory was a thin woman with long, curly hair, Mom was now pleasantly plump, her hair a curly bob.

But nothing had changed the amber color of her eyes, watery as they were. Nothing had erased the way she said "my beautiful girl" with all the reverence of prayer. And nothing had changed that grip. Once upon a time, that hug had been stifling and suffocating, but today it felt like heaven.

She glanced beyond Mom to Dad. He looked infinitely older. Not just in wrinkles and weight and gray, but just all-around like an old man. And still, when she looked at him, shiny blue eyes and that kind of pained hope on his face—so much like when she remembered waking up after the transplant. He'd looked at her just like that.

And when she moved to hug him, and his arms tightened around her shoulders, he smelled exactly the same as she always remembered. Peppermint and grease. It was comfort and home and she breathed it in deep.

She could have stayed out here all day, just being held by them, crying over them, but it was freezing and they weren't wearing coats. "Let's get inside before everyone freezes to death."

Finally, she glanced at Marc. Her big brother. They'd never been especially close considering she'd been born a sickly blob of problems that he'd always been cautioned to be careful with. So this reunion was a little more awkward. Plus there had been the whole their-parents-separated-because-of-her thing.

"Hey, sis," he offered, a corner of his mouth quirking upward. "You look…well, all grown-up."

She had to swallow to speak. "I hear that happens in ten years." He looked grown-up, too. At four years older, he'd still been only twenty-two when she'd left. Just a year out of the police academy. At the time, he'd seemed so old and put together and just frustratingly in charge of himself, but ten years apart made her realize even if he had been those things, he'd still been baby faced and young.

Now he was thirty-two, his dark hair still cropped short, little lines around his amber eyes, so much like Mom's. He was a man. A man she knew even less than the older brother who'd always been something of a silent enigma.

"It's good to see you looking well," he said, so formally it hurt her heart. But as he stepped inside her house, he gave her shoulder a squeeze. And, hey, it was something.

"I do okay these days." She shed her coat and kicked off her shoes, remembering at the last minute to put them in the closet instead of haphazardly in the entryway. "So, um, come in. It's a bit of a work in progress. The house had been abandoned for about ten years when I bought it, so, you know. Some things are still a bit of a mess."

Mom's arms linked with hers. "It's lovely. My goodness, how handy you are. Well, I assume your man helped."

Leah had to focus not to tense. "Yeah, Jacob helped a lot."

"I love the name Jacob. Such a sturdy, solid name. When do we get to meet him?"

"He's coming for dinner tomorrow night." How were they already talking about this?

"What's wrong with tonight?"

"Oh. Well, I thought you'd want to settle in. Get used to everything. You know…" Get reacquainted. Be a family.

"Nonsense. He's responsible for all this, isn't he? He should be here."

"Responsible?"

"Don't think it escaped my notice that you didn't really reach out to us until you had him in your life. I need to meet him immediately." She squeezed Leah's arm. "I absolutely need to meet the man who brought you back to us."

It took great pains to swallow down the words she desperately wanted to say. *I'm the one who brought me back to you.* "He probably has plans, Mom. I had hoped—"

"Doesn't hurt to ask. Why don't you go call him up while we unload?"

"Mom. I…" But what was the use? Wasn't that the *point* of using Jacob? The fact she knew she couldn't get it through her mother's head that she did not *need* a man. A man had not *fixed* her. That was just what Mom thought. There was no getting around it.

"All right. I'll call him." She forced her mouth into

a smile. This was part of it. Her penance for the hug. For leaving. For everything. She would just have to grin and bear this little point she and her mother did not agree on.

Because, at the end of the day, that hug had been worth it. Feeling her mother's arms around her, hearing her say "my beautiful girl." It was worth it. That love, that care was worth the things she didn't agree with.

She took a deep breath and let it out, then pulled out her phone and called Jacob.

IT WAS WEIRD to be nervous. Jacob couldn't help it. This was not real in any way, shape or form, but his palms were kind of sweaty and his stomach was definitely uneasy.

It was just the lying part. The acting part. Sure, he did a decent job, but it was still nerve-racking. So many ways to slip up. Of course, none of those really affected *him*. This was Leah's lie, and if her parents found out, there were no consequences for him.

Except Leah's disappointment. Which, because they were friends and not for any other reason, would bother him. Deeply.

He pulled his truck against the curb in front of Leah's house. Though it was dark, he could make out a hunched figure on the porch. He stepped out of his truck, frowning at Leah's pacing form. "What are you doing out here?"

"Waiting for you."

"It's freezing, Queen Whack Job." He hunched in his coat. The wind was bitter cold. He didn't want to be out here to walk from truck to house, let alone skulking.

"Hey, Assy McGee, what if my parents hear you calling me that?"

"Assy McGee is way worse than Queen Whack Job." But as he approached he could already tell she wasn't irritated with him. She was distraught. Miserable. Not a good start to the family reunion, then.

"Hey." He reached out for her arm, holding her in place so she'd stop pacing. "What's wrong?"

"Nothing. I just…needed some air."

"It's that bad?"

"No. Yes. I don't know. Hard." She shrugged, looking suspiciously as though she'd been crying.

"You expected that, right?"

"Yeah." She rubbed her hands up and down her arms. Obviously even with a coat she'd been out here too long.

"Let's get you inside." He went to open the door, but her words stopped him.

"You shaved."

He wasn't sure why that sounded like an accusation. "Well, yeah. Wouldn't want your parents to think I'm a dirty hippie."

She snorted and *almost* smiled, but that died after a second. "She's never even met you and you're already the savior."

"Huh?"

Leah shook her head. In the weak porch light he could see the anguish on her face. "She thinks hooking up with you, like, magically cured me of my ran-away-from-home ways. That you're the reason I reached out to them. She's never even met you, and yet you have all the credit and praise and I'm still the girl to be handled. Maneuvered. Saved and fixed."

Jacob didn't know what to say to that. Obviously her request for him to come over a night earlier than planned wasn't just some spur-of-the-moment suggestion. It was something much bigger than he knew what to do with. At least without knowing the full story.

And as much as she'd told him, it was all vague half stories. Nothing concrete. Nothing to understand this.

"I don't have to be here."

She shook her head, a rough not-at-all-happy laugh escaping her lips. "It doesn't matter."

"You're acting like it does."

"Nope. It doesn't. Ten years didn't magically change anything, and you know what? I deserve it. I deserve to have to bite my tongue. This is my due, and I'll suck it up and take it. That was the lesson I was supposed to learn. Grow up. Be an adult. Bend over backward and think about other people more than I think about myself. Right? That's how it's supposed to work. So let's go in there and pretend we want to do each other."

"Um…"

But she was already stomping inside, guns blazing, shoulders back. *This is my due.* Damn, that seemed sad. Maybe there was some way he could smooth it over for her. Clearly he was missing pieces of the puzzle, but even more clearly her parents did not understand Leah.

Handled, maneuvered, saved or fixed were the last things he thought she needed.

"Jacob's here," Leah called, grim determination set in every line on her face. A plump woman with curly hair and a tall man with a grizzly mustache appeared, smiling broadly.

The woman crossed to him and wrapped him in a tight hug. It was something *his* mother would do to a perfect stranger, so it was hard to mind. "It's nice to meet you, Mrs. Santino."

She pulled away, cupping his face with her hands. "And aren't you handsome, young man. My girl has good taste."

"Um, thank you." He turned to the man. "Mr. Santino." Thankfully the man extended a hand instead of offering a hug.

"Nice to meet you, son."

"And that's my brother, Marc."

Marc cut an imposing figure, and his handshake seemed a little tighter than necessary. He also didn't say anything, just gave a vague nod.

And yes, this was officially awkward. But Jacob knew how to deal with awkward. You smiled. You asked questions.

So that was what he set about doing. And it wasn't hard. Mrs. Santino talked enough for all five of them on her own. He'd barely answer a question before she was moving on to the next. When she went to the bathroom to "freshen up" and was gone for fifteen minutes, none of them seemed to know what to do.

"Now, now, now, we need some dinner." Mrs. Santino returned and clapped her hands together. "Marc, did you bring the cooler in?"

"Cooler? I told you I'd feed you," Leah said, looking genuinely upset over a cooler.

Mrs. Santino waved it away as Marc disappeared out the door. "Of course I brought food. You never would let me teach you to cook."

"You wouldn't let me stand for more than five minutes."

"But if you'd sat there and listened—"

"How can I learn if I can't see?"

"There's a lot to be said for listening, and I always—"

"Here you go, Mom." It was the first time Marc had spoken, carrying the cooler into the house, and the effect was an end to Leah and her mother's argument, which Jacob couldn't make sense of. Not let her stand for more than five minutes? What was this?

"Now let me get dinner started." Mrs. Santino was already walking in the kitchen, pulling the giant cooler-on-wheels behind her. Leah followed, still protesting, so Jacob did the same.

"Mom, you had, like, a seven-hour drive. Besides, you're my guest and—"

"I'm your mother. And look at this." She tsked the contents of the fridge, which contained a lot more fruits and vegetables than it had the other night. Obviously Leah had planned ahead, but apparently it wasn't enough. "I knew you'd need to be fed some real food."

"Mom, I told you—I take care of myself. That wasn't a lie. I look good. I *am* good. Don't start…" Abruptly, Leah clamped her mouth shut. That expression from outside returned. Distraught. Miserable. *This is my due.*

"You know what—I'll help. I'll help with making dinner, and Leah and I will do cleanup. That's a good compromise, right?"

Leah shook her head. "Sure. Yeah. Compromise. Bend."

"You can cook, young man?" Mrs. Santino demanded.

"I can. And I'm very good at following orders." He smiled as charmingly as possible under Mrs. Santino's intimidating glare, even when Leah snorted. Mrs. Santino's expression melted into a smile easy as you please.

"Oh, I do like you. Leah, go rest and catch up with Dad and Marc. Your man and I will heat up some ravioli in a jiff. And don't worry. I brought you a special cheeseless batch."

"Right. Sure." Her smile was pained, but she went.

And Jacob was left with the whirlwind of energy that was her mother.

"First up, get me two pots."

Jacob followed instructions without having to make small talk, glad he knew enough about Leah's kitchen to make it seem he'd spent ample time here. Mrs. Santino talked about her family recipe for sauce and how her mother had made the ravioli from scratch but there wasn't time for that anymore.

Then, just as Jacob was relaxing into being told what to do, Mrs. Santino leaned real close, her voice low and serious.

"You're taking care of my girl?"

If she had asked him that before he'd witnessed the dynamic between mother and daughter, he'd have automatically agreed and assured because that was what Mrs. Santino wanted.

But it killed him to watch Leah bite her tongue and fold into herself because she thought it was her due.

"You know, one of the things I…" he kind of stumbled over the *L* word because it made things… weird…but he knew he had to say it "…love about Leah is how strong she is. Resilient. I'd wager to guess she takes care of me more than the other way around."

Mrs. Santino frowned at that, glanced toward the living room, where the rest of the group were. "How much has she told you about…her health?"

Jacob focused on dumping the Tupperware container full of sauce into the big pot. "Oh, you know, everything." Which he had a feeling was a lie. Sure, he knew about her allergies and her asthma, but the way Mrs. Santino said "health" seemed a lot more dire than either.

Although, maybe that was a mother's perspective. It had been scary to see Leah get all gray with her asthma issue the other day, and that was just as a friend. And Leah had been fine.

"She takes really good care of herself."

Mrs. Santino pressed her lips together. It was an expression he'd seen on Leah often enough. Express disapproval.

"My girl needs taking care of."

"Well—"

"And don't I look well taken care of?" He glanced back at Leah standing in the opening of the kitchen. Her expression had gone beyond miserable. He didn't know what it was anymore, but it made his heart hurt.

"Now, how am I supposed to grill him if you're always popping up?" Mrs. Santino replied, waving a wooden spoon she'd had packed away in her cooler.

"Don't poke at him. He—" She glanced at Jacob, that pink tinge he'd started looking for, examining, possibly even dreaming about, crossing her cheeks. "We want him to stick around, don't we?"

"Well, he is quite handy—I'll give him that. Now, why don't you set the table for us? We'll have a nice hearty dinner all ready for you in a second. I'm not saying you don't look well. I'm only saying you could look better. You're pale."

"It's December."

"She works too hard. Doesn't she? I just know she does."

Jacob couldn't get a handle on the situation. In many ways, Mrs. Santino reminded him of his own mother, but there was a kind of manic force driving Mrs. Santino. As though if she stopped talking or doing or pressing, everything would spin out of control.

Jacob felt complicit in it, so he moved over to Leah and slung an easy arm over her shoulders. Something he'd done in the name of friendship a million times, and yet they were supposed to be more than friends. So, how did he make it more than friendly? He didn't know. "I don't think she works too much. Besides, she's brilliant. We'd be lost without her."

Mrs. Santino paused to look at them, her eyes getting shiny, her hands clasped under her chin. "Look at the two of you. Makes my heart sing."

He wondered if Mrs. Santino had any idea that Leah's smile was anything but happy. Sad, hurt. He pulled her a little closer, just enough that she could easily lean her head on his shoulder. Surprised the hell out of him when she did. Even as her father and brother entered the room, her head rested on his shoulder.

He could smell her shampoo, feel strands of hair brushing across his neck. It was…strange. Like all those other moments, only weirder because he was pretending and it felt very unpretendy.

"Leah living alone for so many years just worried me sick, but I knew me pushing wouldn't help any. I'm so glad she finally saw I was right."

Leah didn't stiffen, but she didn't need to for him to know the words hit her hard. He was a little familiar with being underestimated or misunderstood. Oh, sure, it was done with love, but it seemed certain things just clung to you when it came to your family, whether it was true or not.

His family thought he was a jerk to women. Leah's family apparently didn't give her credit for being the kick-ass person she was.

"Now we need to discuss the very obvious elephant in the room, young lady."

This time Leah did stiffen, every muscle contracting underneath his arm as she lifted her head. "What elephant?"

"It's very sweet of you to try and spare my feelings, but I know this is how these things go these days."

"Mom, I… What 'things'?"

"It's very obvious to me that Jacob has been living here with you."

"What?" The simultaneous response of shock didn't deter Mrs. Santino.

"This young man has been your boyfriend for a year and there is not one scrap of evidence he even exists aside from that picture." Mrs. Santino pointed to a picture of the MC crew in front of MC a few years ago. "I poked around while I was freshening up and not a hint this man spends any time here. Which can only mean you purposefully rid it of his influence. I know in the past living in sin is something I might have frowned upon, but we are here because we support you 100 percent no matter what."

"Mom…" Mouth hanging open, she looked helplessly at Jacob.

"That's nice of you, Mrs. Santino, but I don't mind clearing out for the week. You guys should have family time." Sometimes a little white lie couldn't hurt, especially in the midst of a hundred others.

Leah's helplessly open mouth turned mutinous, but her mom was going on, not giving her the chance to argue.

"Nonsense! Who knows, maybe you'll be part of our family someday."

"Oh, my God," Leah groaned.

"Candace, this is what I warned you about," Mr. Santino muttered, patting his wife on the shoulder.

"I'm just…" She sighed. "Well, anyway, I just want you to know, it won't bother us if you're here, Jacob. Not in the least. So, you should move your things back in and go on as you do when we aren't here."

"Well, I—"

"No. No, that's not—"

He glanced at her and she was glaring at him. "You can't—"

"It's okay—"

"Excuse us for a second," Leah said through gritted teeth, and her death grip on his arm was anything but loving.

Yeah, he *really* doubted he was about to get thanked.

CHAPTER NINE

"Are you high?" Or maybe *she* was. High on some kind of… What the living hell? "Seriously, are you whacked out of your mind?" She glanced at the shut door to her bedroom, hoping her voice wouldn't carry back to the kitchen.

"Hear me out, Leah."

"Hear you out? Hear you out? You don't honestly think you can just move in here. You don't… You can't…"

"Are you ready to calm down and listen?"

"No! No, I won't calm down, asshole. I'm biting back every damn word for my mother, and you do not get the same luxury."

"All right." And then he did the most infuriating thing and plopped himself on her bed, folding his arms behind his head and resting against the wall. "I'll wait."

She wanted to pummel him, and honestly, if her parents weren't a hallway and a room away, she would. She'd punch him as hard as she could. Well, first she'd make him get the hell off her bed. "What we're doing is already too far. Pretending we live together? It's—"

"It's not any different from what we're doing. We're lying. All this means is we keep lying."

"It's a new lie. And it's crazy."

"No crazier than being in love with each other."

Ouch. Why did that pinch? It didn't. No, that was something else. Hunger, maybe. "Please, for the love of Pete, be serious for one second. Just one."

And then the ease slipped off his face and she saw the intensity behind that, and, oh, wow, her stomach did a little flip. Not a sexual you-are-so-hot flip, more of a… Okay, it was a total sexual you-are-so-hot-and-on-my-bed flip.

But that was neither here nor there. Really. And when he unfolded himself off her bed and stalked toward her like… She didn't even *know* like what, because angry, intense Jacob was so beyond her understanding she just felt like a cornered animal.

"I think you need backup."

"Wait. What?"

"You need backup. Support. And if I move in, you'll have it."

She didn't understand. Anything. The look. The words. The desire manifesting itself in her midsection. And lower.

Oh, jeez, so not the time.

"I get it. I get why this was so important to you, why you'd lie and pretend. Because they, at least your mother, don't see you. And she's walking all over you. And you're miserable. And I don't like it. So I'm moving in."

"How does you moving in solve anything? She's just going to sit there and keep making comments about you being part of the family someday and thanking you for saving my sorry ass."

"No. She's going to see. Because if I go home tonight and only come back for another meal or two, all she is going to see is whatever she wants. She can keep telling herself I stepped in and made things different. But if I'm here a lot, she's going to see the way you kick my ass on a regular basis. She's going to see that you do everything on your own. She's going to see that you're the most independent, able-to-take-care-of-herself woman I've ever met."

Oh, *God,* what was he trying to do to her?

"If I stay, you don't have to bend. And you shouldn't bend. I don't care what happened when you were a teenager. You should be you. They should see *you.* I'm pretty accustomed to people… dismissing parts of me. And it sucks, and I hate seeing it suck for you and we're going to fix it."

"By sharing a bed?" Which, really, should be the last thing she was concerned about, but said bed was right there and so was the idea of being in it with him. And that fierce, determined look with those heart-melting words and, oh, oh, it was all she could think about.

Jacob glanced at the bed and some of that take-charge determination left his face. She would not allow herself to think the softening was consideration.

"It'll be like camping."

"How?"

"Remember the time we went camping and you couldn't get your tent together?"

"It was missing pieces. That's not me not being able to put it together."

He gave her his patented sarcastic *sure* look. "You couldn't put it together and you lost pieces because you went on a rampage about plumbing."

"Okay, so I'm not outdoorsy, but this isn't like camping." She gestured to her bed. Sure, it was a queen bed, but his parts and her parts in pajamas and asleep and nope, nope, nope. She would combust.

"We shared a tent."

"We were in separate sleeping bags." And it hadn't been exactly an easy night of sleep. Between the hard ground and Jacob's breathing. Even knowing Henry and Susan had been in tents right next to them hadn't changed how many things she had imagined that night.

A week of it?

"So, I'll pack a sleeping bag. It can be the Walls of Jericho."

"What?"

"If you would get over your aversion to black-and-white movies, you'd have some semblance of a clue as to what I'm talking about. *It Happened One Night* is a movie—"

"Jacob. Just… I need you take a step back. I need to think." She needed five seconds of quiet to think. To figure out. To come up with a plan that did not involve Jacob in her bed. In her house. For seven straight days.

With her family.

He took her shoulders, and even though she didn't want to, she looked at him. The fierce determination was back, earnestness in every line on his gorgeous face, every point of pressure of his fingertips in her shoulders.

"Let me help you make them see you. You deserve for them to see you. All the things you've done to try and get them back into your life. It should work. Let me help. I want to help."

"Why?"

"Because you're my friend."

"I wouldn't do the same for you."

"You know, I don't think that's true. I think you'd do almost anything I'd ask if it was something like this. Because you care. I care."

She blinked at him, and he was right. She would do anything for him if it meant what this meant to her. But words like *care* and his hands on her shoulders… They muddled everything. Mostly her ability to speak.

"We're friends," he repeated.

"Yes."

"A second family. MC is a second family. So I'm going to do this for you."

A second family, yes, although more like a first the past few years. And as this family had started pairing off and procreating, it made her want her own back, because nothing could change blood. Not even bad behavior and running away.

She swallowed down all the emotion clogging her throat and managed to look Jacob in the eye. Steady Jacob. Caring Jacob. *Fucking hot Jacob.* No. Not that. "You're going to do this…because you care."

"Yes."

"I don't do well with caring."

"You do okay with Grace. How am I different?"

"You mean, aside from the penis?" Oh, God, *why* had she said that? She had not meant to say that. "Not that I think about your…" Oh. No. No, no, no.

She closed her eyes against the sight of his wide-eyed look of surprise. "Forget I said that. I didn't mean it like…that."

"Well, regardless, my penis has very little to say in the matter."

"Great," Leah croaked. "Fantastic. Moving on…"

"Are you agreeing?"

"Jacob—"

"Agree."

"Yes, it's such a great idea to tell me what to do. I love taking orders."

He grinned. "Would you prefer endearments?"

"No, I'd prefer…" A million other things over this, but maybe he was right. Maybe alone she'd never convince Mom she was okay on her own, that it was preferable. Maybe if Mom really saw how little influence Jacob had on her life up close and personal, things could change.

Could they really change? She was starting to think they couldn't.

"What do you have to lose, Leah?"

Aside from him? Nothing. She didn't want to risk him, or herself over him, but in the fight between her family and herself, it was probably time her family started winning.

"All right."

"Great." He squeezed her shoulder and when he bent to kiss her cheek she didn't even flinch.

"You're getting better at that," he said with a grin, linking hands with hers. "Now, I'm starving and whatever was in that stuff your mom brought smelled amazing."

"It is. I'm sure it is."

"So we'll eat, and then I'll go grab some things."

Leah nodded, swallowing down the ball of fear in her throat. Sure. Move in. Take over. Share her bed. Yeah, this was going to be so, so, so fine.

Uh-huh.

JACOB'S RIGHTEOUS ANGER propelled him all the way through dinner, all the way back to his bedroom at MC, all the way through throwing some stuff in a duffel bag. It didn't sway or defuse until he came face-to-face with Grace.

"What are you doing?"

He looked at the bag in his hands and realized he hadn't thought this through at all. But, well, his friend needed help and he was damn well going to give it to her even if some people didn't approve.

"I'm...going to Leah's."

"What's in the bag?"

"Some stuff."

"Like?" She crossed her arms over her chest, effectively blocking his exit.

"Mind your own business."

"Leah is my business. And so are you."

"This isn't."

Grace frowned, lines stretching across her forehead. "What are you doing, Jacob Stuart McKnight?"

"Do not full-name me."

"Spill the beans, or I call Mom."

"Seriously? You're thirty years old and you're going to call Mommy on me?"

"Damn straight. You may not be afraid of me, but I know you're afraid of her. So spill it. What's going on?"

"I'm going to stay at Leah's while her parents are here." Because Grace had one thing right—he *was* scared of their mother. Of what she might deduce in her psychoanalysis. Pass.

"Please tell me you're not."

"It's just the pretend boyfriend thing."

"Jacob."

"Yes. I know. You're worried I'm going to devastate your best friend. Hey, who knows, maybe she'll devastate me or maybe we're adults and this will all be fine."

"I don't want *anyone* devastated." She glanced at the bag. "Just let me look."

"What? Why?"

"Because I need to check something."

"Over my dead body."

"Jacob." She fixed him with her best big-sister glare, but since he had no idea what she thought he had in the bag, there was no way he was handing it over. Until he knew for sure she'd be wrong.

"Fine, we'll do this the hard way. If there are condoms in that bag, I am going to lock you in here."

"Jesus Christ. There aren't condoms." Not that it hadn't crossed his mind. You know, just for…safety. Or something. But he didn't have any. Having condoms on hand would have been cruel and unusual punishment while taking a six-month sex break.

Which he still had two weeks left of, and he should do well to remember that.

Right, because Leah's going to jump into bed with you.

She did mention your penis.

Yeah, don't think it matters.

Jacob shoved a hand through his hair. Arguing with himself over the likelihood of Leah letting him do anything with his penis was about the bottom of the barrel of pathetic. Especially with Grace watching him like a hawk, casting suspicious glances at his bag.

"Look, I'm going to help her, not seduce her. So, what is this terrible thing that could happen?"

"What if she falls in love with you?"

His heart pitched, and not in the scary kind of way it probably should. "She won't." *Keep that in mind, heart and penis.*

"But—"

"But if she falls in love with me she'll soon see whatever is wrong with me that every other woman has already seen and that will be that. Right? I suck at this, so what if something changes? She'll dump me and I won't be bitter about it and everyone will be fucking fine."

"That's…not…"

"That's not what?"

Grace stood in his doorway, hands having fallen down to her sides, mouth hanging open and no words coming out.

Yup. Exactly. "I'll see you at Mom and Dad's on Christmas Eve," he muttered, brushing past her.

"Jacob…"

But he kept walking and in the end she didn't have anything to say, did she? Because he was right. He'd screw it up one way or another, but he wasn't going to hurt anyone because that was not what he did.

He was usually on the receiving end of the hurt, pretending it didn't. Pretending nothing mattered. So, on some weird offhand chance things went a little sideways with Leah, well, he'd deal, and everything would be fine.

Which was possibly the most dangerous conclusion he could come to considering he was going to share a bed with her tonight—Walls of Jericho or no Walls of Jericho.

He drove through downtown Bluff City to Leah's small house on the other side of town. He tried to focus on all the ways she irritated him, all the ways he sucked, but he kept thinking about her cheek under his palm, the sharp intake of breath. The way her hand had felt in his as he'd led her back to the kitchen after they'd made their decision.

Right.

Which was dumb and wrong.

Irritated with himself, he grabbed the duffel and strode toward the door. What was he supposed to do? Knock? Barge in?

But before he could decide on either, the front door flew open. "Hi, sweetheart!" Leah's cheery greeting was super creepy. Almost as creepy as the endearment.

"Are you okay?"

She leaned in close. Too close. "I spiked my hot chocolate," she whispered, a little off-kilter. "Probably more than was wise. It's been a while since I had hard liquor. I must have misjudged, but damn, it's making this whole evening easier."

"You're drinking?"

"I know. Terrible idea. Not supposed to. Blah,

blah, blah. But Mom started talking about you proposing and I found this bottle of vodka one of our clients gave me and plop. Into the hot chocolate."

"Vodka and hot chocolate?"

"Surprisingly tolerable when you're trying to placate your mother's insane need to see you married off."

"Leah…"

"Mom and I are watching *White Christmas* while the boys snooze on the couch. Christmastime tradition number one." She walked to the living room, swaying once before righting herself.

He followed her, not at all sure what he was supposed to do now. Drunk Leah. Sharing a bed with drunk Leah. This all seemed infinitely more dangerous than it had before, and he'd been scared then.

Now he was downright petrified.

But she plopped onto the unoccupied corner of the couch, then patted the floor in front of her. "Come here, honey."

Dear Lord, was she blitzed off one shot of vodka? He surveyed her family as he crossed, but none of them seemed to notice. Uneasily, Jacob slid into a sitting position on the floor in front of Leah.

She looked happy, and he didn't think it was all the booze. With the movie in the background and not much conversation going on, things seemed to have calmed down. Mrs. Santino was watching the movie with avid interest, Mr. Santino was snoring next to her and Marc was reading on his tablet.

And Leah was drunk off vodka she'd slipped into her hot cocoa. And he…he had slipped into another dimension, apparently. Probably the other night when he'd kissed Leah.

As if she could read his mind, she shifted, her knees bumping his shoulders while Bing Crosby crooned about blessings. Then her fingertips brushed the back of his neck and his brain went a little dim.

He had the craziest thought he should reach back, rest a hand on her leg, act as cozy as she was acting.

But where on the leg did a pseudoboyfriend touch? Everything seemed too…intimate. Every inch of her seemed too intimate. So, he just sat there, some part of Leah's body occasionally coming into contact with his.

When the movie ended, Mrs. Santino sighed dreamily. "Oh, I could just watch it a million times. But maybe I should get your father to bed. Likely he'll be up at five, inspecting your car." She stood and looked at him and Leah, the same teary-eyed joy as when they'd been in the kitchen earlier. "You two really are just so handsome together."

"Like peas and carrots," Leah said in what he imagined was some attempt at a Forrest Gump voice.

"You're exhausted, baby. Let's get you to bed, too."

Leah narrowed her eyes at him. Apparently not drunk enough to miss the "baby" he tacked on. Or was it the "let's get you to bed" part. Well, regardless, he needed to get her out of here before she raised any eyebrows.

But Leah seemed to get that because she pushed to her feet. Slowly, but without any swaying or stumbling.

"You sure you'll be all right out here, Marc?"

"I'll be just fine," he said, patting a pile of blankets next to his chair.

Mrs. Santino nudged Mr. Santino to his feet and they shuffled down the hall to Leah's guest room.

Leah followed. Slowly. Jacob picked up his bag, glanced at Marc, who was watching Leah's *very* careful walking with an unreadable expression on his face. Jacob didn't know what else to do except follow her.

Once inside the room, he dropped his bag, closed the door and just stood there. Awkwardly. What came next?

Leah didn't look at him, didn't say anything. She walked into her little en suite bathroom and closed the door. The lock clicking into place seemed very... loud.

Sooo. What was he supposed to be doing? Getting ready for bed. Sure. He glanced at Leah's bed. It had been made, but it was still wrinkly. And small. The idea of sharing it with her was...

It was a lot of things. Most of them he couldn't afford to wonder about. So he focused on his bag and finding some sweatpants, which he draped over his shoulder. He wasn't going to risk switching pants when she could walk in at any minute.

He grabbed his toothbrush, but he needed a sink for that. Contacts and contact solution, needed a mirror. Mainly he was just standing around waiting for her to give him use of her bathroom.

When he'd stormed out of MC all "things are going to be fine," he hadn't really pictured…this. And this was reality. He was going to lie next to Leah on that bed and somehow pretend he'd never pictured her naked. Never wondered what it might be like to—

The bathroom door swung open and Leah marched out wearing slouchy sweats and a determined expression. "I set anything you might need on the sink, so don't poke through my things or I'll kick your ass to the curb."

"Yes, ma'am."

Not that he'd planned on snooping, but he wasn't going to argue with her here in weird world. He was going to brush his teeth, take out his contacts and change clothes.

Which he did, only occasionally tempted to poke through her medicine cabinet. As friendly as they were, he realized he'd never been in her bathroom and had only occasionally been to her house before this week. They spent almost all their friend time together at MC, with the other MC employees, so this was like…

It was different, and he really needed to stop analyzing that different.

He shuffled out of the bathroom. She was already on the bed, staring up at the ceiling. Her eyes were open, but she didn't turn to look at him.

"I, uh, left my stuff on the sink. You know, in case your mom goes snooping around again."

"Uh-huh."

Slowly, he advanced on the bed, not sure why his stomach was doing acrobatics. After all, this was just like…camping.

He stood a few steps away from the bed. A bed he was going to lie on next to Leah. Yeah, this was not like camping.

"So you want to do the Walls of Jericho thing," he said, pointing to his sleeping bag he'd wrestled into his duffel. "Or…"

She shrugged, finally looking at him. She wrinkled her nose. "You have glasses?"

"Well, yeah…" And then he grinned. "See, you don't know everything about me."

"How have I never seen you in glasses?"

"I don't really like them, so I only wear them before bed, when I have to take my contacts out."

"Oh."

For some reason that made him feel a little more at ease. As if he wasn't an open book and she couldn't read his every awkward or impure thought. He reached behind him to pull the sweater off.

"What are you doing?" she screeched.

He stopped with his sweater halfway up. "Taking off my shirt."

"You can't take off your shirt."

"Why not?"

"Because…because…" She pointed at his stomach. "Abs."

At his raised eyebrow she shook her head.

"That's not… I don't…" She flung her arm over her eyes. "Ohh, I'm drunk. Leave me alone."

Leah was perturbed by his…abs? Well. And she was also drunk. So. Yeah, maybe he should leave his shirt on, even if it was a sweater not exactly meant for sleeping. He left it in place, and when he edged onto the bed, he did it carefully, gingerly.

He was all but on the edge, but none of their… selves were touching. Anything.

She peered over at him through one eye, one arm still flung over the other. Then she sat up and began arranging pillows and blankets between them.

"That might be the most ineffective barrier I've ever seen."

"You cross the Walls of Jericho, you die. Effective?"

"Yes." Maybe. "You…"

"I what?"

He didn't know what to say, actually, because everything he wanted to say seemed to shift underneath his feet. Besides, he was tired and she was drunk. So. Nothing. He should say nothing.

"Night, Leah."

"Night," she grumbled, turning so her back faced him.

Jacob stared up at the ceiling. He had a feeling he was in for a bumpy one.

CHAPTER TEN

LEAH WOKE UP to a low-level headache and a slightly sloshy stomach. Good Lord, who knew a shot of vodka in her hot chocolate could almost knock her on her ass.

Well, at least not enough for her mother to notice. That was a lecture she didn't need. Another plaintive plea that Jacob take care of her.

Jacob. Right. She opened her eyes and he was lying right next to her. Well, yet another plus to the liquor, she'd drifted off without angsting too much last night.

Hello, angst. Because with his eyes closed and him just lying there inert, she could appreciate how perfect he was. Visually. Open his eyes, start talking, it ruined the whole effect because it was such a reminder that as much as she *liked* who he was, it would never work with who she was.

Unless he could pretend all that health stuff wasn't there, like he did with his mother.

Leah closed her eyes and swallowed down a groan. Why was she even thinking about that? Did she honestly think that was (a) plausible and (b) she'd just throw herself at Jacob and he'd...catch her?

Not if history served.

So, it didn't matter if she wanted to run her hands over his mussed hair or draw her fingertips across his enviably long eyelashes. She wasn't going to run her palm across the stubble on his cheek or find out what his neck smelled like in the morning.

Because while her body might be all hot and bothered at the thought, her mind was not a total idiot.

She scooted herself down to the foot of the bed so she could escape without crawling over him. Scrubbing a hand over her face, she walked to the bathroom. If anything would put a stop to any lusty thoughts, it should be her morning ritual.

Over the years, the amount of medication she had to take daily had diminished. She hadn't been lying to her mother when she'd said she was good. She was absolutely the healthiest she'd ever been.

But nothing would change the fact that someone else's heart beat in her body, and that it was a ticking time bomb.

Way to be morbid, Santino.

She popped the pills, ran through the shower, refusing to linger on the long white scar on her chest. It was faded, barely noticeable, but she could still see the marks from the stitches, the nasty pink. She could remember every time a guy had recoiled and every time a guy had backed away for fear she was too delicate.

She'd had her rib cage cracked open and taken on a new freaking organ. She was anything but delicate.

"Get it together," she said aloud to her reflection when she stepped out of the shower. The fact of the matter was, most days she could all but pretend this stuff didn't exist. But her family here was a constant reminder of what had been, and Jacob sharing a bed with her was a reminder that things would never be easy.

She couldn't even get through the first night of spending time with her family without spiking her drink. A few hours and she'd been desperate. Because things hadn't changed. Leah thought there had been some understanding over the past year, some growth, but apparently Mom being in her orbit meant back to old habits.

Habits that made Leah want to crawl out of her skin. Made her want to scream. Worst of all, made her want to cry. Why couldn't they look past all the health issues and see *her?*

Mom hadn't asked about her job, hadn't complimented her on her place. No, just Jacob, Jacob, Jacob. And Leah didn't know how to make it different.

But you're not going to give up. You're going to keep trying. Because you want a family and you want them to see you. She stared at herself in the mirror for a long time, long after the mirror completely cleared of fog. Then she gave herself a little nod and got dressed and stepped back out into her bedroom.

When she did, Jacob was sitting up in bed, pulling the sweater over his head, expressly as she'd asked him not to last night. He had a T-shirt on underneath, but it rode up as he pulled the sweater off. She could see the abs she'd idiotically mentioned last night. Guh.

"It's friggin' hot in here," he muttered, tossing the sweater toward his duffel bag. On the floor of her room, all unassuming and normal.

"I...I told you not to do that," Leah protested, wishing the words back in her mouth the minute they escaped. Because the reasoning she'd given him last night was super embarrassing.

Abs.

He had them, but a normal person didn't go around pointing them out. Especially to the friend you were trying to ignore your attraction to for the very sake of your friendship.

"You really can't trust yourself to keep your hands off me?" he grumbled, scrubbing hands over his face.

She clamped her mouth shut because, well, sometimes she wondered. There had been a time she hadn't denied herself anything she wanted, and she may have grown up and out of that, but it had taken a life-threatening relapse. Even with that in her history, there were times...times she wished she could go back to being that girl who did whatever she wanted.

Nope, not these times. "It's just weird."

"Because you want to jump me?"

"I most certainly did not say that." *Just thought it.*

He stopped stretching and fixed her with a considering look. "You know, it's not like I've never thought about it."

"What? Thought about what? No. Don't answer that. Just stop talking. You woke up…delirious or something."

"I'm just saying it's not like you're unattractive. So, yeah, I'm not immune, either. It isn't all one-sided."

"Why? Why are you saying that? I like my one-sidedness. Not that…there's…" Seriously. This was an alternate reality. Maybe that shot of vodka was still working.

"Is it a crime?"

"What?"

"To be attracted to one another?"

"Crime? No. Stupidest thing on the face of the planet? Yes."

"That seems harsh."

"Why are you talking?"

He shrugged. "I need coffee. I slept for shit. In this hot room on a bed next to someone that, yes, on occasion I have thought of naked. Hearing Grace tell me I'm going to hurt you over and over again in my head and what the hell am I pretending so hard for?"

Leah blinked at him, her face likely so red she could match that idiotic dress in her closet. And she thought about that red dress, and the times she'd worn it, and the past five years, and it all centered in her gut as anger. Anger at what, she didn't know, but she clenched her fists and the embarrassment faded away.

"You know what, Jacob? I call bullshit."

"What?"

"That's all...you. I'm here and I'm convenient and you've been on your little women break. You're lonely and I think you've built this lovely little fantasy where you've given a crap about me in a romantic way and it's all bullshit."

His forehead wrinkled as his eyebrows drew together. "You're not serious."

She angled her chin because she was. So serious, and it hurt, but she knew she had to be right because for five years, five years of her pathetic unspoken lust for him, he had not given her any indication he felt remotely the same. So, this was exactly it. Lonely and bored and she was here.

"I'm attracted to you. Sorry, you can't excuse that away."

"I don't believe you."

He stood, scowl etched so deep, lines bracketed his mouth. When he took a step toward her, her whole stomach flopped to her toes. She wasn't sure what it was jittering through her. Fear? Frustration? Nerves?

Arousal?

Oh, no, not the last one.

"I have been attracted to you always," he said through gritted teeth, and he took another step toward her, and because she had nowhere to go, except to hide in the bathroom, she stood there.

Because she was strong. She was in control of this. And she was right. "As I said before, bullshit."

"Five and a half years ago, you came into my falling-apart office with this smile, like you were about to conquer the fucking world, and I wanted you." Another step. "You had your résumé in this ridiculously frayed leather folder thing, and your hair was in a braid that was already falling apart, but you waltzed in like the job was yours."

Okay, she was starting to regret not running to the bathroom. Especially as he took two more steps. Steps so that they were now only an inch or two away from toe to toe, him glowering down at her like… like…

She didn't know. Some hot-guy glower that was making her brain go all squishy.

"And it was like a zap of electricity. But MC is the most important thing in my life aside from my family. You were the only candidate with everything I needed. So, wanting you? It couldn't matter. And I haven't let it matter in all this time."

He was really close now. Like, you know, possibly kissing close. Like how he got when he kissed her cheek, but this was not that. Not because they weren't practicing, but because that was not a cheek-kiss look.

And as much as a part of her downright *longed* to know what a not-cheek kiss, a real not-cheek kiss, might feel like, how that look translated into a kiss would feel, she knew it would flatten her, and she didn't have time to be flattened right now. Not with her family sleeping under the same roof.

"Why are you saying all this?" she demanded, not as fearless and steady as she'd hoped.

"Because I need some damn coffee," he muttered, pushing past her. "And your bed is shit." He stepped into the bathroom and slammed the door behind him.

Leah let out an unsteady breath and leaned against the now-closed door. Oh, God, what was that?

WHAT THE HELL was that? He gripped the sink and tried to figure out what kind of stroke he'd just had.

But she'd been standing there with curly wet hair *looking,* and he *wanted* her to, and damn if he wasn't a little cracked.

It wasn't as if it wasn't true. It was all painfully the truth, just probably a truth he should have kept to himself.

He scratched fingers through his hair, then turned to the shower and flicked the nozzle to Hot. Well, it was too late to keep it to himself, and so what? So he'd told her. Grace had told him Leah had a thing for him, so Leah could damn well deal with it, too.

He stepped into the hot spray of the shower and tried to fully wake up. Anything to get his brain to engage. Because apparently it was a bike without a chain...or some other less lame metaphor.

He tried to scrub some sense into his body, all the while ignoring the frustrating morning erection that was less biology and more like having to smell Leah all freaking night. Listen to her breathe. All but see her chest rise and fall.

Shitty shit shit. If he wasn't afraid Leah would think something kinky was going on he would have beat the wall in frustration.

Instead, he leaned his forehead to the tile and took a deep breath of hot, steamy air. So he'd said some uncomfortable truths. So what? It wasn't as if keeping them secret made them any less true.

Yup. Shit.

He wrenched the water off, then stared at the foggy bathroom around him. He hadn't brought in any clothes. Luckily Leah's towels sat on a rack, sloppily folded.

He grabbed one and dried himself off and tried to figure out what to do. There was a temptation to go back into the room with only a towel wrapped around his waist. After all, she very well could have gone. Hopefully to make coffee.

But something about that felt different from innocently taking off his shirt. Stomping around in nothing but a towel struck him as a dick move... literally and figuratively.

So he opened the door a tiny crack. "Um, can you throw my bag in here?"

She didn't say anything, but after a few seconds the bag was shoved in his direction.

He got dressed, irritation and frustration boiling through his bloodstream. Because he didn't know what to do. He didn't know how to blueprint this, how to troubleshoot this problem into submission.

And maybe Leah was a teeny tiny bit right that he tended to, on occasion, do that with relationships, too.

She, however, was not going to be easy to troubleshoot. Scratch that. Impossible.

So, he'd just…pretend. That was what they were doing anyway and apparently they were both experts. They were friends. Buddies. Pretending to be lovers, but not a sexual thought between them.

Yes. That was it. The answer. The key to get them to next week, when her parents would be gone and life would go back to normal. Work and friendship and no all-encompassing, reality-warping lust.

Determined, he stepped into her room ready to pretend his ass off, but before he could do anything, Leah fixed him with that determined glare.

"We're just going to pretend this morning didn't happen. For the sake of MC and…everything."

"Yeah, sure." Why her desire to do just what he'd decided made him itchy, he had no idea.

She had hands dug in her pockets and her hair was pulled back now. She looked like the Leah he always saw, and yet they were in her bedroom, and they'd shared a bed last night, and damn it, he wanted to kiss her. So…

"Would it really be so awful?" Really *that* awful?

She glanced at him warily, a kind of rawness in her expression that made his gut twist. "No. It wouldn't be. But it wouldn't end well, and that would be awful."

"How do you know?" He kind of liked half that answer, but the other half itched, too.

She rubbed a hand over her chest, something she always seemed to do when she was sad. "Just trust that I am not the girl you're going to maneuver into marriage and babies, and that's what you want."

Okay, so, yes, that was the plan, and in order to complete that step in the life plan he needed to be married by thirty, which gave him only a little over a year. Because he wanted a year or two of being married without kids, but he didn't want to be too old when he had them. The—

Christ. Why was he thinking about this?

"Maybe you shouldn't be staying here and—"

"I'm seeing this through regardless. Because, regardless, we're still friends." That was the bottom line, and it always would be. He didn't back out on friends. He didn't let people down.

He took her by the shoulders because he needed her to look at him and see the truth. "Sorry if it's weird sometimes, but it is what it is. And regardless of weird, at the end of the day, I want you to remain my friend."

She swallowed. "O…okay. I mean, I want that, too. To be your friend."

"Good." Here was the part where he, as her friend, should give her a bit of a squeeze and then release her shoulders. Step back and away. Stop examining the curve of her bottom lip. Yes. Stop that.

But he didn't.

She turned her head away, eyes squeezed shut. "Don't kiss me."

"Okay." It would be stupid to argue that he hadn't been about to do just that.

She opened her eyes when he didn't release her shoulder. "Don't look like you're *thinking* about kissing me, either." She gave him a little shove and he released her, but he couldn't help grinning.

"That I can't do. I *am* thinking about kissing you."

"Jacob—"

There was that sad look and chest rubbing to match the exasperated exhalation of his name, which made him really, *really* want to kiss her. Hold her. Tell her there was nothing to be sad about. He wouldn't make her sad.

Unless he did without trying or meaning to. Ouch. That was a crap thought. But when her eyes met his, she didn't look so much sad. Especially when her gaze dropped to his mouth.

"Hey, if I can't think about it, you can't think about it."

"I wasn't."

"You're a hell of a lot better at denial than I am, Leah." Which gave him a boost. Because it *was* denial, and that at least meant he wasn't crazy. "I can't promise to stop thinking about it, but I won't actually do it." And then he grinned again because he knew it would piss her off just as much as his next words. "Until you ask me to."

"I will not be doing that."

"Suit yourself." He sauntered over to the bedroom door. Strangely enough, he left the bedroom light and happy and not at all convinced she wouldn't eventually ask just that.

CHAPTER ELEVEN

"GOODNESS. WHAT A giant house! Jacob did this all on his own?"

"No, Mom, not on his own. He had help." *Like mine,* Leah wanted to scream, but instead she swallowed it down and worked on her best smile as she approached MC with her family. And Jacob. *Wonderful* Jacob. Strong, perfect Jacob.

"Oh, he's all kinds of amazing." Mom smiled broadly at Jacob walking behind them. Leah wanted to roll her eyes. All of this praise and complimenting aimed Jacob's way was bordering on the ridiculous.

And the fact her own mother couldn't see *her* that way? It…hurt. Yes, it did.

"Don't be so modest, sweetheart." Jacob's arm came around her waist and she knew she should put her arm around his and walk into the house all lovey-dovey and pretendy, but she didn't want to.

She wanted to get the hell away from him. Because all that stuff this morning? It was too damn tempting for any kind of comfort. And all this stuff with Mom right now made her want to shove him like a little kid desperate for attention.

"Leah did all the wiring. There wasn't anything we could salvage. It's kind of amazing, really. Everything I do is so aesthetic. I can look at it and say 'Hmm, this doesn't look right,' and as long as I'm within code, I can do whatever I want. Leah has to get every little wire in just the right place without the luxury of tearing everything down."

"She certainly inherited her father's skill with all that mechanical stuff."

"Right, because nothing I've ever done has been of my own doing. It's all been spurred on by someone with a penis," Leah muttered under her breath. Mom wouldn't hear it, but with Jacob hip to hip with her, he no doubt would.

He squeezed a little harder around her waist and she knew it was an admonition, but she didn't care. She was getting beat down by Mom being so quintessentially Mom. And it made her sad and mad and the morning with Jacob had done the same and basically…basically all her lies and planning and determination were crumbling around her.

And it made this whole pretending thing pointless, because this new suffocation from Mom wasn't about needing a man to take care of her, but it felt the same. Effusive praise of everyone but her. Well, so long as they were male.

It prompted those age-old feelings. Flip the bird. Do what you want. *Run away.*

It was all so useless she wanted to cry. Wanted to yell, "I am here! I am capable! I am worthy!"

But she didn't. Maybe because as here and capable as she was, worthy was something she had her doubts about.

It was easy to forget ten years later, so she had to keep reminding herself what she'd caused. Parents' separation. Debt. Pain. Worry. So being worthy of Mom's praise, of Mom seeing her for who she was? Yeah, not so much.

Which did not make her any less sad, but it did stop her from letting any mad leak out. It stopped her from yelling it was all a lie. Because Mom was so *happy.* Downright giddy over Jacob, and Leah wasn't going to take that away from her.

She'd just deal. And maybe someday she'd have the guts to tell her mom the truth, or maybe someday she'd find a guy as decent as Jacob.

She shot him a sideways glance and he winked, his arm moving from her waist, hand traveling up her back until it reached her shoulder, and then he squeezed.

That did *nothing* to her. Not a zap, not a pinch of heat, nothing.

She used to be so much better at lying to herself.

They entered MC through the front, which *was* pretty impressive. Considering she could remember when the entryway had moldy drywall and peeling ceilings.

Now it was all gleaming wood and curved candelabra light fixtures Kelly had found and Leah had rewired.

"This is really amazing. Really. And you're so young. What an accomplishment."

"I was exceptionally lucky. I couldn't have done it without the people Kyle and I have found to join us. Really, it's such a team effort."

They stepped into the parlor, big and open, a mix of modern and Victorian decor. Leah didn't often *think* about how much they'd done. How she'd painstakingly removed the old corroded setup and replaced it. How Jacob and his team of laborers had turned this from musty, falling-apart decay to a livable, beautiful piece of architecture, and then Kelly had swept in and designed it into this. And with the small, fat Christmas tree winking with white lights and wooden ornaments, it felt as much like home as a showpiece for MC Restorations.

And all this was, this home, it had been a team effort. A team effort of family, however far removed in genetics they might be.

Though she took great pride in her work, her skills, she tended to forget to look back and remember what she had done.

It soothed some of the pockets of insecurity and self-pity she'd walked in with. She'd had a part in doing this; she'd built this life for herself out of sheer determination. She wasn't so badly off.

"Have a seat. Take a look at our book. It really shows how far this place has come. I'm going to go check and see if Kyle and Grace are here. I'll be right back."

Mom and Dad settled on the fussy couch, Marc in one of the puffy armchairs. It was strange to have them here, but nice. So she sat next to Mom and pulled the book off the coffee table.

"We show this to customers so they can see what we can do." She opened the first page. "This is what MC looked like when Jacob bought it. It was our first project. He actually did some work on it before I was hired, so even I didn't see it this bad."

Mom glanced at it quickly, then to where Jacob had been, as if to make sure he had left. She leaned close, resting her hand on Leah's knee.

"You're going to marry him. I just know it." Mom squeezed her knee, eyes gleaming with joy.

Any good feelings she'd managed leaked right out of her. "Mom, I'm not getting married. Ever."

Mom waved her away.

"It wouldn't be fair to…whoever. I've…always felt that way." It was bad enough she couldn't do the whole kid thing for the stress it would put on her heart, but having a heart transplant at thirteen cut her life expectancy a decent chunk. Add that to all her other issues, and she'd never planned on tying herself to someone that would have to lose her before it was fair. Friends were one thing. Spouses and kids? That was a whole other minefield of hurt.

Mom leaned in. "He'll change your mind. I know he will. He's so perfect and he loves you. And just because pregnancy would be dangerous doesn't mean there aren't other options. Surrogacy. Adoption. Jacob does not strike me as the kind of man who'd be hung up on—"

"Mom, stop."

It shocked the hell out of Leah that Marc was the one who spoke. Those words had been in her brain, but she hadn't been able to voice them because of all the pain clogging her throat. Babies and love and, oh, damn, it all hurt.

"I'm talking to your sister."

"And you're upsetting her. And Dad. Just...take a step back."

Leah glanced at Dad as Mom did; he had a grim look on his face but he didn't say anything. Marc had barely said ten words the whole two days, but he'd stepped in and stopped Mom. Huh.

"I don't know why on earth it's upsetting. What's upsetting would be her living alone, but she's not anymore. She has a good man to look after her and keep her on the right path, keep her healthy and safe. And I think it's fairly obvious Jacob wants to marry her, if only she'd—"

Jacob cleared his throat at the entrance to the room. His smile looked pained, but Leah had a feeling he looked way less mortified than she did. Grace and Kyle stood behind him, looking a lot more like she felt.

"Mrs. Santino, this is my partner, Kyle, and my sister, Grace," Jacob said, stepping farther into the room.

"Leah's told me a bit about you two," Mom said,

smiling. Though Leah had to give her credit for looking at least moderately embarrassed. Everyone stood and exchanged handshakes and introductions.

Jacob stepped in and led the conversation. Away from marriage and babies and futures, but it couldn't make Leah forget, unclench the tension in her stomach.

She'd never been one for forward thinking. The future held little promise; all she could count on was the now. But Mom's words stuck the way an electrical shock still buzzed over her skin moments after she'd pulled away from the current.

For who knew what time today, Jacob's arm slid around her. Shoulders this time, but the gesture was becoming normal almost. Comforting, yes.

Her heart hurt, so she leaned into him, against all her better instincts. Her head against the crook of his neck. It felt good there. And it felt good to lean, because really? She'd never leaned before. Not really. As a kid, leaning would mean Mom would take away her already limited outside-the-house time. As an adult, leaning meant letting someone all the way in, and she hadn't done that.

Not even with the people at MC, the people who'd become her family over the past five years.

The bottom line was Jacob wouldn't let her down. Even with...whatever weirdness between them, he wouldn't drop her. But he might suffocate her, just like Mom.

Not if he doesn't know everything.

Insidious thought.

"I need some air. I'll be back in a few." She had to escape, and it wasn't fair to leave Jacob holding the reigns, but she couldn't bring herself to care.

SHE WAS NOT back in a few. Jacob glanced at his phone. It had been at least ten minutes. Grace and Kyle had made their excuses to head out to Carvelle and he needed to do the same. Christmas Eve, and he wanted to be home. Where things made sense. Where he wasn't going to blab things to Leah he had no business blabbing.

Because something about *talking* about all that, especially about the kissing, had led to a whole lot of *thinking* about kissing. And *thinking* about the fact he'd been celibate for five months, three weeks and four days. And kissing. And same bed at night.

And now he was thinking about that in front of Leah's parents and brother, which was all kinds of wrong, wrong, wrong.

"Maybe you should go check on her. She wasn't happy with me." Mrs. Santino smiled sheepishly. "Can't say it's a first. I hope you're not—"

"I'll go find her." Jacob forced himself to smile his smooth difficult-client smile. One he wouldn't be able to force if he thought about what he'd walked in on.

I think it's fairly obvious Jacob wants to marry her...

Weird on a whole lot of levels, none of which he

wanted to ruminate on. "Feel free to roam. We routinely let clients tour. Any room with an open door is fair game. I'll be back in a few."

"Yes, all right."

He wasn't sure where Leah would have gone, but if he had to guess, he'd go with her workshop. It was private, and she would have had to go outside for "air" to get there.

He walked across the lawn, shoving his hands in his pockets against the cold bite of chill. When he reached her shed, he didn't hear any music, but he still had the sneaking suspicion she was in there.

He could knock, possibly should, but since she'd ditched him with her family, he didn't feel very magnanimous at the moment.

Until he stepped inside. Her back was to him, and she was leaning against her stupid Joe Mauer poster, but he didn't miss the sounds of crying. Not sobs or anything. Just a hitch to her breathing, some sniffles.

He honest to God hadn't expected that. "Are you crying?"

She sniffled again, not turning to face him. "No, me and Joe are just having a moment." Her voice was squeaky. Yeah, crying.

"You're crying into your Joe Mauer poster's shoulder."

She sighed. "Joe understands. And he doesn't try to cop a feel. Not that I'd mind from Joe." She patted the crotch region of the poster, causing Jacob to cough out a laugh.

But when she turned to face him, he lost any and all humor. Her eyes were red-rimmed. Her cheeks were splotched red, too, and not in the alluring way they tended to be when she was embarrassed.

"Leah."

"I just need a few more minutes," she croaked out. "To…to…get it…together."

It killed him to see Leah, of all people, crack like this. He'd never thought she was…crackable. Not Leah. He'd figured she'd destroy whatever was in her path first.

"Leah." He touched her shoulder. Comfort was something that usually came rather easy to him, but there was something unsettling about comforting someone he'd always viewed as…way stronger than himself.

Until she turned her head into his shoulder, crying. Then the comfort came as easily as it usually did.

"Oh, baby, it's not so bad." But his heart ached for her, so he ran his hand over the length of her braid, rubbed the other up and down her spine, let her cry against him because she obviously needed it.

"Why do you keep baby-ing me? You have never once even accidentally called me anything related to a stupid endearment." She inhaled but it became more of a hiccup, and her head never raised from its spot against his shirt.

"Yeah, well, you've never cried in front of me."

"Touché." She sniffled, and in possibly the oddest

moment of his life, she burrowed in. Leah Santino, the woman who he'd always figured would chop her own legs off before she did a thing like need, was resting against him for comfort.

He swallowed at the tightness in his throat. Some mix of fear and concern and...well, enjoyment. Yeah, he was a dick to enjoy her pain, and he didn't enjoy that, but he did enjoy the fact she was giving a part of that to him, seeking comfort in him.

"I need to stop leaning on you," she said in a croaky voice, still pressed against him.

He rested his cheek against her hair, because it was there. Because it was kind of nice. "Why? I don't mind. Lean away."

"I mind. Leaning is..." She didn't ever come up with an ending to that sentence; she just kept leaning. Her cheek resting against his collarbone. Her slowly evening breathing making the rise and fall noticeable considering she was indeed against him.

Which meant it took a lot of noble thoughts not to think about her breasts.

She kind of pulled away. Kind of because he didn't let her go and she didn't make him, so there was some space between them. But his arms were still around her and her hands were still resting on his chest.

She looked at him, eyes shading toward blue in the murkiness of her shed. It was a long look, but not the kind a man interrupted. Not if he had any sense.

And when her gaze dropped to his mouth, he didn't let himself breathe. It might spoil it.

She leaned again, but this wasn't into him so much as against him. Her body pressing to his, trapping her hands between. When her mouth touched his it wasn't anything like that first time.

Her mouth remained on his, and because he wasn't stupid, he returned the kiss. Since she'd initiated it, he didn't feel the least bit guilty about kissing her back, drawing her closer. If somewhere in the recesses of his brain he knew this was wrong, his brain didn't speak up. His mouth, though? It spoke metaphorical volumes.

Because he trailed his tongue across her bottom lip, and then her mouth parted and he didn't hesitate to taste. To linger. To discover. He smoothed his hands up her neck, cupping her face, inching his fingers into her hair.

It was a kiss that did none of the things he'd thought it might, because Leah was right. Usually he had a plan. An endgame. A blueprint. Right now all he had was the softness of her lips, her hands grasping his shirt. Liquid heat, desperate want, and it wasn't just screaming for sex or release; it was begging for Leah in particular.

Something changed. Maybe she could read his mind, but she ended the kiss, pulling her face away from his. He couldn't summon enough brain power to let her go, and she had to be at least somewhat similarly affected because her hands were still fisted in his shirt.

She blinked up at him, lips parted, cheeks pink, hair tousled. He opened his mouth to say something, or maybe it was to kiss her again. Who was to say, but she released his shirt and stepped away fully, shaking her head.

"Crap."

"That wasn't crap from where I'm standing." No, everything about that kiss was good words.

"Jacob—" She glanced at him, looking rueful, and it made him grin because she had kissed and kept kissing him, touching him, pressing up against him. It had been...big.

Screw whether it was a good idea or not; it was definitely smile worthy. "I mean it was kind of the opposite of crap. If the opposite of crap is awesome and hot."

She pressed her lips together, but the corners of her mouth hitched up. "That...was a bad idea."

"Really? Felt amazing."

"Okay, so maybe it was those things, too, but it was a bad idea. We are a bad idea, and, quite honestly, this is what I do."

"Kiss people?"

She took a deep breath, squaring her shoulders, building herself back into the Leah he recognized. An odd transformation, but one that did nothing to undercut the painful erection he had going on.

"I seek out things that are bad for me when I feel…suffocated."

She looked sad again and his chest ached. He couldn't blame her for that feeling. He understood too well what it was like to have your family look at you as something other than what you really were.

"She can't force me to marry you," he said gently. "No matter how much she insinuates to either of us. She can't change your reality."

"It's not…that. It's…that she'll never believe I can handle things on my own. My life. My health."

And he didn't have any words for that because he couldn't fix it for her. She was right. Mrs. Santino wasn't going to magically stop doing those things if ten years of separation hadn't.

But what she said, the way she referred to her "health," it poked at him. All those pieces not quite a clear picture. "Speaking of…"

"No, I—" For the first time since the kiss, she turned her back to him.

"I'm missing some of the story, aren't I?" Quite honestly, the question scared him because…he didn't want to know. Whatever it was. Whatever obvious big picture he was missing, it would change things. He could tell. It wasn't just the asthma or the allergies. It was bigger, and it was the core of the issue she had with her parents.

And he'd asked, but he really, really didn't want to know. Because the only thing he wanted to change was the fact he'd never seen Leah naked, but whatever this was, he had a sinking feeling it wasn't going to lead to that.

CHAPTER TWELVE

LEAH KNEW A lot of curse words. She was educated and trained in a male-dominated industry and for a while there she'd hung out with a pretty sketchy crowd. Curse words were like commas to her.

All of those words failed to express the magnitude of what she'd just done. And the achy longing somewhere around her lady parts was worthy of a lot of magnitude.

What on God's green earth was she doing? That was…that was…well, in Jacob's words, hot and awesome. But also bad. Bad, bad, bad. Kissing him. Oh, such good kissing.

"Leah."

Ugh, he wanted to know about her health issues, and that pretty much killed any lady-parts action. "It's just not important." It wasn't, because aside from a few lifelong complications, her day to day was pretty much normal, healthy adult. Minus all the trigger-avoiding she had to do.

"Right." Silence settled over the shed and Leah had to clamp her mouth shut. Words she'd never wanted to speak threatened and only remembering how things would change kept them inside. Sure, Jacob was great for leaning on, for a favor, for kissing—oh, boy, was he—but how would that change if he knew…everything?

Maybe it wouldn't.

She went for the door, ignoring that voice because it was the same one that used to say, *What's one drink? What's one cigarette? You deserve to be normal.* "Jeez, we really need to get back. We just ditched my parents and—"

Jacob folded his arms. "I told them to look around. We probably have a few minutes left. Your mother understood you were upset. I think they'll give us some time."

"I don't want her to understand I'm upset." She squeezed her eyes shut because, damn it, she felt like crying again. Because even with all her mother's ridiculous notions, Leah didn't want Mom knowing how bad it made her feel, how it felt as if she was being shrunk into nothing. Overlooked. Ignored. Waved away.

Her body was faulty, so she needed a keeper. A male keeper. Jacob the Great. Why couldn't she just roll her eyes and say, "Sure, okay, Mom," and do whatever the hell she wanted? Why couldn't she just not care or care enough to change or anything other than stand there in a pool of her own misery?

Well, sadly, the answer to that was easy. She wanted her mother to love her again. Unconditionally. Like when she'd first started acting out. Mom had been there. Sure, she'd tried to lock her up in the house and keep her from trouble, but no one else had been blamed for her bad behavior.

Jesus, this was a level of self-analysis she wasn't at all comfortable with.

"Leah, talk to me."

"I can't," she choked out.

"Why not?"

"Because. Because…I…I don't know what to say or how to say it. I don't know how to process all this…" She gestured to her chest because that was where everything squeezed and ached. "Feeling crap. I don't know what…how… I don't know!"

"Shh." And he was holding her again and she was leaning again.

"Damn it, Jacob." She kind of wanted to punch him because he was being all understanding and sweet and she didn't have the defenses for that right now.

Maybe it would feel good to tell him. Maybe it would be okay. Maybe it would ease some of this pressure. "I was born…with a defect."

"Defect?" His body tensed, arms tightening around her, and she immediately regretted saying anything.

Ease the pressure? Jacob knowing she was a ticking time bomb would do nothing but cause more problems when her parents left, and she couldn't give up the life she'd created for herself. If she had to stifle everything for her family, she wasn't going to have to do it with her second family.

She pulled away from Jacob's tight grasp. It had lost its comforting vibe. Now it was worry. Concern.

Yuck, blech, nope. She had to get herself and this situation under control.

"It's…complicated medical jargon." Which was a lie, but close enough to the truth. "I had surgery to fix it when I was thirteen. So, I'm good. I'm fine."

Some of the tension on his face loosened, smoothing out the deep groove across his forehead.

"If you're fine, why does your mom want to see you married off?"

"After my surgery, and I was better, Mom still hovered and wanted to keep me home from school. She suffocated me, but I was better and a teenager, so I…I did a lot of things I shouldn't and put my health in danger again, and I put my family through a lot of crap, emotionally and financially. So, whatever my mom does to me now, however I feel when she does stuff like that, I just…deserve it. And I need to learn to live with it. Some way."

He didn't speak right away, and the usually easily readable Jacob had a supreme poker face on.

"Okay, here's what we're going to do."

The laugh escaped her easily. "Blueprinting already."

He grinned. "You love it. Now, when whatever your mom's saying starts bordering on too much, we'll come up with a signal. Then I'll change the subject. We'll be more careful about alone time and just try to minimize the times when she, you know, brings you to scary, scary girlie tears."

"Scary? I think you did pretty well."

"I'm exceptionally brave."

Now she was smiling. Tears barely dry on her cheeks and she was laughing. Oh, he was going to ruin her, wasn't he? "That really is above and beyond."

"I'm pretending to be your live-in boyfriend. We've already exceeded above and beyond. Let me help you make this what you wanted it to be. A reunion that will help right some wrongs, and if the only way to do that is for me to step in and change the subject from time to time, easy enough."

Gah, that got her right in the heart. "Why are you doing this for me?"

"Because you're my friend and I care about you."

Leah swallowed. She knew that. Of course she did, but when he said it so *earnestly* it really did crawl under her every last defense.

"All right, so let's talk signal. Your mom starts hinting marriage and you pat me on the ass and I'll swoop in and change the topic to baseball."

Leah choked out a laugh. "You want me to pat you on the ass?"

He took a step toward her, and she tried not to notice there was a wicked intent in his expression.

"I would very much not mind your hands on my ass." Another step and Leah had to step back. She didn't believe in retreat, but holding her ground wasn't going to do her any good with him…getting so close.

"Or vice versa."

"J-Jacob." Was that her? Stuttering and backing away and—bump—there was the wall. Then there was his hand, pressing against the wall right next to her face. She was trapped, only she didn't want to escape this trap. She wanted to rub against it.

Bad. No.

Hot. Awesome.

"Ask me to kiss you," he said, his mouth so close to hers it felt as if he *was* kissing her.

"I already… I kissed you. And it was a bad idea, and I'm not doing that again."

"Well, this time I'll do the kissing. But I said I wouldn't kiss you unless you asked." His body moved against hers, but she was at the wall now, so she was just pressed against him more firmly. "So ask."

But she wasn't going to ask. That kiss had been an unrepeatable mistake. Bad choices to deal with disappointment, her pattern. So she would not ask him to kiss her. She would not kiss him. She would just…

Die of longing and lust.

His fingertips brushed along her cheekbone, those dark brown eyes never leaving hers, intense and determined and, oh, shit, hot. "Ask, Leah."

She did not take orders. And she most certainly didn't like bossy people. But something south of the

border was not listening to her brain's admonitions.
"Oh, just do it."

"Do what?"

"Kiss me, jackass."

"Say 'please.'"

"Oh, fu—" But before she could finish, his mouth
was on hers. Not tentative like her initial kiss. Not
brief like his. This was...hungry, damn it, and so,
so, so *good*.

The hand that had been leaning against the wall
and the gentle fingertips across her face all moved
and morphed into possessive grabbing. And she
liked it. The way he gripped her neck before releas-
ing, then slid his palms down her back. His tongue
in her mouth, his erection very noticeably pressed
against her stomach.

Jacob was kissing the hell out of her and hard because of it and, oh, screw bad. She would take this.
This was, perhaps pathetically, the best damn kiss
of her life. Might as well take what she could get.

She trailed her hands down his chest. He wore a
sweater with one of those preppy button-up shirts
underneath, but she'd caught a glimpse the other
night and had spent enough summers around him
to know what was underneath.

Muscles. Rangy, work-hewn, completely lickable
muscles. Which usually she tried to ignore, pretend
she'd never seen.

Well, to hell with that, too. She ran her palms

down sweater-clad abs and only stopped at the waist of his jeans because his hands had slipped under her shirt.

Rough palms edged across her sides, to her belly, and upward. She arched against him because the heat, the ache was all too much. She wanted more. More with Jacob McKnight, and the fact it was actually within her reach wasn't nearly as scary as it should have been.

JACOB HEARD THE knock a few seconds before his mind engaged enough to withdraw his hands from Leah's shirt, just centimeters from breast territory. Damn it all to hell.

"Leah? Jacob? Are you in here? I can't—"

Kyle's voice cut off abruptly, presumably when he saw what they were doing. Even though Jacob's hands were free, he hadn't quite disengaged his mouth until Leah hopped away.

Disheveled, beet-red and so damn beautiful he wanted to growl at Kyle to get the hell out in some ridiculous hope there was anything left to finish.

But this was something of a situation one didn't just wave away. Kyle's expression remained neutral but he stared at the ceiling. "Grace can't find the present for your mother. She asked me to come find you since you weren't answering your phone."

Right. His phone. Had that been the buzzing he'd

heard? He was so sure that had been his brain disintegrating into lust.

"Bottom right drawer of my desk," he managed roughly.

"All right." Kyle turned as if to leave, then paused. "Leah, your parents are waiting for you."

"Yeah, yeah. We were…we were done." She glanced at him briefly, flicking her gaze away the minute he made eye contact. She took a step toward Kyle's already retreating back. "Kyle, please don't tell Grace."

Kyle pressed his lips together, giving Leah a disapproving look over his shoulder. Her cheeks were red again and she didn't meet Kyle's gaze any more than he met hers.

"I'm sorry. I can't promise you that." He gave a curt nod, then exited the work shed.

She looked at her shoes. "We should get back," she mumbled, her cheeks still bright red, everything about her demeanor screaming regret and embarrassment.

Which made him feel like crap, for a lot of reasons. Partially because he'd been pushy. Partially because…well, did she really have to act as if it was the worst thing in the world? "You don't have to be quite so embarrassed."

She stopped at the door. "I'm not embarrassed. I'm…"

"The color of Santa's suit, honey. It's okay. I get it." He brushed past her and into the frigid cold of the December afternoon. He should have brought a coat. He should have brought his brain.

"I don't think you get it at all," Leah returned, following after him.

"I pushed you. Kyle caught us. Horror. Embarrassment. Et cetera." Maybe it was the still-not-quite-killed erection, but those were *not* the feelings he had. Who cared if Kyle saw them? Who cared if they did whatever? It was only his and Leah's business and he was tired of anyone acting as if they had a say besides him and her. So, no, he wasn't embarrassed and he didn't regret a damn thing except that they'd been cut short.

"You're a fantasy, Jacob. So, no, I'm not embarrassed, but I'm not exactly picking out my wedding dress, either. There's a reason we spent five years not doing…that."

"And it is?"

"We're oil and water. Put business or friendship soap between us and we do okay. Take that out, we're back to repelling each other."

He turned to face her, halting her progress. "Or we're people who have found each other attractive for a very long time but were too afraid to act on it for a wide variety of reasons. And while we might not have killed off that fear or those reasons, we certainly find ourselves in the circumstances to look beyond it."

She blinked up at him, mouth hanging open. "That's…"

"A lot more realistic than your idiotic oil-and-water

analogy?" He couldn't place the source of his anger or what exactly he was angry about. Maybe it wasn't even anger. Maybe it was disappointment and...something a little too close to hurt for him to want to examine closely.

"No, because you forget to mention we annoy the hell out of each other."

He shrugged, shoving his frozen hands under his armpits for warmth. "Maybe that's our thing."

"Our thing?"

"Maybe we annoy the hell out of each other to show interest."

She shook her head, and because he'd had his hands in her hair not all that long ago, the strands that had escaped framed her face. "That's ridiculous. And warped. And ridiculous."

"Do you ever watch TV?"

"We're not a TV show, Jacob." She started stomping her way back to the main house. "We're two people with a lot of baggage."

"I'm pretty baggageless, sweetheart."

"My ass." She whirled on him right in front of the back entrance. "See? We're fighting. We always resort to disagreement. That is us. You want to kiss me now?"

He crowded her, because apparently that was a thing he did now. "Yeah, I do. And the more I do it the more I want to do it and a whole hell of a lot more than just an amazing-as-all-get-out kiss or two."

"I... You... Oh, you're just saying that."

"You want me to be plainspoken, Leah? I want to kiss you. I want my hands on you, all over every last inch of you. I want to have sex with you, even when you're being so clueless and stubborn. Because I think you're hot, because I like you. And I get there are some practical issues that may be…complicated, but I kind of don't give a shit knowing you feel the same. Because I'm not afraid of hard work."

She crossed her arms over her chest, her nose getting red from the cold. He wanted to push her inside and finish the argument, or finish something else, but her family was in there and that was probably not okay.

"I'll give you that, Jacob. You may even love hard work. But are you not afraid of ruining our friendship or our partnership?"

It softened him a little because, well, both those things *were* important and he didn't like that he might be giving the impression he thought they weren't. "How about this? You break my heart, I won't hold it against you."

Her throat moved and her direct gaze shifted to beyond his shoulder. "How about vice versa?"

And then he *really* softened because that was the absolute last thing he wanted to do. "I don't hurt people. Haven't you heard? The women do the breaking up in my experience." He tried to grin, but figured it didn't come out very convincing when her response was a frown.

It wasn't her usual angry scowl when they were

arguing. This had a softness to it. Pity, if he was being honest with himself, but he wasn't interested in being that at the moment.

"I won't be blueprinted or maneuvered. I've got enough of that. And if you haven't noticed, I don't handle it well."

"I've noticed, baby."

"Lay off the 'baby' or you're going to get a boot to the ass, which, let me tell you, is not going to be like your fantasy of my hands on your ass."

"I haven't even begun to tell you about my fantasies."

"Go home, Jacob. Enjoy Christmas with your family. All this...other stuff we'll figure out some other time."

"My stuff is at your place. Your parents think I live with you."

"Right. Well, I'll tell them you always spend Christmas Eve and Christmas night at your parents'. I'm sure your parents have an extra toothbrush for you. You have clothes upstairs. Problem solved."

"Afraid to share a bed with me?"

She blew out a breath. "I'm afraid of a lot of things."

And that little admission, so unexpected from Leah, had him stepping back. Nodding. Okay, he'd give her her space because he didn't want to make her...that. "All right. I'll...see you Tuesday, then, I guess."

She nodded, a little too emphatically. "Yup. Later."

She disappeared inside, and though he was freezing, he gave her a few minutes. Gave himself a few minutes.

He needed a plan. That would solve everything.

CHAPTER THIRTEEN

LEAH DROVE HER family back to her house in silence. She didn't know what to say. Not about anything. So, what option was there but silence?

She pulled into the driveway, trying to muster... something. Christmas cheer or family togetherness or...anything but the sort of numb feeling she had going on at present. A mix of Jacob and Mom and... the state of both her lives right now.

She was supposed to be repairing the old one, not in the hopes it'd mesh with the current one, but more in the hopes they could exist side by side.

But the present one was being knocked all topsy-turvy thanks to Jacob and his kissing and his words and his touching and his...everything.

"I want you boys to go to the store," Mom said, turning in her seat to look meaningfully at Dad and Marc in the back.

"Well, I can get whatever you need, Mom. You guys hop out. It's Christmas Eve, so only a few places will be—"

"I want the boys to go to the store."

Translation: confrontation ahead. Well, good,

maybe Leah could work out some way to feel or deal or…whatever. Get past the numb. Get past those feelings that had caused her to run away in the first place.

Dread pooled in her stomach, but this talk was probably necessary, so she gave Marc directions to the grocery store she thought might be open and Mom told Dad two unnecessary things to buy.

"LET'S FIX SOME DINNER," Mom said brightly, marching into the house with a singular kind of purpose that made Leah almost wonder if there wasn't going to be a confrontation.

Mom gestured to one of her kitchen table seats. "The roast is already started but you can peel the potatoes for me. Then we'll do the cannoli."

It was strange to do all this stuff in her little house. The routine came back to her easily as Mom set a bag of potatoes, a peeler and a bowl in front of her. Helping Mom in the kitchen with the least labor-intensive tasks. Always sitting.

But it was her kitchen now, not the brightly colored one in Minnesota. And she was an adult, still eaten up by the same old issues.

Well, at least she wouldn't sneak out tonight to find a party to make bad decisions at. Which oddly make her think of Jacob. *Afraid to share a bed with me?*

Yup, 100 percent shaking in her boots because after those two lady-bits-scorching kisses, she didn't trust herself to keep her hands, mouth or those lady bits 100 percent to herself.

Leah looked at the potatoes and sighed. It was really hard to remember that kissing Jacob was her adult version of the drinking and the smoking and the partying she'd indulged in as a teenager. He just...said all the right things, did all the right things. How was she supposed to remember it was all such a very bad idea? Something she'd been remembering for five years?

"Did you and Jacob have a fight?"

"No. I told you, Christmas with his family is very important to him." *And I cannot be in the same room with him without getting lusty thoughts, apparently.* Leah grabbed a potato and started peeling.

"But he didn't come back in with you."

"His sister came and... Look, Mom, things with Jacob are fine. Really."

"And things with us?" Mom asked without looking at her, instead fiddling with her pot roast.

Leah took a deep breath. "We're good. Really. I just... I don't like the marriage-talk stuff. I'm almost thirty. I've spent a lot of time thinking about this, and I know what I want. It would... I would feel so much better if you could respect what I want." There. She'd said it. All adultlike and without crying or throwing herself at Jacob.

Although that simply might be the case of not having an opportunity to do so right this very second.

Mom slid into the chair next to her and pushed

the potatoes gently out of the way before covering Leah's hands with hers. "I can't stand the thought of you alone and helpless."

"And I can't stand that you think so little of me." It was the first time in ten years she'd spoken so honestly with her mother, and Leah couldn't make herself look up. She stared at their hands and held her breath.

Maybe it could be the start of something honest and healing. Maybe if she said this, put it right out there, they could unwind the past and forge something new.

"I don't think so little of you. I love you with all my heart, but you don't think straight when you're in a bad place, Leah. Your aunt was absolutely the last person you should have run to to take care of you."

"I stayed with her *because* she wouldn't take care of me. Because she let me do whatever. And I needed that space to really grow up. To figure out what I wanted to be and how I could fix myself." She wanted to add the part about how her leaving fixed everything. Mom and Dad got back together instead of separation leading to divorce. They paid off their debts. Everything had been fixed because she'd taken herself out of the equation.

Mom shook her head. "You don't look at the big picture. You're like your father and put things off until it's an even bigger problem, and with health like yours, that's terrifying as your mother. It's not loving you less to think you need someone to help you, to watch out for you when you hit the rough patches. That isn't thinking little of you. It's caring about your well-being."

Wasn't it both? Leah didn't know. Maybe it wasn't. Maybe she was wrong. All she knew was she was tired, and apparently she wasn't getting her new beginning by being honest. So, she let out her held breath and didn't argue.

"Don't push Jacob away. You need him."

Ouch. She didn't even *have* Jacob. *Except for all that stuff he said earlier.* Yeah, she did not have the energy to figure all that out right now. "I need a boyfriend because I'm not reliable enough to take care of myself."

"*Reliable* isn't the right word." Mom pushed away from the table, back to lining up ingredients. Ingredients she had brought. Pans and utensils she'd brought. Because Leah wouldn't possibly have thought to have any of those things.

"So what is the right word?" She didn't know why she was pushing or, God, hoping something would give, but she was, she did.

"Finish those potatoes so you can help me make the cannoli. Your father will simply cry if we don't have cannoli for Christmas Eve. Though Lord knows why I go through the effort when the man can't even stay awake for midnight mass one day out of the year."

Leah didn't know what else to do besides go along with it. To pretend. Help Mom with the cannoli. Watch *It's a Wonderful Life,* get choked up when everyone shows up to save capable, resourceful George.

Oh, she'd get saved if she were in trouble, but would anyone just…let her save herself? Her own way?

"I CAN'T BELIEVE YOU," Grace hissed, handing him a dripping wet plate.

Jacob took it and dried it off, setting it on the counter of his parents' kitchen. "Would you keep it down?" Jacob glanced at Mom and Dad on the couch in the living room as he and Grace hunched over the dishes. His parents were laughing with Kyle, *It's a Wonderful Life* on the TV screen in the corner.

"You kissed her," Grace whispered, leaning in. "After everything I've been saying. After everything you've been saying. You kissed her and don't try to bullshit me about it being for her parents."

"Shouldn't you be out there with your boyfriend minding your own damn business?"

"Why won't you listen to me?"

"As I recall, you weren't exactly listening to me when I warned you off Kyle, were you?"

"That was so incredibly different."

"You're right. I was trying to protect you. You could give a shit about me."

"Is that what you really think?"

She looked so hurt he wanted to take it back, but damn it, she was pissing him off. "I think you need to take a step back and remember how happy you were with me when I was meddling with your love life."

"First of all, you didn't just meddle. You punched Kyle because you were being a grade-A dick. Second of all, you do not have a love life with Leah. Unacceptable."

"Why? Why is that so unacceptable and what business is it of yours? I think she's fully capable of determining whether she wants to have a love life with me or not and vice versa."

"Right. You're so capable in the love-life department."

Jacob looked at his stack of dry dishes, ignoring that feeling that seemed to be popping up lately. Hurt? What did he care if everyone thought he was a failure in the women department? He *was*. But the fact his family couldn't see…well, anything past that sometimes. That did not feel particularly good. "If it helps, she kissed me first." A joke soothed all hurts after all.

"That makes it worse, and just like when you were trying to warn me off Kyle, you aren't listening to what I'm actually saying. She has feelings for you. Of course she kissed you. You kissing her back… are you thinking at all?"

So much for joking. "What if I have feelings for her?"

"You don't even know her!"

"I've known her longer than you. Spent more time

with her than you. I damn well know her, Grace."
Only the fact that his parents were in the next room,
completely viewable from his place at the sink, kept
him from slamming the dishes into the cupboard.
Kept him from letting the anger and frustration he
felt spill out.

"You know her, huh? Okay, why does she always
wear high collared shirts?"

"What?"

"Have you ever seen her expose anything below
the collarbone?" Grace asked, hand fisted on a
cocked hip.

Jacob stopped what he was doing. "What are you
even talking about?"

"Have you ever seen this portion of Leah's self
exposed?" she demanded, gesturing wildly at the
scoop neck of her own shirt.

And because he couldn't think of a time he had,
his stomach sank. Point one for Grace. "So what?
She's…modest."

"Yeah, that red dress she wears to parties showing off a mile of leg is so modest."

Jacob swallowed. "So, I have to understand a
woman's insecurities to know her?"

"Maybe you should understand them before you
go around kissing her and confusing something
that's already confused for her."

"So, what is it? Why doesn't she wear anything
lower cut?"

Grace turned back to the now-empty sink. "I don't know," she grumbled.

"Say again."

"I said I don't know, either, but I've noticed it." She pointed a soapy finger at him. "And you haven't. So. There."

"You know what I think?"

"Oh, enlighten me."

"You're not worried about Leah, and we both know you're not worried about me. You're worried about you."

"What?"

"Yeah, Leah's your best friend these days. And you're afraid that if anything happened with Leah and me, it would change things for you. And you'd lose your best friend to me. You might hide it all under not wanting to see Leah get hurt, but I think it's hiding the fact you just don't want things to change because of how that might affect *you*."

"That's…"

"It's what?"

Grace's eyebrows drew together and she dried her hands slowly on one of Mom's Christmas-themed towels.

"Because tell me, Grace. Tell me really. Why would Leah and I be so bad for each other?"

"I don't think you would be in the short term, okay? But I'm afraid you're both too stubborn to work through the hard stuff, *and* I think Leah… I think she keeps parts of herself hidden from us and

I don't think you'll take it very well when you find out what those pieces are *or* if she won't let you see those parts. And I think that will hurt you both, but I think you'll get angry and she'll just be hurt."

"We're both adults. What do you care?"

"I care that my brother and my best friend might not be on speaking terms and that might affect both me as a person and the business my brother and my boyfriend have built and care very deeply about. It isn't like you to risk MC for something so…"

"Something so what?"

"You know what? You're right. I didn't like it when you did it to me, so I'm not going to do it to you."

"Good."

"But keep in mind this isn't a joke. Leah is not some woman you can just discard when she no longer suits you."

"Why do you think *I* do the discarding? Has it escaped your understanding I'm not the one doing the breaking up? It's them."

"But it's a pattern and you're the common denominator, Jacob."

"I must be a really horrible person."

"Being bad at relationships doesn't make you a horrible person. I think you'd make an amazing boyfriend if you just… You're selfish sometimes. You're the baby, and sometimes you're so wrapped up in *you* you don't see anyone else. How long did you know Kyle without really knowing what was going on with him?"

"He didn't want me to know. And I don't feel like I need to push everyone into confessing every damn thing to me if they don't want to. Maybe you're selfish needing to know everything about everyone."

"It's Christmas. I don't want to fight with you. I love you. You're an amazing brother. I just think you need to start taking a step back from...yourself."

"Well, thanks for the advice, sis."

"Don't be mad."

He forced himself to smile. "Of course not."

"Jacob. Listen to me. You are wonderful. You are. But you have a tendency to be a little...careless when you're set on something, and I can't sit by and not say anything when that carelessness might affect my best friend."

"Yeah, no, I get it. And I'm not mad, and we should go watch the movie."

She looked up at him plaintively, so he did his absolute best to look at ease, to reach out and squeeze her shoulder affectionately even though he didn't feel it at all. "Really. I get it. Let's just agree not to talk about it anymore, okay?"

"Okay. Christmas truce," she said with a rueful smile. She turned and headed for the living room, but Jacob stayed behind. He needed a few minutes to...work on making the smile, the ease real.

He stared at the dark night outside the window in his parents' kitchen and tried to believe Grace's words. He could be selfish. He wouldn't say *careless,* but he could get wrapped up in himself, but Grace was off base. She really was, and it wasn't the first time someone in his family looked at him and didn't see what was ticking underneath.

Usually he threw his restlessness, his...insecurity or whatever the hell it was, into work, but there wasn't work to be had on Christmas Eve. There was only his family and...

Leah. There was Leah. Who understood, in a weird way, what it was like to have your family look at you without...seeing.

Grace thought he was going to hurt Leah if he pursued this. Mom thought he was selfish when it came to girlfriends. And Dad, well, he didn't think Dad had much of an opinion on his dating life. Kyle thought he couldn't stand to be alone, when the truth was he just knew what he wanted. A wife. Someone to be there. He wanted that next phase of his life to start. On his timetable.

And Leah had come the closest to understanding, closer than even him in his six months of no dating.

He was trying to plan it all out. Blueprint a future. And while that worked fine for him, he couldn't do it to other people. But maybe now that he understood...

He took a deep breath and forced himself into the living room lest Grace think he was brooding or upset. He finished the movie, mimicking the favorite lines with his dad like always. He might not feel the Christmas cheer, but he could certainly fake it like nobody's business.

So, he faked the smile and hug he gave Grace as

she and Kyle headed out to spend the night in their almost-finished house down the street.

"You can go home, too, if you like," Mom said. "I know your old bed isn't very comfortable. We can do a late brunch instead of breakfast." Mom smiled. "It isn't as if we have any little ones eager for Santa."

"Hey, make those comments around Grace. She's the one with the steady boyfriend. In fact, make those comments around Kyle. I'd love to see his face."

Mom's smile was thin, and Jacob noticed not for the first time she looked tired. "You okay?"

"Oh, that stupid flu I had last week is lingering. I need a good night's sleep and I'll be fine." She gave him a little push toward the door. "Go home. Sleep in tomorrow morning, and I'll be sure to make the hash browns nice and crispy, just how you like."

He leaned in and gave Mom a kiss on the cheek. "All right. Night, Mom. Merry Christmas."

"Merry Christmas."

And when he stepped outside, he knew he wasn't going home. Maybe it was wrong, okay, yes, it was wrong to go back there when he was all…broody. When he was without a plan or any idea what to do about him or her or them.

But Leah understood what he was feeling. She had kissed him when she was feeling this way, so, hey, turnabout was fair play.

CHAPTER FOURTEEN

When Leah stepped out of her bathroom, she screamed.

Jacob, sitting on her bed as if it was *normal,* winced. "Sorry. Didn't mean to scare you."

Leah pressed a hand to her heart, the hammering almost tangible underneath her long-sleeved henley. "Christ on a cracker, Jacob. What the hell are you doing here? How did you get in here?"

"You might want to go make sure you screaming didn't wake anyone before I answer those questions."

He was right, so she stalked over to the door and poked her head out the doorway. Down the hall, the door to her parents' room was still closed and dark. In the opposite direction, the living room where Marc slept on the couch remained quiet and dark, as well.

Leah turned back to Jacob still sitting on her bed. "How did you get in here?" she asked, her breath still coming a little fast, the scare still pounding in her veins. If she was alone, she might take a hit of her inhaler, but she didn't want Jacob giving her *that* look. She wasn't up for that look from anyone right now.

"Well, I was going to knock, but you know, if I

live here I should probably have a key. You weren't answering your phone, so I remembered you left a key for Grace in the old mailbox a few months ago and, shock, it was still there."

She blinked at him, trying to make sense out of any of it. "But…why? It's Christmas Eve. You're supposed to be with your parents. Why did you…? Why are you…?" She fisted her hands on her hips, trying to be stern. Trying to…ignore the fact he was on her bed. And they'd…done stuff this morning that could lead to…bed stuff.

Dear Brain, NOPE.

"Why are you here?"

He shrugged, idly tracing the pattern on her comforter. "Well, Mom wasn't feeling well, so she sent me home, so to speak."

"This isn't your home."

He met her gaze. "Yeah, I know."

"So…"

"So, Grace and Kyle went to spend the night in their new house, and I didn't feel much like spending the night at MC alone, but your bed is a hell of a lot more comfortable than my old mattress that hasn't been replaced in twenty years at my parents' house."

She relaxed her stance because even though him being here seemed…dangerous for her sanity, she felt sorry for him. He looked lonely, she realized. Lonely and restless, and the normally cheerful, affable Jacob being melancholy always got to her. It was rare, and she was a sap.

When it comes to him.

Oh, shut up, self.

"Okay, so, you came here."

He nodded, fixing his gaze on her. Not her face this time, but her chest. She flushed and crossed her hands over her breasts. Since she hadn't been expecting him and had been planning to go right to sleep, she'd taken off her bra.

She intensely regretted that decision. In fact, she might never take off her bra again. Just to avoid another moment like this.

"Why do you wear high collared shirts?" he asked, still staring despite her crossed arms.

"Huh?"

"Even your pajamas in this hot-as-hell room are all the way up to your neck."

"I…I get cold easily." She wrinkled her nose at him. "What do you care about my fashion choices?"

"So, you cover up to your neck even when it's July and 100 degrees out? Because I've seen you sweat your ass off in a room with no AC, decidedly not cold, and still never seen you wear anything less than fabric all the way up to your neck." He gestured to his collarbone.

"Why are you…?" She swallowed, feeling panic squeeze her heart. "What made you even think of that?"

"Grace noticed. She noticed you do that and she asked me why. Because she says I don't know you, and maybe she's right."

That explained some of his restlessness, she supposed. Kyle must have spilled the kissing beans to Grace and Grace had lectured Jacob, and here he was. On her bed, on Christmas Eve, feeling alone and as if he didn't know her.

Since she'd been on the receiving end of her own version of a shitty lecture, she felt sorry for him. But more than that, she didn't like him thinking he didn't know her. Even if things were getting weird with them, he was still her friend. And for all her secrets, he and the whole MC crew knew *her*. The her she'd built. The her she actually liked.

"You know me," Leah said firmly. "You know the now me, who is the me I want to be. So you and Grace and Kelly and Susan and even Kyle to an extent, you *know* me. I hate to disagree with one of my best friends, but she is wrong in this case."

"Then why don't I know this? Why didn't I even notice this?" He stood, frowning at her. "I hate thinking she's right."

"She's not." Leah looked beyond him because his intense glare was doing things it should not be doing to parts that had no business being involved in this conversation.

"Then tell me." He crossed to her, eyes intent on hers so she couldn't keep looking away. Her heart raced all over again. His expression was so serious, so…frowny, not at all sexually charged and yet things south of the border didn't seem to pick up on that.

He put his hand at the center of her chest. His palm right over where the scar, faded and white, all but pulsed beneath the fabric of her shirt and the warmth of his hand. "Tell me what I don't know."

"I have a scar." She closed her eyes because it felt as though she was opening Pandora's box. Even if she didn't tell him everything, which she wasn't going to, it felt like letting out evil spirits that would ruin her. But the words tumbled out, the truth. The little sliver of possibility that could change everything.

And she wasn't even all that upset about it, because his hand was on her and he was looking at her and it was all very...*guhhh*.

His brows drew together. "Does that have to do with the surgery you were talking about? The defect? It's all connected, isn't it?"

She nodded despite the initial instinct to deny, to lie. She couldn't force those words out. The truth felt like an entity or inevitability she couldn't fight. And his hand was undermining any effort for self-preservation. His hand felt like salvation.

Oh, she was *such* an idiot when it came to him.

"That means...if you're covering up... The defect, the surgery... That means it was your heart."

She nodded again because, well, an argument would be pointless now. There weren't a whole lot of scars she could have in this particular spot that could be chalked up to a defect.

So, he was putting it all together, she couldn't

deny it, and everything would fall apart. And for what? This idiotic chance to have her family back that wasn't going remotely the way she'd wanted.

"Why would you hide that?"

"Why do you think?" she snapped, not at all pleasantly. But it was an unfair snap because she certainly wasn't angry at him; she was pissed at herself.

"I don't have a clue."

"I've spent my whole life being…poked and prodded and fussed over. Worried over. 'Don't do that, Leah. It's too strenuous.' Well, I wanted a life without that, so I built one where it didn't matter." Because she was feeling defiant along with her anger, she fixed him with a glare. "And it doesn't fucking matter."

"You said you were better. The surgery fixed that."

"It did and I am, but that doesn't stop people from perceiving me as weak because of it."

Finally, finally, his hand left her chest, because that was really getting distracting, but instead of staying away or giving her space, he stepped in. Crowding her. She wanted to hate his apparent new habit.

But instead what she really wanted was the body-pressing, brain-killing kiss from this afternoon.

Wrong, wrong, wr—

His hands cupped her face—God knew why. He wasn't reacting at all like she'd thought he would in the few times she'd allowed herself to consider this. The truth.

Well, part of the truth. Heart surgery and heart transplants were two different things, but she wasn't about to concede the whole thing. Let him think she'd had her heart fixed, not replaced.

"I'm not sure I could ever think you were weak, Leah."

Oh, oh, *hell,* that was smooth. But she needed to put a stop to this. To him and them and something. Because thinking was a thing she wasn't doing and she needed to.

"Look." She put her hands over his in an attempt to remove them, but he wouldn't budge and in the end her hands just rested there, on his wrists.

Maybe he didn't have all the details, but he wasn't looking at her as if she might break. He wasn't demanding to know the details of her health. He wasn't saying she needed someone looking after her otherwise she'd make bad decisions and ruin herself. He was just looking at her. Right in the eye. As if he was searching for something on her face.

"I've never done anything wrong when I feel this way." His voice was quiet, soft, but she recognized an undercurrent there. She'd felt that undercurrent. A confused kind of desperation to make sense of things.

She felt it now.

"Maybe I've had too much to drink on occasion when I'm particularly pathetic. But I don't seek out bad things when I feel like no one sees me or whatever this is. I pour myself into work. Into what I can control."

"I…"

"Your way…I want to do it your way. Because that sounds like it would feel…good. I would like to feel good. What about you?"

"Yes." Oh, she hadn't really meant to say that. What she'd meant to say was "Maybe you should go home." Or "How about a drink?" Or "Go to bed, Jacob."

Instead, his mouth was fused to hers, her arms around him and her back pressed to the wall. And she didn't want to stop it, or pull back, or to find her senses, or to be interrupted.

No, this time she wanted everything, and if there was a way to get it, well, why the hell not?

IT WAS STRANGE, but everything seemed to right itself with Leah's mouth on his, her hands hitching up the back of his sweater.

He stepped back to remove the bulky garment.

"Are you stopping— Oh."

Jacob grinned, pulling the sweater over his head and dropping it on the floor. It was impossible to not feel like grinning when she was watching him unbutton the shirt underneath with avid interest. When he could see the peaks of her nipples against the fabric of her shirt. "Not stopping." He dropped the button-down shirt, then nodded at her. "Your turn."

She hesitated and he belatedly remembered what had even brought them to this point. Her and her high collared shirts. Her scar. Her surgery.

He didn't like how…distant it all made him feel. As if he was standing shirtless in front of a stranger. But she said he knew her, so he was going to believe he did. Because he needed to. He needed to believe he wasn't a totally self-absorbed asshole.

Before he could suggest losing her sweatpants instead, she tugged the shirt up and over her head, revealing a long torso of fair skin, interrupted by a white scar between her bare breasts.

He wanted to press his hand to it. Travel the length of the whitish line from top to bottom. He wanted to ask a million questions, but she was stiff, tense, and it was a secret she'd painstakingly kept for five years. So doing any of those things was off the table. He had to pretend as if it wasn't there, because that was what she wanted.

Something weird and uncomfortably heavy settled in his chest. That disconnect between being labeled selfish and careless and yet always feeling as though he was doing what someone else wanted.

Before he could work on pushing those thoughts away himself, Leah eradicated the small distance between them and put her hand to his belt.

"Now pants," she said firmly.

"Be my guest."

She didn't lower her gaze as she undid his belt, but kept it steady on his face. He groaned when she unzipped his pants because she took her sweet time lowering the zipper, giving a little tug, so the jeans lowered from hip to leg to floor. He stepped out of them, toward her, pushing her back up against the wall.

He liked her there, with nowhere to go, feeling as if he had some kind of power or control even though this was completely beyond both.

He kissed her, sucking her bottom lip between his teeth. She shuddered a breath against his mouth, any of the tension that had been in her shoulders completely gone.

He wouldn't think about what it said about him, but there was some secret thrill in making Leah, practical, kick-ass Leah, all breathy and pliant.

She pressed her hands down his back, drawing her short nails lightly against the skin, dipping into his boxers until she cupped his ass. And then she squeezed. Hard.

He laughed and then she did, too.

"Sorry. You have no idea how long and how badly I've wanted to do that."

"Tell me. In great detail."

"You know, we have a job with a lot of bending over and scooting into small places and…well, your butt is in my face a lot."

"Yeah, well, so is Henry's. Don't tell me you're fantasizing about his ass, too."

"Oh, ew."

"That's my girl."

"Let me make one thing perfectly clear," she said, squeezing his butt again, although not nearly as hard. "I am not, and never will be, your girl. I am my own person."

"Leah." He slid his fingers under the waistband of her sweats, tracing her waist around to her back, her ass, palming the curve as he inched the sweatpants and her underwear down. He went with them, kissing thigh, knee, calf as he lowered the sweatpants to the floor. And then looked up at her. "I am very aware of that fact."

She didn't say anything to that, just watched heavy-lidded as he kissed his way back up. Ankle. Kneecap. Hip. Belly button. And then, because regardless of her scar because he couldn't ignore them, he kissed each breast, then eased his tongue around each nipple, repeating both gestures until her head fell back against the wall with a thunk.

"We might want to move this to the bed."

"Yeah, yes, let's do that."

He chuckled to himself, then stopped abruptly halfway there, realization dawning on him like a bucket of cold water. "Oh, shit, do you have condoms?"

"What? You were the one…" She shook her head, scrambling out of his grasp. "Hold on. I think so." She stalked to the bathroom, apparently completely at ease with being naked.

"You think so?" He settled onto her bed as she rummaged around in her bathroom.

"It's been a while."

"How much of a while?" He lounged on her bed, comfortable. Happy. That oppressive weight was gone. Whatever madness it was, he was damn well going to enjoy it.

She returned to view, a condom—thank the good Lord—in hand. "Do you want to talk about the last guy I had sex with or do you want to *be* the last guy I had sex with?"

"Option B please." He tossed the pillows and blankets she'd stacked between them last night at the end of the bed. "Goodbye Walls of Jericho."

"You and that movie," she grumbled. She held the packet under the weak light of an old lamp.

"What are you doing?"

"Checking the expiration date."

"That long, huh?"

"It can be longer." She fixed him with a glare that made him laugh, because for all the ways this was new, uncharted territory, she was still Leah, and he was still him.

"Get over here."

"Let me make a second thing perfectly clear. I do not take orders."

Jacob grinned. "What if I took that as a sexual challenge?"

She pressed her lips together but her mouth quirked upward. "You can try. But I tend to be rather contrary."

"Okay. Then stay over there. Way over there. And

don't you dare come near me." He pushed his boxers off, folding his arms behind his head.

"You are awfully full of yourself, McKnight." She held the condom up between two fingers. "I bet I could have you on your knees in five seconds."

"Undoubtedly. My knees would prefer the bed, though."

She walked over, no bones about making it slow. But he liked watching her. The way she moved, the way she tried not to smile. The round slope of her hips and the little birthmark on her thigh.

The only difficulty was keeping his eyes off her breasts so she never got the impression he was staring at her scar. He had a feeling that would end this pretty darn quick, and he wasn't doing anything to jeopardize this chance.

Maybe he'd veiled it as a bad thing to deal with crappy feelings, but right now it felt more like a chance. A starting point. A maybe. And he damn well was going to grab that with both hands. Figuratively. And a little literally as he grabbed her by the waist and pulled her onto the bed, leveraging himself over her in a pretty smooth move, if he did say so himself.

She pressed her palm to his cheek, rubbed. "FYI, I liked your beard. Bring it back, please."

"Well, I can't summon it this minute, but if you have patience, your wish is my command."

Her hand covered his dick, stroking lightly. "Just how patient do I have to be?"

Holy hell. He had to clear his throat to speak. "Well, let's find out."

CHAPTER FIFTEEN

LEAH COULDN'T BELIEVE that she was doing this. Or that it was easy. Or…anything. But she was giddy with that disbelief. Giddy with the freedom to do whatever the hell she wanted. It was an old giddiness, one she'd spent a lot of time eradicating from her life.

With her hand on Jacob's length, it was hard to care. No, not hard. Impossible. She wanted this with every last breath. She wasn't big on feeling desperate, but this kind of desperation was so mixed up with longing and desire, she couldn't even dislike it.

He didn't look at her scar. He didn't get weirded out by it or feel the need to mention it or ask her if she was up for anything. He'd just…taken the news and moved on.

There was seriously nothing sexier than that.

So, she squeezed, causing Jacob to hiss out a breath. Yeah, this wasn't desperation; it was power. And she was going to take all the power she could get.

She stroked and watched him as he watched her hand. Oh, man, that was hot. Then his hand grazed across her belly and lower, cupping her, sliding a finger inside.

She stopped watching, because she couldn't keep her eyes open as he slid his finger in and out, drawing her desire to a sharper and sharper point. Until she couldn't take it anymore and grabbed the condom she'd dropped on the mattress and tore it open.

This might be stupid, but she wasn't afraid. She didn't do fear anymore. So she held his gaze as she rolled the condom on, as she guided him to her entrance. Her hands were steady even if her breathing was a little ragged. With one arm, he leveraged himself, the other gripping her hip as he slowly slid inside.

It *had* been a while. A long while since she'd felt this. The intimate connection of body to body. And of course, this was a man she knew, better than just about any man in the world, and that made it different. More important or something.

He kissed her collarbone, her jaw, nuzzled into her neck before withdrawing and slowly thrusting again.

Leah arched to meet it, linking her arms around his neck. He'd already brought her close with his hand, so this wouldn't take long for her. Part of her wanted to hurry, but her body couldn't get that message to her brain or to Jacob, because she accepted each languid thrust, each aching pull of wanting more.

It wasn't until the tempo of everything picked up that he pushed deeper, harder, and she was so close she dug her fingertips into his shoulders, trying to take some of the power, set some of the pace.

He didn't fight her. Instead, they found some common ground. Some equal frequency. His hand, rough palm, long fingers slid up her torso, a heavy caress, pressured as he palmed her breast.

It was a possessive gesture, something she wouldn't have considered in her list of sexy, take-me-over-the-edge attributes, but apparently Jacob broke a lot of the molds she'd set for herself because the orgasm washed over her as she arched to meet it, him.

He pressed his forehead to her shoulder, each movement inside of her becoming more frenetic, until he let out a low groan and pushed deep one last time.

It wasn't her experience to hold on after the deed was done, but she couldn't unwind her arms from his neck, and his one hand around her waist didn't loosen. They lay there, basking in the last dregs of the orgasm, until he kissed her, eyes wide-open, watching her.

Which did something weird to her heart. Weird and not at all welcome, because now that the ill-advised sex was over, the consequences would have to be dealt with.

Stupid consequences.

"So." He cleared his throat, rolling onto his side. "Merry Christmas."

The laugh bubbled up so unexpectedly, she had to cover her mouth to keep it from being too loud. "I don't think you're supposed to say that when you're naked. It seems really wrong."

He grinned, then kissed her again, this time just a quick peck. "Hold on—I'll think of something more appropriate to say." He pushed off the bed and disappeared into the bathroom for a few seconds.

Leah took a deep breath, staring at the ceiling, the uncomfortable thought that she could get used to *all* of this making her stomach cramp.

Nothing to get used to, Idiot McGee.

She shook her head and got out of bed, finding her underwear and sweats and pulling them on quickly. Jacob stepped out of the bathroom as she picked her shirt off the floor.

So now she'd seen him naked. And Jacob naked rivaled every fantasy she'd ever allowed herself to have, which wasn't many. Still, he was all taut muscle and he even had the tiniest hint of those ridiculous hip dip things that, yes, very much made a girl go dumb because she was ready to drop her pants all over again.

Instead, she held her shirt to her chest, covering up her scar. The scar he hadn't touched, hadn't stared at or considered. He'd made it feel as if it was nothing.

Which made her emotional because that was all she'd ever wanted.

"So, um, that was fun."

He quirked an eyebrow at her. "That's one word for it." He sauntered, seemingly not at all self-conscious, to where his duffel bag sat in a corner. Before they'd actually done everything, she hadn't felt at all weird being naked in front of him. Hard to feel insecure when the guy was all but a cartoon character with a tongue hanging out, but now...

Ack. Weird. For her. Apparently not him. Which figured.

"I have a few other words for it, too." He stepped into his sweatpants and lifted them to his hips. Then he grinned. "Wanna hear them?"

She smiled back even as her brain admonished her not to. In the aftermath, they needed to set up some ground rules. Understand that that was a one-time thing, and now it was...over. It was their bad-feeling therapy or mistake or whatever, and now it was done.

End of story.

Jacob taking a seat on her bed, shirtless, self-satisfied smile on his face, did not say "end of story." It said... well, things she couldn't think about.

"Look." She took a deep breath and crossed over to him. She'd made this bed, so to speak, so now it was time to lie in it. One-time deal. As awesome as it was, meaning nothing.

Nothing except now you know what it's like and will forever picture him naked. Forever and ever. Amen.

Oh, crap, but yes, amen. Naked Jacob. Sex with Jacob. All very worthy of hallelujah status.

"Let's be clear that—"

She should have known better. Should have known that getting close enough to touch meant he would touch, tug, pull, until he'd somehow maneuvered her on top of him, still clutching the stupid shirt to her chest.

She was on his lap. Oh, she shouldn't be on his lap. He tugged the shirt from her grasp. She should have held on tighter, but it slid from her fingertips.

Still he didn't look at her scar. Didn't touch it. Didn't ask questions about it. And it didn't even seem purposeful. It was as though he seriously didn't care, and that was so, so, so dangerous to believe.

Then she might believe other things.

But when his mouth met hers, gentle and coaxing, her defenses were already gone. Melted. She leaned into the kiss, sighing contentedly when his palms brushed down her bare back.

God, he was good at this stuff.

When his hands reached her hips, he pulled her closer to him, flexing his hips so sparks of heat centered low in her belly.

He wasn't seriously hard again, because that could lead to…round two, which would lead to forgetting her whole one-time policy of screwing up.

He pulled her forward again. *Ohhh.* Surely twice couldn't be any bigger mistake than once. Surely. Surely.

He kissed her neck, concentrating on the space right below her jaw that made it hard to do anything but arch against him.

"What was the expiration date on those condoms?" he murmured into her neck.

"What? Why?"

"And how many were left?"

Oh, God, she had to stop this. She did. In a minute. "Jacob."

"I'm just wondering, should we hurry up and use them all before they go to waste? I'd hate to see you lose a few dollars when they could be well spent. Very, very well spent."

"Should there...should there really be more times?" Which was a stupid question when she was tilting her head to give him better access to her neck. "I thought this was a bad-decision-to-make-crappy-feelings-go-away-type deal?"

"I'd like it to be more."

Ah, crap. Bucket of ice water right there. She could ignore a lot of things for these pleasant downstairs feelings, but not that. Not...leading him on. "Jacob."

"Oh, are you going to be sensible now? Because that sounds terrible."

"I just don't want you to think..." She wiggled off his lap because she could not think with his erection pressed all that close to where she would very much like it to go, even with layers of clothes between them. "You said you wanted some good, or whatever, because you were feeling bad. So, this isn't starting anything."

He reached out, twirled a strand of her hair around

his finger. How she wanted to lean into that. To cuddle. Which was an alien enough feeling that she pulled away instead.

"So, what would be so terrible if it was the start of something? Because obviously we're compatible." He gestured to the space between them. "We have a lot in common, and before you bring up the fact that we argue all the time, consider that despite that we've been good friends for five years."

"You're right."

"I'm sorry. Can you repeat that?"

She shook her head. "I'm not going to argue that we aren't a certain amount of compatible...and, short term, it would probably be nice."

He wrinkled his nose. "Nice? Nice?"

"But long term...we don't want the same things." And she didn't like how hard that basic truth was to formulate in her brain, because all worked up, she had a hard time thinking beyond *Sex. Good. More.*

But there wasn't more for them. There couldn't be.

"Like?"

"Like..." Leah scrubbed a hand over her face. "Like, you want to find a wife and have 2.5 kids in a house with a dog and a white picket fence. For starters, I'm allergic to dogs."

"So, we'll get a cat."

"Allergic."

"Fish. Turtle. I'm pretty flexible in my pet plans."

"Jacob." She took a deep breath and looked at the ceiling. "I don't want to get married. To anyone. Ever. And I don't want kids—2.5 or otherwise. I don't...want those things for my life. So, like, pretending this could ever be more is just stupid."

He was silent. Completely still and silent. Her stomach jittered and she had to swallow past the nerves and fear in her throat. She didn't go around telling people those things. It tended to bring up a whole slew of responses she didn't feel comfortable dealing with.

Because it wasn't about anything more complicated than a faulty heart, but she'd rather people think it was feminism or independence or selfishness over fear.

The silence stretched on and she couldn't stand it any longer, so she looked at him. He had his poker face on, but he was staring at her. Intently. What he was thinking, she didn't have a clue.

"Is it, like, you don't like the institution-of-marriage thing? Or something else? Give me something to go on here," he finally said.

And the way he asked—no, demanded—put her back up. "Why? So you can try and change my mind?"

"No, so I can understand why something this good isn't an option."

"Don't try to conquer me, Jacob. I don't want to lose your friendship, and if you try to take me over, that is what will happen." She had no doubts about that.

JACOB FROWNED OVER at Leah. Shirtless and gorgeous and irritating the hell out of him in just seconds. "I'm not trying to conquer you by wanting to understand."

"Why do you need to understand?"

"Because..." He stopped himself before he could say what he really wanted to say. Which was "so, if you're wrong, I can show you you're wrong." But that was not the way to win over Leah.

Not that he knew the way. She made it all sound so final. No marriage. No kids. And not that he was ready to make that kind of leap, but she was right to say that was what he wanted for his future, and if they weren't ever going to agree on that...well, then this...

"Jacob. It's just... It just is. It is the way it is. We want different things and no amount of great sex is going to change that."

"It was pretty great." He forced himself to smile, to not let that depth of frustration and, hell, maybe hurt show. "So what would be the harm in a few more greats?"

She got that pained look on her face again. Pity or something way too close for him to be able to look at it. "Hey, I'm going in eyes wide-open. This isn't leading to till death do us part. Got it. But, the way I see it, I'm still your fake boyfriend for a few more days and as long as Grace is lecturing me about how I'm too selfish and careless to be with you, I might as well enjoy being with you briefly."

"She didn't really say that."

He gave her a doleful look. "Her words. Exactly. Selfish. Careless."

Leah's eyebrows drew together and she inched a little closer. "You know, I love Grace, but she doesn't see past your mask."

"My mask? I thought I was an open book." He grinned, without any feeling whatsoever. Okay, so maybe occasionally he donned a bit of a mask, but what was the point of pouting or acting hurt? It didn't change anything.

Leah rested her hand on his shoulder, gingerly. He didn't like that tentative touch from someone he'd just had sex with. It grated, but he didn't let his mouth curve downward, and if that was a mask, so fucking be it.

"All the jokes and the smiles and affability? That hides a man who cares, maybe a little too much."

He shifted because that was…uncomfortable. Wrong. It was wrong. *Then why are you squirming like a kid in the principal's office?*

But she just kept going, her hand sliding closer, giving him a little squeeze, her leg brushing his. "And that, along with wanting to control everything and believing right should be rewarded and wrong should be punished… Well, that's why you flip out when bad things do happen. Like with Grace's… situation this year. You can't hide that or pretend to laugh it away, so you go all lunatic."

"See, here I thought you were coming to my defense, and now you're calling me a lunatic."

"No." Her hand slid up his neck to touch his cheek, resting her palm there, her thumb dragging across the edge of his chin. "I'm saying you're not selfish, because you care about how other people feel. Like right now, you're pretending you're fine and smiling when I know you're irritated with me."

Well, it was hard to keep smiling through that truth. And extremely uncomfortable she could see through that.

"And you're not careless. You pretend to be, lest someone see how much you care. How much you want everyone to be happy. And that only slips when really bad things happen. So Grace is wrong. You're the opposite of those things, but you give her reason to think that, because that's the version of yourself you show."

He looked at her, wondered that…she could just crack him open like this. See through him in a way he wasn't even sure he saw himself, but she was right. He could feel the rightness of her words like a physical punch.

"Look, you spend five years with an idiotic crush, you notice things about a guy." She shrugged, obviously uncomfortable. "And I wouldn't have a crush if you weren't a good, decent guy. But crushes are crushes and bad decisions are bad decisions, and bottom line, what we want is what we want, and it's not going to change."

"Yeah, and what's another week or two of sex going to change?"

She bit her lip, chewing on it as she stared at him. "It seems like a bad idea."

Probably the worst idea, but he didn't care. He wanted to be with her again. A lot of agains. Besides, he knew how things went. He got involved. It didn't work. Female party said adios. That was how his relationships worked. So he'd go into this one knowing that was what would happen.

He tugged her back onto his lap. "Indulge in a few more bad ideas before you kick me to the curb, baby."

She frowned at him, but she was in his lap, straddling him, her hands back on his face. Her breasts pressed to his chest.

"For what it's worth…" She took a deep breath, looking him right in the eye. The blue and green meshing together in a kind of swirl he could lose himself in for hours. "If I wanted different things for my life, for my future, you would absolutely be my first choice."

That did nothing to make him feel better. If anything, it twisted the knife deeper. "How the hell is that something I want to hear?"

She smiled ruefully. "Isn't it better than me saying you're forgettable at best?"

"I'm not sure." But he covered her mouth with his, because he was damn well done with talking, with feeling anything other than lust and orgasm.

She sank into him, and he knew he shouldn't say it. Shouldn't think it. Shouldn't feel it. But he couldn't help himself. "For the record," he said against her lips, "you'd be my first choice, too." In fact, quite honestly, all future choices seemed as though they'd pale in comparison.

CHAPTER SIXTEEN

LEAH COULDN'T REMEMBER the last time she'd woken up with someone. Maybe…Steve? And, jeez, that had been at least four years ago. The last time she'd dared hope something would…go somewhere.

A hope long gone. For good reason. She had to remind herself of that sometimes. Remind herself what she was doing by swearing off marriage and kids and all that…junk.

Saving those people who might be involved in those things from suffering the same fate as her parents. She thought she was older and wiser enough to make amends there, to keep herself separate enough from making them miserable, bankrupt, apart.

But lifelong relationships that required people live with her and depend on her… It would not be fair to those people. The worry, the cost, the just *shit* they'd eventually be subjected to.

The bad stuff that couldn't be controlled, that wasn't fair. Those things that flipped Jacob's unreasonable switches.

Last night had been weird. Articulating all the things she'd observed about Jacob in the past five years had crystallized them, made it even clearer how bad this was. Because she'd known all those little pieces, but until he'd looked all sad and upset over Grace calling him selfish and careless, until she'd realized how little Grace understood…well, she hadn't put all those little pieces she understood about him together.

And now she had, and her heart hurt. Because she understood him. She wanted him. They were… so weirdly good together, and yet, it couldn't work.

All because her body was faulty to the extreme.

Which was a dangerous line of thinking. Because blaming her body had led to the whole almost-died-after-the-transplant thing in the first place. She wouldn't go back there. Not for her parents or even for Jacob, but because she would be there all too soon without helping the transplant along its way to early doom.

This was her life. Good behavior or bad, so she'd just do what she wanted. That was how she'd operated since running away from home, and she wasn't about to stop.

Jacob stirred, his hand brushing against her thigh before his eyes even opened, his fingers walking up her side as his mouth slowly spread into a smile.

"Are you sleep feeling me up?"

"Is that a problem?" he asked in a gravelly voice. Oh, that voice was yum. Of course, so was the rough fingertip tracing the outline of her underwear, back and forth.

"Nope."

"Excellent."

His mouth curved into a smile before he opened his eyes. Pretty brown eyes. Not a very manly description, but apt. The color reminded her of the polished wood at MC, all rich and complex. She reached out to touch his face, then wished she hadn't when he rested his cheek against her palm. They really needed to focus on lusty sex heat not…warm, gooey affection.

"Now I am awake feeling you up," he said, his hand venturing toward the apex of her thighs. "I assume that's okay, too?"

"As long as turnabout is fair play." She slipped her hand into his underwear, closing her fingers over the hard, hard length of him.

It took no time at all to have each other breathing heavily, and then Jacob withdrew his hand, rolled over her and reached for the box of condoms on the nightstand. He grabbed a condom and tore the packet open in what seemed like one fell swoop.

"You really don't want those condoms to go to waste, do you?"

He rolled the condom on himself. "I care very, very deeply about your bottom line." Then he slid inside until she sighed. "Waste not, want not and all that."

"Uh-huh." He withdrew, slowly teasing her with tiny thrusts that did almost nothing in the sensation department. And the almost was kind of driving her crazy. So she pushed him over and climbed on top, guiding him inside and deep, just where she wanted him.

She took his wrists and pinned them to the bed up near his ears, but he only grinned. "You know I could flip you in a second flat, right?"

"Try me."

"Mmm, let's just keep doing this."

"Or we could do that." She moved against him, slow and deep, again and again until his eyes fluttered closed. It so did something for her that she could make him do that. Close his eyes, lose control. She was doing that. To Jacob.

So wrong. So damn right.

She increased her pace, chasing her own pleasure as fast as she could. He gripped her hips, meeting her thrusts, pushing deep.

"Leah, baby," he whispered into her ear.

And she wanted to hate herself for orgasming over *baby* when she hated that endearment, but, well, her body wasn't listening.

Then he did flip her, in about a second flat, and thrust deep, holding her tight.

She was a little afraid he was going to sex her into acquiescence, but there was too much at stake. So she'd take the sex and leave the rest. Yes, she would.

He grinned down at her, her wrists still pinned to the mattress by his hands, her body pressed hard against it by his. "Merry Christmas."

She closed her eyes. "You have to stop saying that

naked. I'm going to get dirty thoughts every time I hear it now."

He chuckled against her neck. Oh, she liked his mouth there, the shivery feelings he managed to elicit with just the lightest of touches. A breath, a kiss, a nibble.

He rolled off her, then the bed, whistling "We Wish You a Merry Christmas" as he disappeared into the bathroom.

When he reappeared, she fixed him with her sternest glare. "Do not take this as a compliment."

"Take what as a compliment?"

She reached over and grabbed her inhaler off her nightstand, shaking it, then drawing in a breath.

He grinned, but she saw that flicker of something else before he did. Worry. And that was all she needed to know she was making the right decision here. He might pretend her scar didn't exist, he might pretend this didn't bother him, but it did. And it would build and build until...

Well, she wasn't going to let that happen.

"I guess we should go a little slower next time." He said it like a joke, but it wasn't. Not even a little.

"I haven't had an asthma attack that sent me to the hospital since I was a kid. I grew up and out of the severity. The inhaler just helps me breathe a little easier when things get tight."

He plastered one of those blank smiles on his face. The kind of smile that didn't fool her, even when she wanted it to.

"I need coffee." She stepped out of bed, pulling on the pajamas they'd discarded after the second bout of pantlessness last night.

"I'm going to run through the shower. I should try to beat Grace and Kyle back to Mom and Dad's."

Leah nodded, pulling on her socks, then stepping out in the hall. She could still hear Dad snoring, but the light in the living room was on and she could smell food and coffee. Well, there was one nice thing about having Mom around after all.

She stepped into the kitchen. Mom was standing in front of the coffeemaker, already done up for the day. Bright red Christmas sweater. Green elastic-waist pants.

Tears stung Leah's eyes unexpectedly. She'd forgotten Mom's ridiculous Christmas-outfit tradition. She'd forgotten a lot of things, really, in the past ten years.

Sniffly, and maybe a little relaxed from all the ill-advised sex last night, she went over to Mom and gave her a hug from behind. "I'm glad you're here." Ridiculous assumptions, insinuations and straight-out wrongness all seemed to fade away.

This was what she'd wanted. This was what she'd been working for. Getting back family. Because no family was perfect or right all the time, but they had traditions and moments when things *were* right.

"Merry Christmas, sweetie," Mom said, patting her arm. "I'm glad I'm here, too." She turned her head and smiled up at Leah. "Christmas hasn't been the same without you." Mom's eyes got a little watery, but she waved her hand in front of her face. "Well, none of that. I'm making a big old breakfast. Sit down and I'll tell you my trick to making the perfect bacon."

Leah didn't even mind being admonished to sit down. "Where's Marc?"

"Oh, he went on a run. A *run*. Can you believe him? It's snowing and icy and he won't listen to any of my warnings. Oh, I'll just never understand him."

"And Dad's still sleeping."

"Snoring like a log. That man." Mom tsked, pulling an armful of items out of the fridge.

"Now, the first trick to perfect bacon, even turkey bacon, is rinsing each piece individually. It's a pain in the tookus, but so worth it. Your father has not complained about my bacon in thirty-three years of marriage."

Leah smiled. No marriage talk was going to pop a hole in her happy Christmas spirit. Tomorrow? Maybe. Today, she was determined to be Ms. Cheerful no matter what.

Jacob stepped into the kitchen, hair still damp. He had on a chunky red sweater over some ridiculous green plaid shirt. Like a damn Christmas poster. He was so cute it hurt.

Mom's smile broadened. "Oh, Jacob. I thought you spent last night with your family."

"I was going to, but I couldn't stay away." He grinned at Leah, and like an idiot, she grinned back.

Sure, this wasn't a thing, but having sex three times in the past twenty-four hours earned her a grin, right?

"But I do have to go. Brunch with my family. You guys have a merry Christmas and maybe I'll see you tonight if you're up when I get back."

"Oh, well, at least take some coffee." Mom gestured to Leah, so Leah found a travel mug and handed it to Mom. She poured, then handed it off to Jacob. Naturally, then she also pinched his cheek and pulled it down for a smacking kiss.

Jacob chuckled. "Merry Christmas, Mrs. Santino." Of course, he wasn't looking at her mother when he said it; he was looking at her. All...smirky and evil, because she was definitely invaded by dirty thoughts.

Jerk.

Then he leaned down and kissed her on the mouth. Just a quick peck, but still. She was getting sunk fast. Thank God for Christmas and separation.

"Merry Christmas, baby," he said quietly and then also kissed her on the cheek.

Oh, jerk, jerk, jerk, because she was smiling and blushing like a moron, and he'd done it on purpose.

Jacob disappeared and it took Leah a minute to realize she was all but mooning after him. Oh, ugh, she really needed to get that B.S. under control and fast.

"You two made up," Mom said, clutching a spatula to her chest.

"We weren't fighting."

"You were...tense yesterday. Today you're happy."

Mom squeezed her shoulders. "Has he given you your Christmas present yet?"

"Uh, no." She hadn't thought about that. They'd done a secret Santa at work, but neither of them had had each other in the drawing. Crap. Maybe she could find something in her room to pretend to be a gift.

"Maybe it's an engagement ring."

Well, there went any and all good feelings. *Thank you, Mom.*

JACOB WAS WHISTLING when he walked up to his parents' house. Amazing what a little sex could do, even when it would probably end up causing more problems than it solved.

But for today, for Christmas, he was just going to enjoy the fact he'd had sex for the first time in months, with a woman who...well, a woman he didn't have a clue what to do about.

He'd figure it out. There was a first time for everything, but he always figured things out in the end.

He stepped inside. "Winter isn't kidding around this morning," he called.

"Come into the kitchen. Nice and toasty," Mom returned.

Jacob shed his winter gear and walked through the home of his youth. Not much had changed. He admired that about his parents, the way they kept things. It was who they were, this place, their steadfast dedication to their family, their town, the school they both worked at. The students Mom had counseled still sent her emails; some of Dad's former baseball players sent Christmas cards. They had made their mark, and as small as this town was, the mark was important.

He very much admired that about them, tried to emulate it in his own life.

Why that made him think about Leah and her no-marriage, no-kids outlook, he wasn't sure. But it was there, curling up in his brain, eating away at any enjoyment.

Well, screw that. It was Christmas, and he'd made Leah smile and blush this morning. Oh, and there was that little thing of also giving her an orgasm. It was a great damn morning and no bad thoughts allowed.

He stepped into the kitchen and frowned. Mom was standing by the stove, but she was kind of leaning against Dad. Dad had his arm around her and looked worried—that was, until he saw Jacob and smoothed the worry into a smile.

"Merry Christmas, son."

"Merry Christmas. Everything okay?"

Mom smiled at him. "Oh, still feeling a bit puny is all, and Dad's being a worrywart."

"Not worry-warting if it's warranted."

Mom waved a dismissive hand. "I'm fine. Really. The flu is hitting people hard this year, and I'm no exception even with that stupid shot. And it is a drag to be sick over the holidays."

"Maybe you should go back to the doctor."

"If it's still bothering me Monday, I will." She patted his cheek. "My sweet boy. Don't go worrying about me."

"I'll worry about who I want." He kissed her cheek. It felt a little cool, which he wasn't sure was good or bad or in-between. "Here, you let me finish up. I can't make too much of a mess of things at this point."

He nudged her out of the way.

"Oh, you know you could probably do a better job than me. All those classes you took."

Jacob ignored the way the niggle of worry deepened. He'd taken those classes when he was pretending not to know Mom was going through chemo. Home ec and some stupid cooking thing at the Y. Trying to help, pretending as though he wasn't, as though he was into it.

He glanced back at Mom as he pushed the hash browns around in the pan. She looked a little pale, but otherwise fine. She wasn't gaunt or gray like she'd been then.

Overworrying. The flu could be nasty. He'd just keep an eye on her and make sure she did go to the doctor next week if she didn't feel better.

Plan in place, he went back to finishing the brunch Mom had started.

Kyle and Grace didn't show up until he was nearly finished, Grace's laughter announcing their arrival before they shuffled into the kitchen, rosy cheeked and grinning.

"Sorry we're late."

Mom waved away the apology. "Jacob's just finishing up brunch for me. Have a seat. We don't have to be at Aunt Winnie's until three."

"Um, actually we have some news first." Grace grinned back at Kyle, who looked both happy and incredibly uncomfortable, which, really, was pretty normal for Kyle since he and Grace had worked things out.

"So, we got engaged."

"Gracie!" Mom was out of her seat in a flash, ridding Jacob of any last worry about her health. They hugged and laughed and Jacob had to force himself to pry his hands off the spatula, smile, find some kind of...joy.

It caught him a little off guard. He wasn't sure why. Maybe he thought Kyle might ask him first or tell him beforehand, or maybe he thought he'd see it coming, but he...hadn't. They'd been together for months, were moving into their own house. It shouldn't be a surprise, but somehow, wrapped up in his own life, it was a big old shock.

And he would chalk up the weird feeling in his stomach to that over jealousy. Just a little gut-squelching surprise.

When Grace finally escaped Mom's grasp, which landed on poor Kyle, Grace turned to Jacob.

It wasn't hard to muster the smile at this point. She looked so happy, and that was what he wanted for her. Happiness and excitement. She'd had enough of the other crap.

"Hey, now, that is a rock." He took Grace's hand and squeezed.

"It is at that."

He pulled her into a hard hug. "I love you. You know that. And I'm happy for you. Always." Which was the truth. His cheer might be a little off-kilter, but his sister deserved this happiness. His best friend deserved this happiness.

She sniffed into his shoulder. "I know."

He released Grace so she could sniffle over Dad and offered his hand to Kyle as he was released from Mom's clutches. "And a brother." He shook Kyle's hand, then, what the hell, pulled him in for a one-pat man hug. "I couldn't ask for a better one. Really."

"Very much likewise."

Mom and Grace were both teary and sniffling, and even Dad looked a little shiny eyed and had to cough to clear his throat once or twice.

"Well, now. That's quite a Christmas gift, young man," Dad said. "Did I ever tell you about the time—"

"No!" Jacob and Grace groaned in unison.

"Dad, no pig story. Please." Grace leaned into Kyle and Dad laughed.

It was a good moment, and Jacob wanted to bask in that goodness. This light of a future for two of the people he cared so deeply for. And he was happy, but he couldn't squelch the weird not-happy part of him.

"Well, where's the champagne?" he said, clapping

his hands together. "Let's celebrate properly." Maybe if they got over being weepy and hit the happy part, he wouldn't feel so much like his chest was caving in or that the only thing he really wanted to do was go back to Leah's and bury himself in her.

CHAPTER SEVENTEEN

LEAH SAT CONTENTEDLY on the couch, wrapping paper strewn about, piles of unwrapped presents next to everyone in her immediate family. The lights on the small, leaning tree that had given her a weird rash the day she'd brought it home twinkled in the low light of the room. The smell of the veal scallopini they had eaten hung in the air, spicy and familiar and comforting.

Even if the visit wasn't shaping up exactly as she'd wanted, Christmas with her family was everything she'd been dreaming about. It was like years past, except for the two she remembered having to spend in the hospital.

But this was a good day, a good evening, hospital free and all the comforts of family tradition. She'd swallow down the rest for this because this made all the crap worth it.

And that wasn't just the glass of wine she'd had at dinner. It was that Mom hadn't tsked her over it. Hadn't kept an eagle eye on how many bites Leah had ingested. Maybe…maybe there was common ground to be found, if they could just figure out the man thing.

Which had somehow morphed into the Jacob thing.

Leah sighed. Not tonight. She wasn't thinking about that tonight. Or if he'd come to spend the night again. If they'd find a way to use more condoms again. Nope, nope, nope. Not going to think about it. Or hope for it.

"So, time for dessert?"

"Actually, we have one little present left," Mom said, grinning broadly.

Leah looked around her pile, but she didn't see anything unwrapped, and Dad and Marc didn't seem to, either, but Mom only chuckled.

"No, no, not that kind of present. More of a news present. Something that's going to happen." Mom looked at Marc and nodded at him.

He looked incredibly uncomfortable and took a deep breath, looking as if he was on death row or something. The complete opposite of Mom's eager expression.

Then he forced an awkward, tight smile. "I might be moving to Iowa."

The words didn't quite…process or make sense, even as a hard weight settled itself in her gut. "Iowa?"

He nodded, not meeting her gaze.

"Like, here, Iowa?"

He shrugged, picking up scraps of wrapping paper and folding them precisely. "Possibly. I've applied at a few places in the general area. If I get on with State I'd have to go to basic, so it wouldn't be right away or anything."

"And the best part," Mom said, all but bouncing in her chair. "We're going to try to join him in a year or two."

The weight in her gut did a jump, thudding harder against her insides. "What?"

"Well, we considered asking you to move home," Mom began, looking at Dad. "But we know you wouldn't be able to find a job like you have here, and there's Jacob, of course. Then we considered the ties we have in Minnesota, and aside from my sister and Uncle Roy...well, there's just not much keeping us there. So we started saving and getting the house ready to sell. We have a ways to go yet, but optimistically in two Christmases we could live here, too."

Leah couldn't breathe. Or she'd floated out of her body. "What?" She didn't know what else to say because this didn't make sense. None at all.

"We should be together. Now that we've made strides to mend fences between us, it's time we lived in the same place." Mom's eyes had tears in them. Happy tears.

Leah looked at Dad, who was excited and smiling just like Mom, and then at Marc staring way too hard at his scraps of wrapping paper.

"I don't understand." This...wasn't possible. It couldn't be happening. Not...really.

"What don't you understand, sweetie?"

"You don't..." She took a deep breath, tried not to let her panic show. "You don't need to uproot your lives for us to be a family. There's phone calls and visits and—"

"Nonsense. Like I said, nothing is keeping us in Minnesota except the house and money and a few not-close relatives. We tie up our loose ends, and then we can all be together. For all the holidays. And if things happen with you and Jacob, we'll be here. Unless things move faster between you two, which would be fine by me."

"I don't know what to say." And she didn't. Not good or bad—there were no words in her head. Well, except *Nooooooooooooooo!*

"You and your brother clean up and he can tell you a little more about the places he's applied to. I'm going to get dessert started."

Mom and Dad got up and disappeared into the kitchen. Leah watched them go, flabbergasted. Then she turned to Marc. He was picking up wrapping paper, crumpling it all into careful balls.

"Why are you doing this?" she whispered.

"What?"

"Why the hell would you ever move here?" She crouched next to him, picking up a piece of paper and balling it to give her hands something to do.

He shrugged.

"No, I need an answer." Desperately. Why was Marc agreeing to this…this…lunacy?

"Maybe I needed a change."

"Why?"

Marc glanced at the kitchen, then at the front of

the house. "Let's take this out to the garbage can in your garage."

She nodded, scooping up an armful of discarded wrapping paper and following him.

In silence they each deposited their trash, stepped back inside and then discreetly Marc pulled the mudroom door closed so they could be inside without Mom or Dad hearing.

"I know this probably isn't what you wanted," he said, hands shoved in his pockets, eyes locked on the wall behind her. "I know they can be a bit much, but you have to understand how much this means to them."

Leah swallowed. "It's crazy. Parents don't go following their kids around. They don't uproot their lives and move *to* them."

"They're worried about you. They want to be closer to their daughter, who has some serious health problems."

"Always about my goddamn heart," Leah muttered.

"Yes, actually. Which, let me tell you, has been the case since you were born. And you're their child, and maybe you should consider not being selfish for a second or two and put yourself in their shoes."

Leah's jaw dropped. Selfish? Well, okay, yes, he wasn't wrong, but…this was still crazy. "Why are you coming with them? Don't you have a life in Minnesota?"

"I have parents who asked me to do something

for them. Parents who have been through a lot the past almost thirty years. So, to me, it doesn't matter so much what I want."

The implications of all of that, that she was wrong, the bad child, et cetera. And that he was the savior, the perfect child. Well, that reminded her a whole hell of a lot of teenage life.

"Don't..." The anger was so palpable she couldn't fight it anymore. She barely knew her brother, and he and her parents were going to move here and... No. It couldn't happen. She'd escaped for a reason, and she wasn't going back. "You're a grown-ass man, Marc. You can't keep doing what Mommy and Daddy tell you to. Rescind those applications. Cancel whatever interviews. You can't move here."

"Can't I?" He kind of chuckled, but it wasn't a pleasant, amused sound. Not at all. "How about this, Leah. I have spent my whole life helping them clean up after your messes."

She opened her mouth to speak, but nothing came out because... Well, she had no idea what messes he even meant, but more so, as little as she knew him, he'd never directed anger at her. She wasn't sure she'd ever seen him angry. Wasn't sure she'd ever seen anything but stoic standoffishness or stoic vague niceness. Perfect Marc, a statue of responsibility.

Marc was a mystery, always had been, and now he was standing there, the anger vibrating off him.

"You might not care about them, but I do. So, I'm

going to keep caring about them, and if they want to move here, they damn well will. They want me to pave the way? Consider it paved. And you can fight and rage all you want, but you're a grown-ass woman, and you're just going to have to deal with it."

"Why on earth are you mad at me? You should be mad at them for…orchestrating this bizarre idea."

He laughed. Bitterly. "Why am I mad? Because your selfishness has been the leading force of my whole damn life and I'm tired of pretending that it hasn't. You've screwed this family six ways to Sunday, so you do not get to tell me what I can or can't do. I will do what I please. More, I will do what they please, and you have no say."

"I'm not…" She swallowed down the hurt, because he wasn't wrong. She'd done some crappy, selfish things that had adversely affected everyone. She'd just never…given much thought to him. He'd been her aloof older brother.

And now he was all but telling her he hated her.

"If I get a job here, I will move here. And I will help them move here. Because until they have you back, permanently, they can't see anything else."

"I know I sucked. I know that, but I was a teenager with a heart transplant. Don't I at least get a little slack?" She swallowed at the lump because those words felt so…little in the face of his anger. "I left. I left so they could work everything out. And it did, didn't it? Me leaving solved everything."

"Are you that clueless?"

"They got back together. They got out of debt."

"And they spent so many hours planning ways to get you back, it barely mattered. All that mattered was you. Which isn't any different from the moment you were born. And I know that wasn't your fault. You were sick. That wasn't your fault. But your shitty attitude and the shitty way you treated them? That *was* your fault. So, yeah, I'm going to do what they want. Because they should have at least one kid who gives a damn about them." He went to the door, jerked it open and stalked out.

Leah stood there watching the now-empty doorway, barely battling back tears. Well, so much for a merry Christmas.

THE NIGHT WAS CLEAR, sparkling stars dotting the sky. If it wasn't so damn cold, Jacob would be tempted to stay outside. To find some kind of understanding or sense in the vast sky.

But Leah was inside, and that was far more tempting. It was late, and she might be asleep, judging from the dark of the windows of the house, but he wouldn't mind just…sleeping next to her, either.

This was definitely going to be a problem once her parents left, but for now, he'd push off that problem for another day. Christmas and all that.

And a healthy case of denial.

Yeah, that, too.

He used the keys he'd pocketed from her old mailbox last night to open the door. Dark and silence met him. Even the lights on the Christmas tree were off. Gingerly, Jacob crept through the house until he reached Leah's bedroom door.

Judging from the dark at the base of the door, she was asleep, so he did his best to slip in without making too much noise. But she wasn't in bed.

She was curled up on the little armchair in the corner, eyes on the window and the pretty night outside he'd just been admiring. The stars, the colorful Christmas lights from her neighbor winking in the bushes that separated their yards.

She sniffled, and even with the lights out, he had a pretty good feeling she was crying.

"Christmas didn't go well?"

She let out a watery laugh. "That intuitive nature of yours is a real gift, Jacob."

He crossed to the chair, not sure what to do. At this point he'd dealt with Leah's tears, and he felt as if he dealt with them pretty well, all in all. But...he was feeling a little off himself, a little...soft or vulnerable or whatever bullshit word he didn't want to think about.

Still, he rested his hand on the top of her head because it wasn't as if he could disappear the way he'd come. "What happened, baby?"

She stood, flinging the blanket she'd been wrapped up in on the floor. "Everything was great. Great Christmas. Cozy, fun, perfect. I haven't had a perfect Christmas in I don't know how long."

She wrapped her arms around herself, expelling

a loud breath. "And then history served, and shit hit the fan." Her voice squeaked at the end, and much to his surprise she turned to him and buried her head in his shoulder, wrapping her arms around his waist.

He held her there, both because she obviously needed it and because it felt good. Good that she'd lean on him, good that he could offer something.

"Marc hates me." She sniffled. "God, that sounds so stupid. But he does. He hates me. Apparently always has or something. Or at the very least has enjoyed a heavy dose of resentment since the day I was born."

"Hey, hey." He pulled her back so he could see her face, tears streaming down her cheeks, cheeks red and blotchy. "What'd the asshole say?"

She brushed at the tears on her cheeks. "Nothing that wasn't true."

"Still. He doesn't have a right to make you cry."

She shrugged helplessly. "Hell, maybe he does."

"Leah—"

"They want to move here."

"What?"

"They want to move here. Marc's already applying for jobs. Mom and Dad will need a few more years to keep saving and sell their house, but they want to move here. So we can all be together." She pulled away from him, stalking the room. "I should want that. But I don't. And it's not even because I'd have to admit I was lying. I can't… I love them, and I do want us to be close…but not…" She stopped in front of him again. "Is it possible to love her and not want her here?"

"Of course it is."

"She'll smother me to death. And I...I don't want to turn into that terrible person I was. And I feel like I won't be able to help it. God, I'm an idiot. Such an idiot."

"Why, baby?"

"Because I'm almost thirty and I should be able to handle my mother without wanting to...drown my sorrows...in whatever." She looked at him as though he was part of the "whatever."

And he was, wasn't he? Because she'd said this would never be anything more than...good covering up bad. And for whatever reason, that made him think of this morning. Grace and Kyle. That wasn't even a bad thing. Not at all.

But it made his chest all tight. "Grace and Kyle got engaged."

"Huh?"

"I'm not supposed to tell you. Grace wanted to do it. I don't know why I did. It just...popped out."

She swallowed. "Well, that's...great. That's really great."

He nodded lamely. "It is."

"We don't sound very happy for them."

His chuckle was rusty. "No, we don't."

"You're jealous."

"So what are you?"

"Sad."

"Don't be sad." He cupped her face, brushed his fingers over her wet cheeks. "And don't...don't underestimate yourself. Your parents moving here might not be easy, but you aren't eighteen anymore. You're smart and strong, and even if your mother drives you crazy, tries to suffocate the crap out of you, you get to say no. And if she can't handle that no, if she can't handle your boundaries, you get to lock your doors and turn off your phone and hide."

"You make it sound so easy and rational. I just feel like I can't breathe."

"You need time to let it sink in. To make a plan on how to deal with it."

"God, where do you come up with this shit?"

"It's not shit."

"I know. It's perfect and wonderful and the exact right thing to say. Like always. How do you do it?"

She looked at him in awe. Leah Santino looking at him as though he did something wonderful for her. It made him feel all the more off-kilter. Almost in pain.

"She thinks we're going to get married. She's so sure of it. She—"

He didn't want to hear any more. To soothe anymore. He wanted...more than all of it, so he covered her mouth with his, pushing her back to the bed so he could cover her body, too.

"Jacob." The word was a half-assed protest against his mouth.

"Let's just shut up for a while." Because he didn't want to feel this anymore, and this—sex with Leah—

was apparently his new coping mechanism. And it was a hell of a good one.

Her arms went to the waist of his jeans, began to unbuckle his belt. "Yeah, let's do that."

CHAPTER EIGHTEEN

WHEN LEAH WOKE UP the next morning, elbow pressed into Jacob's side, his knee jamming into her thigh, there was a moment of pure, unadulterated contentment.

And that made her sleepy eyes snap open, because that was so something she couldn't afford to feel.

This wasn't a relationship. It was more of a blip, but she was beginning to think it wasn't exactly healthy. They were both struggling with their roles in their families, the way they were seen or perceived or something, and apparently having sex to cope with that.

Fantastic sex, but sex wasn't exactly solving any of their problems, and quite honestly, waking up all warm and cozy curled up with Jacob was probably causing more problems than it would ever solve.

She glanced at him, his face half obscured by the pillow. Dark lashes any woman would kill for, the growth of two days without shaving just starting to be noticeable. The sharp nose and square jaw. Pieces of him she'd memorized for years, working side by side, being friends.

And she'd spent all those years convincing herself it didn't matter. Because it wouldn't work and he wasn't attracted to her and they were too damn different.

Except, the past few days had worked pretty well, and she couldn't ignore that he *was* attracted to her. Unhealthy penchant for having sex after being pummeled by their families aside, this fake relationship was the most comfortable one she'd ever been in.

It felt...right.

Crap.

His eyes fluttered open, the rich mahogany color meeting her gaze. Lips curling into a smile, and her chest tightened even as she involuntarily returned the smile.

It was wrong, impossible, downright stupid, but somewhere in the past few days, she'd toppled the rest of the way in love with him. If this was *before,* she knew she could handle it. Pretend it away.

But this was now, and the nagging belief that he might be able to love her, too, existed. So deep and so palpably real she couldn't pretend it away.

It could be real. This thing. "I'm going to take a shower." She inched to the end of the bed and stepped off.

"Actually, I have a question for you first."

She stopped, her chest tightening again. She wished she could blame that on her faulty body, but it was all fear. "Can't it wait?"

He looked so serious, lying in her bed, shirtless and tangled up in her sheets. So handsome. Oh, ugh, how had this all spiraled so far out of control? She took a step backward toward the bathroom.

"Last night you said I was jealous of Grace and Kyle getting engaged, and I guess that's right."

"I think that's normal, Jacob. You want a family of your own and—"

"And you said you were sad, and I haven't been able to work that out." He scratched a hand through his hair as he moved into a sitting position, making it even more mussed and unruly than it had been after last night's...activities.

Jacob McKnight was sitting in her bed in his boxers. Seriously, *where* had everything veered so completely off path?

When you asked him to pretend to be your boyfriend, maybe?

Right. That. Leah chewed her lip, eyeing him warily as he studied her. She wasn't sure where he was going with this line of conversation, and she wasn't at all comfortable with any of the possibilities. "Well, I—"

"Because they're your friends, and you should be happy. And you don't want to get married, so there's no jealousy. So, why would you be sad?"

Leah looked up at the ceiling, as if the answers might be written there in some secret language. As if there was some answer to this question that didn't put them on dangerous ground. "I don't know. It was just the whole...Marc thing."

"We weren't talking about Marc. You said you were sad in direct reference to Kyle and Grace getting engaged."

"You misunderstood—"

"It's too early for you to try and bullshit me, Leah. I don't have the patience for it." He stood, looking... yeah, angry, frustrated. All those things he so rarely let loose.

Oh, crap, this was going somewhere bad.

"Why did you say you were sad?"

"Because." It was none of his business. Okay, it might be a little bit of his business, but she didn't want to tell him. So that was that.

"Okay, let me change tactics."

"Could your change of tactics involve putting clothes on?"

Some of the tension left his face, just the tiniest eye crinkle and upward curve of his mouth. "Why don't you ever want to get married?"

"Not this again."

"That's your reasoning for us not being a real thing. That we want different things out of our future. So, I think I deserve an explanation. Whatever it is."

"It's not important."

"Actually, it *is* important. It's important to me because it's the thing keeping me from having a relationship with you. A relationship that, for the first time in...ever, I find myself not even trying to maneuver. And, yeah, I get it. Maybe it won't work out, but maybe it could. So, I want to know the thing that's keeping you from even giving it a shot."

Oh, *oh,* that one hurt. He hadn't been maneuvering her at all, and she could be some kind of first for him? Oh, damn faulty heart. She pressed a hand to it, rubbing there. "But…it's not real."

He didn't say anything to that, instead just stared. Stared her down until she felt as if she had to say something. "It's pretend. We're pretending." Lame city.

"We are really, really good at pretend sex. Why, it almost felt real!"

"Jacob—"

"Who knew we had fictional penises and vaginas!"

He was mad. Snarky mad. She wasn't sure she'd ever seen him quite like this. Irrationally angry, yes. Frustrated with a client to the point of pounding his steering wheel? Definitely.

Snotty jokes and direct questions? New territory. And she could not, not, not read anything into or be pleased by the fact she was the one bringing this out in him. Because that…

"I can't."

"You can't tell me why you don't want to get married?"

Even with the panic seizing her lungs, even though every ounce of reason told her to nod, agree. She could not tell him. But she didn't do anything at first.

Because the insidious line of thinking that kept getting her deeper and deeper into this mess was there, whispering at her.

Things were going to hell in a handbasket anyway. Marc would likely move here within the next few months based on his determination to do what Mom and Dad wanted. Mom and Dad would be moving soon enough, judging by Mom's singular ferocity when it came to anything she wanted.

So why keep pretending? Why keep trying to shore up the foundations of the life she'd built in Bluff City? The Santinos were going to storm the gates and sweep it all away.

Because she wasn't naive enough to think she could keep the secret about the extent of her health issues hidden if her family was around full-time. No more so than she could keep pretending to her parents that she was with Jacob.

Unless…

"Stop thinking and say something," Jacob demanded.

"I've been lying to you." The admission made her sick to her stomach. Five years she'd pretended this part of herself didn't exist. It didn't exist to him or to her. It was nothing.

But it did, and no amount of pretending could make it stay away. So, yeah, she felt pretty damn queasy, but there was no other option.

"I didn't just have heart surgery when I was thirteen." She swallowed, looking at him defiantly, because, hell, she was going to be defiant. She was going to be strong. She'd have very little left of the life she'd built for herself after this, but she wasn't going to give up the strength part. "I had a heart transplant."

He stayed very still. In fact, the only movement he made was to drop his gaze to her chest.

She kept going because she was determined to get it all out. To really make him see. There was no room for half-assed explanations anymore, not with him… pushing things he had no right to push, demanding answers for questions he had no right to ask.

Does he really have no *right?*

She didn't want to think about that. "I was born with a defective heart. It was not a fixable issue. The only fix was a transplant. So, I got one."

"When you were thirteen." Nothing in his expression, his stance, gave away his reaction, but the gravel in his voice at least pointed to some kind of emotion.

"Yes. And the thing about a transplant, especially at such a young age, is that they don't last forever."

He stepped forward, a jerky movement, something flashing across his face before he went back to blank and still. Then he cleared his throat. "No one's heart lasts forever, Leah."

"Yes, but it's pretty well certain I'm not going to be an old and gray biddy with eighty-five great-grandchildren at my feet. It's not in the cards for me. And I just have to be okay with that, because, hey, lots of people don't get that, either."

She had to take a second to work through the emotion with saying these words aloud. She'd come to grips with her reality. Learned how to deal with the knowledge that her life expectancy was definitely going to be a little shorter than it could be.

And, sure, she could get hit by a bus tomorrow. Sure, someone else might, nothing was guaranteed in this world, but no matter how many times she accepted her fate—whatever that might be—it was hard to just be okay with so many people having a *chance* to be the little old lady in the rocking chair when she didn't.

"Well," he said, his voice still having that low, pained tone to it. "Okay, so, I didn't know that. But now I do. So. Was that supposed to change my mind?"

"I'm not done, Jacob."

He swallowed, and though his gaze remained devoid of emotion, it wasn't on her anymore. He was staring at the wall behind her.

"Still demanding your answer? You really want to hear the rest?"

He flicked his gaze to her, a hint of emotion there. But she didn't know what it was. She couldn't read him at all. And maybe she didn't want to.

"Yeah, I want to hear the rest."

"Fine. Good." Sure, she'd been hoping that would be enough, but hey, half-assing it was off the table, right? "I watched my parents struggle, be afraid, put everything they had into my health. They didn't have a choice. I was born that way and I was their child.

Shitty luck of the draw and all that. But a spouse and kids of my own… That is a choice I have."

It wasn't an easy one or even one she'd made right away at thirteen. Or even at eighteen, when she'd left. Life had taught her that involving anyone else wouldn't be fair. Wouldn't be right. Sure, she didn't deny herself friends, but friends didn't have to be financially invested. They didn't have to spend nights in the hospital. They were just visitors, bystanders.

A husband. Kids. They were participants. And she wasn't going to deal with the guilt of tying anyone to that. She'd much rather do without.

End of story.

"Don't they get a say?"

"I don't have a husband or kids, Jacob. That's the point. And unless you're proposing, which you're not, no, the fictional 'they' don't get a say. And you don't get a say because I know you, and I don't need your hovering and your worrying and your trying to control something that isn't controllable."

Though he remained silent, empty-expressioned, she knew the wheels in his head were turning. Recalibrating his plans, whatever they had been. Making sense of the whole thing.

The silence twisted her stomach into knots, digging the nausea deeper, sharper. She wasn't sure how much longer she could stand here with his silence. She should make it clear—whatever their blip had been, it was over now. Them, in any way, shape or form, was off the table.

But those were words she couldn't form, couldn't say. *Pathetic, Santino. So pathetic.*

And then his eyes sharpened on her, the set of his mouth going determined, and her stomach unclenched, flipped. Because determined, focused Jacob was a dangerous thing.

And he was focused on her.

"I've done a good job so far, haven't I? Not making a big deal about it."

"Y-yes. B-but…" Why was she stuttering? As though her heart had jumped into her mouth, beating in her words.

Oh, man, she was really losing it.

"I'm good at giving people what they want. I could give you what you want, not hovering, not controlling. I did that for my mother when I was sixteen. Surely I could do it for you now. And as for the rest…well, Leah, life sucks. People die and get sick all the time."

"You should want to be with someone you don't have to try so hard for." And she had a feeling, based on how earnestly he'd asked that initial question about doing a good job, that he'd been trying much harder than she'd suspected. "Someone who has a little better chance of not dying so…early."

"I…" He crossed to her, touched her face. The brush of his fingertips over her temple, her cheek, and then he looked directly into her eyes. "I want to be with you. If you were trying to change my mind on that, you failed. I'm not wanting easy, because easy isn't any kind of guarantee. I want you."

Leah sucked in a difficult breath. She knew she couldn't agree to this, believe in this. It was wrong and it would end badly, sooner or later, but with his fingertips on her face, his eyes on hers, his body so close, his words so damn earnest...

She couldn't think of a single reason why.

JACOB HELD HIS BREATH. Maybe it was silly, but he couldn't find a way to work air in or out until he got some kind of response.

This was crazy. The whole thing from top to bottom. From lie to half-truth to complete honesty. It was all a mess.

But he held his breath and stayed still. On the outside, he was calm, determined Jacob. A skin he wore well. On the inside, he was a storm brewing. Fear, anger, hurt. How she could have kept this from him. How unfair the damn world was.

How the women he loved, Mom and her cancer, Grace and her attack, repeatedly got the short end of the crappy cosmic stick.

The women he loved.

Christ.

That seemed...like too much. You didn't flip a switch and magically love someone after five years of friendship. But maybe that was the thing. Even with this lie, he knew her. In fact, finding this stuff out only reinforced the things he knew about her. Admired about her.

She was so damn strong. She didn't let anything get in her way. And she lived her life the way she wanted.

Toss sex in and…well, wasn't that love? Or was he just some kind of screwed-up weirdo?

"You don't want to get messed up in this kind of stuff, Jacob. Really. My parents separated. They almost drowned under the debt. They… Marc apparently resents the crap out of me. It's…not fun. It's not easy."

But the thing was, she wasn't moving away from his hand on her face. She wasn't looking away or putting any distance between them. She was looking at him, all but leaning into his touch. So…that was something.

"We could go back to the way things were," he said carefully. "Be friends, coworkers. Fight. Go home at the end of the day…apart. We could do all those things."

"Yes, we should—"

He tightened his grip on her face. "Or we could be as brave and strong as you normally are and see if this couldn't be something. You're not walking out of my life anytime soon, Leah. You have a minority share in MC, you work for us and love it with every fiber of your being. Your life is here, mixed with mine, so whatever happens to you would damn well affect me whether we're in a romantic relationship or not."

She took a deep breath, her eyes getting shiny, though no tears fell. He had to clear his throat, something clogging there. Maybe hope or desperation or…fear.

"Give us a chance to be something, and if we're not…we go back to being friends but we end on good terms. We end like this, knowing you could have tried but wouldn't…I'm not sure how good of terms I can be on with you."

"That feels like a threat. I do not respond well to threats."

He brushed his thumb back and forth across her cheek. "Yeah, I know that about you, you difficult, infuriating woman. And I'm not making a threat. I'm just being honest. As damn honest as I can."

Her shoulders slumped a bit at that. "I know. I'd just…hate to think…" She took a shaky breath. "I care. You know I do. As poorly as I sometimes show it, I care so much about you, and I'd hate to see you have to hurt or grieve or sacrifice the way my parents have."

A tear escaped her eye, and he brushed it away. She swallowed, eyes never leaving his.

"You said there's a difference because you have a choice. Well, it is different because I have a choice, too. And if that's what happens, that's what happens. I could just as easily get sick and die, you know. Cancer and strokes run in my family like marathon runners."

"That's different," she said, her voice rusty.

"Yeah, a little bit. But only a little."

"You're really willing to…deal with the potential of all that…just to be with me?"

"Yes. Don't you think you're worth it?"

"Of course I'm damn well worth it." Her tiny smile broadened a hair. "For the right guy."

Jacob stepped closer, so they were hip to hip and knee to knee. He lowered his mouth to just a whisper away from hers. "I could maybe be him." Then he pressed his lips to hers, let his hands cup her face, then tangle in her hair.

When he broke the kiss she blinked up at him and gave an almost-imperceptible nod. "Well, I guess we'll find out."

CHAPTER NINETEEN

"So, um, how exactly are we going to break the news to everyone?" Leah wasn't even sure she'd fully broken the news to herself because this was…nuts.

Wrong. Stupid. Pointless. Other bad words. Et cetera.

Well, the shower sex had been none of those things.

But that portion of the morning was over. They were about to step out of her bedroom, head over to MC and just…be a couple. The postsex haze was wearing off. The post–sweet words haze was wearing off. Panic was setting in.

"This is nuts."

He grinned at her. "I wonder how many thoughts you're going to have."

"Thoughts?"

"Well, you're already past second thoughts and it hasn't even been an hour."

"Jacob—"

"And luckily, I will ignore them all. Because you said yes. No take-backs."

"I'm glad we're treating this situation like adults."

"Always, baby."

She glared at him. Screw him for saying "baby" in a way that made her all warm and squishy inside.

"But seriously, how are we going to tell Grace? Kelly and Susan? Henry?"

Jacob shrugged. "I don't know. Maybe we can throw a Jacob-and-Leah-started-having-sex party?"

"You are not taking me seriously."

"Nope. Sure not." His phone dinged and he pulled it out of his pocket. "We're going to be there with your parents. If anyone else is there, which no one is scheduled to be, they will only think we're pretending. I figure we can tell them once your parents aren't around to wonder why our yearlong relationship is news to our coworkers."

Well, that made unfortunate sense. Or was it fortunate? Fortunate they didn't have to tell anyone that everything they'd basically sworn up and down they weren't going to do was happening. And it had taken only a few days, not even the whole stupid week.

"I hate that they were right," she grumbled as Jacob scrolled through his phone. "Are we sure they were right?"

"Yes, ma'am. But, um, you're going to want to save that rage for another time. I have three voice mails and five emails from the Martins."

"The morning after Christmas? Ugh. Why are they the worst?" They'd had some pretty annoying clients over the years, but the Martins' demands and inability to let go really took the cake. "What is it this time?" When Jacob only made a weird face, Leah began shaking her head. "No. No, no, no. It's not an electrical problem."

"It's an electrical problem."

"Tell them to call a damn electrician."

"They did, sweetheart—you."

"It's only a matter of time before I punch her. You know that, right?"

Jacob began ushering her out the door and into the hallway. "You don't want to do that. Not only have they referred five new people to us this year, but you know she'll press charges. You might even go to jail for assault. And then you wouldn't be able to share a bed with me tonight." His hand slid from her shoulder, down her back, over her ass.

She smacked it away. "You are coming with me, and you are keeping her distracted by any means necessary." She wagged a finger in his face as he wrinkled his nose.

"Ew. Don't say it like that."

"*Any* means. Shake that nice little butt of yours. Butter her up. You keep her away from me." Leah started walking again, but Jacob stopped her before they reached the living room.

"The only butt shaking I will be doing," he began, taking her off guard and trapping her against the wall, "is for you."

Leah bit back a smile, relaxed enough to enjoy the way he did that. All lean, rangy body pressed against hers. She could probably fight him off if she tried hard enough, but she liked this. Being covered by him. It felt good and not just let's-get-pantsless good. It made her feel…powerful or important or desirable. Okay, all of the above.

She had some issues. "Well, technically, you *would* be doing it for me," she said, touching a finger to his top button. Then the next. "To keep me out of jail and all that. I would appreciate it and Mrs. Martin might even tip yo—"

Before she could finish, he cut her off by pressing his mouth to hers. She smiled against it, the silliness of the argument working to melt away some of her anxiety over the whole her-and-Jacob situation.

"Ahem."

Jacob pulled away and Leah blinked at Marc's profile.

"Uh, sorry," she said with a wince as Marc walked past on his way to the bathroom. It was silly to blush, for a lot of reasons. But she really didn't know how to act at all. With this whole Jacob thing. With Marc. Why did dudes have to be so hard to deal with?

And then Mom appeared from the laundry room and she remembered it was definitely not just dudes.

"Don't you two look cozy," she said with a broad grin. "Ready for breakfast?"

"You don't have to make breakfast every morning, Mom. I could pick something up. We could get doughnuts. I—"

"Nonsense."

Of course. Why should Mom let her handle anything? In her own house. "Jacob and I might actually have to do some work today, make a house call. You guys can still come with, but you might be more comfortable to stay behind."

"Of course. We don't want to be in the way. You two do what you have to do. There's some car museum your father wanted to go to, and I could do some shopping. Go. Work. But eat some breakfast first. You know how important it is you start your day off with protein, Leah honey."

Leah smiled. She didn't feel like fighting something so small any more than she liked the overly thoughtful look on Jacob's face.

Was this what she'd agreed to? Her mother would leave and Jacob would step in with the worry machine?

"You know, Mrs. Santino, we really do have to get going. We'll get something at MC. Besides, you've been feeding us so well, I don't know how we'll ever be hungry again."

Mom frowned, opened her mouth to speak, but Jacob was already ushering Leah out the door.

Shoving feet into boots, she glanced at him. "I thought you were going to take her side for a minute there."

"You don't want me to, though," he said simply.

Which was a sentiment that produced two completely different reactions in her. One…joy or relief. Someone was willing to do what she wanted. Which was wonderful.

But the second one was dread. Dread she didn't know whether to listen to or not. Because shouldn't he be not taking Mom's side because *he* didn't want to? Didn't agree?

She wasn't sure which was the right emotion, wasn't sure how to even begin to figure it out. So, she had to do what she always did in the face of a problem. Bulldoze through until something clicked.

It wasn't always the prettiest solution, but what other choice did she have?

LEAH WAS KILLING HIM. Poking around the fuse box, air thick with sawdust and probably century-old mold spores or something. But she didn't put on a mask.

She coughed and Jacob actually bit his tongue to keep from saying anything. He was going to draw blood if she kept it up.

"I told her she couldn't overload this shit system she wanted," Leah grumbled, all but slamming the fuse-box door closed. More dust puffed out and she rubbed a hand to her chest.

"We need to get you out of here." Which, all in all, was one of the more innocuous things he could say. Much better than the things he wanted to say.

Leah waved him away, apparently too frustrated with the Martins to notice that he was five seconds from shoving her up the basement stairs and into some fresh air.

Even if her asthma was mainly under control,

surely the stress couldn't be good for a heart she was concerned about giving out early.

He really could not be thinking about that right now. Leah had a way of seeing through him and he wasn't going to let that happen. They'd just agreed to make this work. He wasn't screwing it up already.

"I hate them. I hate them. I hate them." She rolled her shoulders, coughed again. "Okay, got that out. Now I can face them."

Jacob gave himself a few seconds as she stalked up the stairs. He took a deep breath and let it out. He tried to tell himself she knew what she was doing. And she did. She wasn't gasping for her inhaler or toppling over. She was fine.

Fine.

He made his way up the stairs, trying to ignore the tenseness in his shoulders. Trying not to think about how he didn't want her working in conditions like this. Because they almost always worked in conditions like this, and if he told her she couldn't...

Well, that was a laughable thought.

"Now, honestly, since it was your fault, I don't think I should be billed for this," Mrs. Martin was saying as Jacob crested the stairs.

When Leah's eyes bulged, Jacob stepped between them. "Mrs. Martin, you can't really expect us to not charge you for Leah's services."

"That is exactly what I expect," Mrs. Martin said with a sniff. "Didn't she install the fuse box?"

"I restored your fuse box to your specifications

and explained to you the limitations in your voltage when—"

Since Leah's hands were clenched into fists and her expression had that head-about-to-spin-off-neck look to it, Jacob worked up his best smile for Mrs. Martin.

"How about we'll have Susan send you a bill. We'll only charge you 75 percent of Leah's normal labor rate as a merry Christmas and loyal-customer discount."

"How about a long walk/short pier discount," Leah muttered.

Thankfully, Mrs. Martin seemed to miss the snark and gave Jacob a considering look. "Make it 60 percent?"

"I'm not negotiating with you. I am sorry. But it's 75 percent. That's it."

"You need a lesson in customer service, young man. About how the customer is always right."

Leah took a step forward and Jacob almost had some concerns she was going to throw the punch she'd been joking about earlier. Or not joking about.

"I'll take it under advisement," he said, taking Leah by the arm and leading her out of the Martin house.

"I could...I could..." Leah made a low growling sound and gave the Martins' mailbox a little kick on the way to the MC truck. "She's the devil."

"Just an annoying customer." And really, not as

annoying as the woman he wanted to shake some sense into.

When he got into the driver's-side seat, Leah was already slumped in the passenger seat. "I'm exhausted."

He felt the little flicker of panic and ignored it. Pushed it away, all the while keeping his expression blank and his movements easy as he started the car and pulled it out onto the road.

He wasn't going to let her see what her whole truth had done to him, because she wouldn't like it. The way the worry was already sneaking into everything. The way he suddenly understood her mother's hovering and wished he could do a bit of his own.

Would this happen every time they had to do a job? Would he be able to bite his tongue every time?

He gripped the steering wheel a little harder. It would be fine. He was good at pretending. He'd convinced his family he didn't know about his mother's cancer. That took some serious skill, didn't it? Well, worrying about Leah's asthma or exhaustion or her eating habits or if her heart was okay... He could just as easily keep all that on the inside.

Because it meant having her. Crazy or weird as it might be to think that after all this time he'd been looking for Mrs. Right, and it was Leah. Right there.

But he really thought she could be it, they could be it. Without any of the planning or maneuvering he usually did with a woman and only a little bit of trying to mold himself into what they wanted.

Mostly with Leah, he was himself. This little thing he pretended didn't exist was nothing compared to that.

So he ignored the pressure in his chest that made him want to ask if she was okay or if she needed a nap. Instead, he smiled. "I'm going to have to stop keeping you up so late."

For the first time since stepping foot on Martin property, her lips curved upward. "Hmm. I don't think that's why I'm exhausted."

Again, his panic bubbled up. He didn't know what she was up for. Maybe she wasn't supposed to be having sex every day. Which, okay, that was a weird thought, but he didn't know. He knew jack squat about heart transplants. What he was supposed to do. How he was supposed to treat her. What she was capable of handling, what might be too much.

If she was so worried about dying early that she didn't even want a family, surely things weren't as okay as she pretended.

"I'm just going to say this once, and if you can't get it through your thick skull, we're through before we even got started." She straightened in her seat, glaring at him. "Sometimes I get tired, and it's not because my heart is going to fall out."

"I don't think that."

"You're tense. Your brain wheels are turning so loud I can hear them over here. This was exactly what I didn't want."

"I'm so damn sorry I care, Leah. That must be

really rough for you." This probably wasn't the way to not be over before they even got started as she'd said, but…well, it wasn't fair. He should at least be able to worry at least a little. "But maybe you should think before you do something that stupid."

"Excuse me?"

"You should have been wearing a mask. I know you said your asthma is under control, but that kind of…work can't be good for your…" He trailed off because when he happened to glance at her it wasn't anger on her face.

It was shock. Maybe even horror. He'd let it slip and… Crap. He had to…do some damage control. "I just…"

"You just can't pretend, can you? The whole truth was too much."

"No. It's not."

She let out a bitter laugh. "I won't do this after every job with you, and I don't want you stewing and pretending, either. I knew this is what would—"

"I need more information. That's all. I don't know what kind of limitations you have or if I'm pushing them. I don't have enough information to just ignore it. But I'm not your mother and I'm not going to try and lock you in a bed or tell you not to do your job."

"You'll just berate me after the fact?"

"No." No, there had to be a way…

He pulled into the back lot of MC, trying to get his brain to work. To think. To fix this. Because he wasn't throwing in the towel already. He was not a quitter.

"You could ask, you know? Before you call me stupid."

"Right, because you wouldn't berate *me* for asking if you were okay. Pretty sure we've been there, done that."

She sighed, shifting in her seat so that she was looking out the window. "I know my limitations. I understand my body. I take care of myself. If I start to feel like those things aren't true, I seek help. I have doctors who know me and my many issues. So, note, that if something is wrong with me, I will get it fixed. And I'm not *stupid,* asshole."

He wanted to snap, but he took a deep breath instead. Ignoring the "asshole." Ignoring the stuff that would get in the way of what he wanted. "Will you promise to tell me? That you won't be all guns-blazing Leah. If something is too much, you're pushing too hard, something is wrong, you will tell me. Calling you stupid, okay, that was a dick move, but I need to know you won't hide it from me. That's not about… being like your mother. That's about knowing you've lied to all of us for years."

"Five years where I have lived my life both healthy and without telling you anything. Five years where I was fine." But she fidgeted in her seat, not quite as determined as her expression and words seemed. "If something comes up that concerns you, I'll let you know."

He was glad the answer made him more sad than angry, because getting angry again wouldn't get him what he wanted. Feeling like a sad piece of crap kept him from losing his temper any more. So, he pushed the car into Park and took her hand, and he didn't have to fake the emotion in his voice.

"I need you to tell me, whether it concerns me or not. I don't want to find out something is wrong because I'm scared and trying to figure out what's going on by eavesdropping."

"That's…what happened with your mom when you were a teenager?"

"Yes."

She dropped his hand but reached out, rubbed a palm against his stubbled cheek. He could hear the rasp of her palm against it, and he nuzzled in. Because it felt good and she felt good and this was going to work, damn it. He was going to find a way for this to work.

"All right. I'll be up front with you if something should happen. I… But you have to understand that, for the most part, I am healthy. And I take care of myself. And I need you to be reasonable even if something bad happens. I was stupid about my health once, but never again, and I won't let someone tell me I am."

"It was the wrong thing to say. I just…"

"It's scary."

She looked so beat down, so close to throwing in

the towel, but he couldn't let that happen. "It's only scary because I don't know enough yet, but I will."

"You could trust me."

"I do. I *do*," he repeated when she looked skeptical. "But I need you to trust me, too."

She nodded, chewing on her lip. "Okay. We'll make a deal. You ask if you have a concern and I'll…try not to get bent out of shape about it."

"For you, anything."

She sighed, looking sad. "What about for you?"

"I get a pretty decent girlfriend out of the deal."

She wrinkled her nose. "*Girlfriend* is such a lame word." She pushed out of the truck, so he followed suit.

"Okay, how about love bug?"

"Ha-ha." She walked over to her truck and dropped her electrician box inside.

"Lover?"

"Oh, ew, ugh."

He chuckled, heading for the door. They were going to be okay. If they could work through this, they could work through anything. "You're going to have to pick something, Leah darling, because you are something to me now, and *friend* doesn't cut it."

The snowball hit him directly on the back of the neck, bits of snow sliding under the collar of his coat. He turned to glare at her, but she was just standing there, innocent smile on her face as she tossed another snowball up in the air, from one hand to another.

She was gorgeous. *And mine.* She would not like that thought, but he did.

"You will pay for that, *lover.*"

She squared and threw the snowball. He managed to narrowly dodge out of the way, scooping up his own handful of snow as he did.

"You can't snowball-fight me. I'm weak and damaged, remember?"

Jacob knew a test when he heard one, and while it made him tense, he wasn't an idiot. Luckily, he'd always been very good at tests. "I'll cart you to the hospital later. First, retribution."

Her smile widened, and already he'd gotten an A+. He tossed his snowball, pleased when it hit her leg as he'd intended.

"Lame," she called, hurling another one at him that glanced off his hip as he tried to jump out of the way. They traded a few more attempts, Jacob advancing closer and closer with each dodge, until he was close enough to tackle her into the snow.

She glared up at him, snow on her hat and the hair that feathered over her shoulders. Her nose and cheeks were red, and when he lowered his mouth to hers, her lips were cold.

They should go inside and do this, but when her arms wound around his neck, even with the sprinkles of snow flaking off her coat and onto his face and neck, he never wanted to move.

Cold, wet, uncomfortable—none of it mattered

when Leah was pressed below him, kissing him back eagerly.

She broke the kiss. "This is great and all, but I am, quite literally, freezing my ass off."

He chuckled, but instead of letting her up, he rolled onto his back and pulled her on top.

"Not quite what I had in mind." But she grinned down at him, settling herself so that every part of her was lying on top of him rather than on the snow now seeping into his pants.

The urge to tell her he loved her slammed into his chest. So forceful, so almost desperate he opened his mouth. But, whether she sensed it and didn't want to hear it or just had unfortunate timing, she kissed him, effectively silencing anything he was going to say.

"What in hell's bells are you two doing?" Kelly called out.

Leah closed her eyes, leaned her forehead against his. "I thought you said no one would be here."

"Well, no one is scheduled to be here." Jacob grinned up at her before glancing at Kelly standing on the back cement stoop. "It appears Leah and I have engaged in a romantic physical relationship, from which you must now turn away should you wish to remain unscathed," he called to Kelly.

"Ugh." A sound that came from both women and made Jacob laugh even as Leah wiggled off of him and onto her feet.

Leah trudged to the house, Jacob not far behind.

When they reached Kelly, she pointed an accusatory finger at Leah.

"I told you it was a sex vibe!"

"Well, it wasn't. At the time," Leah grumbled.

"And now it is? You are in trouble, young lady, and you're coming with me. I need details." Kelly began dragging her inside.

Leah looked back at him as if he would step in and help. Instead, he winked. "Have fun, sweetheart." He had some research to do. And some dry pants to find.

CHAPTER TWENTY

"I DON'T FEEL right about poking around Grace and Kyle's closet."

Kelly waved it away. "I texted Grace and she told me just where— Aha." Kelly pulled out a pair of sweatpants and a sweatshirt. "Change, Ms. Snow Angel."

Leah groaned, but did as she was told. Her clothes were cold and wet, so she didn't have another choice that didn't involve Jacob's clothes. Which would be fine, except she'd have to go around smelling him and being ridiculously turned on.

Grace's sweats were a little too short, and her shirt was somewhat tight, but they were just fine.

"Come on."

"Where are we going?" Leah asked warily.

Kelly led her down the hall to the guest room that had been Grace's until she'd started cohabitating with Kyle.

"Now." She closed the door behind them and settled herself on the flowery coverlet. "Tell me *everything*."

"What, how the sex is?"

"Oh, no, penises. Ick." Kelly grinned. "How did it happen? When did it happen? Why did it happen?"

"Oh…that."

"And what does it *mean* that it all happened?"

Leah clasped her hands together. This was why she'd asked Jacob how they were going to tell people. Because…she didn't know what to say. Even though Kelly had been one of her closest friends for the past few years, Leah'd always kept this Jacob thing on the DL. As far as she knew, only Grace had ever suspected anything more and, okay, maybe Kyle by extension of Grace.

How did she explain…any of it?

"Why are you being so tight-lipped? You've always talked to me about your dating life. Why is this different?"

"Because it's Jacob. Our…boss."

"Leah does the boss. You could be your own porno!"

She laughed, even if it was a terrible, ridiculous joke.

Grace burst in the door. "Did I miss it?"

Leah drew her eyebrows together, looking from Grace to Kelly. "Miss what?"

"Oh, I called in the cavalry," Kelly said, walking over to the window. "Susan's just pulling up now. We *all* need to hear this."

Leah glanced at Grace, nervous. She hated that. Nerves in front of her best friend, but Grace had already made her disapproval known and…well, Leah didn't want things to change. Didn't want to explain the change. She just wanted to live in the fantasy world where she and Jacob were a thing separate from real life. "Just so you know, I'm not talking about sex in front of your baby."

"My in-laws are watching Presleigh. Which, let me tell you, is a great sacrifice I'm making, as they think babies should never see the light of day or sleep on their backs or any of the things our *doctor* told us to do."

Damn, Leah'd really been hoping the baby excuse would work.

"Besides, as long as I'm here I really don't want to talk about the sex portion," Grace added, looking pained. "That can remain a mystery. Forever and ever."

Footsteps sounded on the back staircase, and then Susan burst in on a loud exhalation. "Did I miss it?"

"Jeez, you'd think I was revealing state secrets or something. What are you all so afraid to miss?"

"Why suddenly our Leah, the Leah who gives Jacob the hardest time out of any of us, including Grace, his sister, has found herself in a sexual relationship with the guy." Kelly closed the door. "His words. Not mine."

"I don't know. We…we just did." And she didn't need her friends making her feel self-conscious about it or, worse, changing her mind. Because things were kind of tenuous, even with the nice snowball-fight moment. She wasn't…sure. That outburst after the

Martin job. But he'd promised to ask and she'd promised not to be so snappy. So maybe she was sure but not confident. Not certain they could exist in the reality of the situation. Maybe "they" could exist only in pretend.

He'd called her stupid. Just like Mom did with every insinuation she couldn't handle herself. And even if they'd talked through it, how did she know a similar situation wouldn't crop up again? How did she know this wasn't the fight they'd replay over and over until they couldn't get past it?

Until she knew or understood or felt certain or whatever, she didn't know what to say or how to say it to her friends, people who would want to help and support. "I'm not talking about this."

"Why not?"

She pointed at Grace, not afraid to throw a friend under the bus. "Because Grace is engaged."

"What?" Kelly and Susan shrieked in unison.

Grace scowled. "The rat bastard told you. I told him I wanted to be the one to tell you!"

"Ring, ring, ring!" Kelly snatched Grace's left arm and then there was much oohing and aahing. Leah knew precisely nothing about jewelry, but the ring was sufficiently unique and sparkly, just like Grace.

"He did so good," Susan said reverently.

"I thought for sure he enlisted Kelly's help," Grace said, looking so happy Leah felt bad for shutting them out. For turning the tables. Grace was happy, and she really deserved it.

"I had no idea," Kelly was saying, turning Grace's hand back and forth so the diamonds winked in the light. "Kyle picked this sucker out all on his own, as far as I know."

Grace cradled her hand to her chest. "Aww." She sniffled, her eyes getting shiny. Then Susan sniffled.

"Ugh. Crying. I'm out." Leah bolted for the door, but Grace was too quick and blocked it.

"Not so fast, little missy," she said, waving her finger in Leah's face. "Time to face the Jacob music. And remember," she said, softening, "we're asking as friends. Not as coworkers or overprotective sisters. We just want to know what's going on so we can be a part of your life."

Which Leah knew and even understood, but sometimes it was too much. Because then she'd be tempted to cry over how lucky she was to have found this group of women and, ugh, she didn't want to be a blubbering mess.

"We just…are dating, I guess."

"Real dating, not pretending-for-your-parents dating?"

"Y-yes."

"How did that happen?"

Leah clasped and unclasped her hands. "I don't know. We just… I guess all the forced-proximity stuff and fake-relationship stuff and then I kissed him and things kind of…escalated from there."

"Sex-calated," Kelly giggled.

Grace pointed a threatening finger at Kelly. "None of that in my presence."

Kelly stifled the rest of her laughter. "Yes, ma'am."

"Well, it was kind of that at first," Leah mumbled, feeling weird. She didn't like being the center of attention like this, but it felt oddly...good to be telling people. Even if she didn't tell them everything.

"But, I don't know, Jacob seems to think we'd... do okay together."

"Oh, Jacob seems to think. Well, the Leah we know and love is so inclined to do what other people think out of the goodness of her heart."

Leah stuck her tongue out at Susan. "Okay, so I think that, too. And yes, I have feelings for him and want to be with him and blah, blah, blah. Can we be done now?"

Kelly slung an arm around Leah's shoulders. "Aw, I think someone's falling in love."

"Oh, ew, no, don't say that."

"It's cute. You two. Strange, but cute. They were making out in the snow when I found them."

"Aw," Susan said, leaning against Kelly.

Leah made a disgusted face then turned to Grace, who was studying her thoughtfully. Leah winced. Nothing good ever came from thoughtful expressions. "What?"

"I know I was...not exactly a supporter at first," Grace said carefully.

"You weren't?" Susan asked.

"No, I was worried Jacob might...be a little careless. Not on purpose. I just wasn't sure he would have as much invested as Leah."

"I think you underestimate him."

That made Grace smile. "I'm glad you think that, really. And what I'm trying to say is, no matter what happens, we will be here for you." Kelly and Susan nodded solemnly next to Grace.

And Leah supposed she should smile and say thank-you and group hug, but…she couldn't shake the feeling… "As nice as that sentiment is, why do I feel like the subtext is we're doomed to failure?"

The three women exchanged glances before they started to protest, but Leah saw it. The hesitation, the consideration.

"You guys don't think it'll work out." Not a question because she knew that was what she saw on their faces. They supported her, yes, but only because she was going to fail.

"It's not that."

"It's just…"

"Well…"

Leah looked at her three closest friends in the world. The women who'd kept her sane and happy the past few years. Friendship. Real, strong, lasting friendships like ones she'd never been able to make as a sick kid with an attitude problem.

And they were trying to be nice about it, but no one really thought she and Jacob could make this thing work. Whether it was because of their arguing or Jacob's track record or her not-so-Suzy-Homemaker skills, they looked at her and the man she was, yeah, kind of in love with and saw a mismatch.

A bitter pill to swallow. But what else could she do? Wasn't she a little unsure herself? "Maybe we could switch subjects? Summer wedding, Grace?"

No one jumped right into the chatter, but they eased into it. Discussing Grace and Kyle. Moving away from the uncomfortable topic of Leah's doomed relationship.

Maybe if she had more faith in it herself it wouldn't feel so damning, but there was an annoying piece of her brain that wondered if her heart had made a big fat mistake.

LEAH DIDN'T TALK much the rest of the day. She smiled when he told a joke, told some innocuous stories about her childhood over dinner with her family, but she didn't seem…tuned in. It was all very detached.

Jacob had half a mind to call Grace and demand to know what had happened in her and Kelly and Susan's little powwow in the guest room this afternoon.

Unless he was the problem. He thought they'd moved beyond his outburst after the Martins, but maybe…

"I think I'm going to go to bed," Leah said, pushing away from the table. She gave her mother's shoulder a squeeze. "And please don't worry. I just have a little headache." Leah left, everyone frowning after her.

"Is everything okay with her?" Mrs. Santino asked in a hushed whisper.

Jacob forced a reassuring smile. "Oh, we dealt with a difficult client all morning. Nearly impossible to escape without a headache or an ulcer. I'll make sure she takes some ibuprofen and lies down."

Mrs. Santino looked horrified. "Ibuprofen? That isn't recommended for transplant recipients. Is she—"

"I misspoke," Jacob interrupted, trying to backpedal without screwing everything up. "I just usually take ibuprofen. I know Leah can't. More important, *she* knows she can't."

Mrs. Santino rested a hand over her heart. "Don't scare me like that. Goodness. We really can't move here soon enough."

Jacob debated his next words, how much it was his business. But he and Leah were real now, so maybe he owed it to her to say something. Because as much as he had concerns, Mrs. Santino's seemed above and beyond. "You understand how well she's doing, right? How healthy she is. It isn't…dire." He had to believe that or he'd turn into the outburst guy too often and ruin everything.

"Yes, well, I understand how you can think that, Jacob, but I don't have that luxury. Because I've watched her almost die too many times to not worry about every step she makes. And she's finally let me back in her life. I won't let that slip out of my fingers again."

"I'm…" Sorry, speechless, sad for all of them. He couldn't formulate a word in response to that.

"You should go check on her."

Mrs. Santino had turned away, and Jacob looked helplessly at the other men in the room, but they both stared at their hands. So, there was no other choice but to walk away.

Floored. Hurt. Embarrassed. Scared.

He tried to breathe through the overwhelming emotion, but as he stepped into the hall, he saw Leah standing there, just outside her bedroom door.

He approached, not sure if she'd heard or what he should say or…anything.

"Still so sure about this?" she asked in a voice thick with tears.

"Yes." Well, at least that word came out without a problem. Mrs. Santino's words would haunt him, he imagined. *Watched her almost die too many times…* But it didn't change his feelings or his determination he could give Leah something her family couldn't. He would. He would *not* be Outburst Guy. He was going to be everything she wanted.

She kissed him and then pulled him inside. "Thanks for that."

"You heard?"

"Most."

"I'm pretty sure I shoved my foot in my mouth."

Leah smiled. "Maybe, but I appreciate it." She let go of his hand. "I'm going to get ready for bed."

"Hey, about today…"

She stopped at the bathroom door, shoulders tensing. "Look. I know I'm being emo about the whole us thing. I just... It's a lot at stake. It's a big change. I don't take risks like this. Not anymore, and when I did take risks, it never ended well."

"I'm the best risk you'll ever take."

She smiled a little ruefully. "Well, probably a little less dangerous, anyway." She examined the door frame as she spoke her next words. "I'm just still kind of working things out in my head. Everything is fine, though. I promise."

"You can work things out with me, you know. I hear that's how relationships work."

"Well, I've never been any good at that." She finally looked over at him as he settled himself on the edge of her bed. "I just... It's one of those things where if everyone thinks you're crazy, shouldn't you consider that you are?"

"Not in this case."

"Why not?"

"Because it isn't about us. It's about them. I mean, that's what started your working things out, right? Whatever Kelly and Susan and Grace said?" *Not me. Don't be about me.*

"Partially."

So partially about him. Well, that he couldn't fix with words. He'd have to show her. Be more careful. But the Grace et al thing? Well, he could ease her worries about that.

"Whatever they said, whatever doubts they put

in your head, they're not really about us. Trust me, ever since Grace made her displeasure known, I've been working it over in my head. Trying to figure out why she would feel that way when she loves us both. And the only logical conclusion is it's them."

"Them?"

"Yeah, and I know that makes them sound selfish, and I don't mean it like that. It's just…when I was all…not taking the whole Kyle and Grace thing very well, it was partially because I wasn't dealing well with the threats to Grace from her ex, but partially, if I really examined it, it was because I was afraid of the change. My best friend and my sister were now closer to each other than they were to me, and it's a crap way to view things, but it was my initial gut reaction. Grace is doing the same. Kelly and Susan are thinking about work. And after they get used to it, they'll come to see…what we see."

"You're always so reasonable. So…smart. With Mom, with this."

She seemed irritated by that, so he went for a little mood lightening. "That's right, baby. Now, why don't you come here and hop on." He patted his lap with a grin. He was tired of…emo. He wanted to get to the good part. The part where it was just them and everyone else could screw off.

"I take it back," she replied with a smirk. "You're an idiot."

"I figured you would. Come here." She scowled at

him, so he smiled. "Please? You said you can't say no to my 'please.'"

"And I will regret saying that every day for the rest of my life." But she crossed the room. And when she stood in front of him seated on the edge of her bed, he took her hands.

"A lot of baggage sits between us, and they only know you fail at relationships and I'm prickly. Not the heart stuff. Maybe they aren't wrong to think... to doubt."

"Do you doubt?"

"Honestly? I have a lot of pretty deep-seated doubts. I think we're a hard sell, but the chemistry is good enough you're ignoring it."

"You're here with me, agreeing to it. So, if I'm ignoring, what are you doing?"

"Stewing."

He smiled. "You know, I've been thinking about the failed-relationships thing, too. What I did so wrong, and what you said about the maneuvering thing was right. Partially. But I also think, maybe, at least somewhat, it didn't work out with all of those other women because a part of my heart was already yours."

"Oh, shit, don't be romantic." She blinked a few times. "I suck at emotional crud."

"You'll get better." He tightened his grip on her hands. "You'll have to get better at it, because...I think...I l-love you, Leah." That was a lot harder to say than he'd planned. He thought it would roll off his tongue, smooth and easy. Because the words were true. He'd known her too long and too well for it not to be true.

She was perfectly still, and even though he'd never seen real, deep-seated fear on Leah's face, he knew that was what he saw now. Fear, he could work with. Hell, fear he understood. He was scared out of his mind, but it didn't change the reality.

And as much as he'd hoped she might say it back immediately, he also understood that she had a lot more baggage to get over than he did. He could be patient. He was excellent at patience. "You know what we need?"

"What?" she asked creakily.

"We need to go on a date."

Leah wrinkled her nose. "We're all but practicing living together. You're being all—" she waved a hand in front of his face "—that. I'm not sure a date is totally necessary."

"Sure it is. Getting moderately dressed up, as in you not wearing jeans and a sweatshirt, us going out of this house and MC, you letting me buy you a meal. See a movie that's 75 percent sex because this time we can come home together and have it."

Her throat moved as she swallowed. "We're doing this all kinds of backward."

"It just might be perfect, then. Oh, you know what? The New Year's Eve thing. You be my date, wear your red dress, and I can enact one or two of the many fantasies I've had of you in it."

"Fantasies, huh?"

"Well, there's the obvious on my desk back at MC."

"Obviously, but that's kind of vague." She knelt in front of him, which he was pretty sure eradicated every brain cell he owned.

"Vague," he repeated, his voice cracking like a prepubescent.

She rested her hands on his knees, blinking up at him innocently. "Yes, vague. I need more detail to get the full…impact."

Her hands inched incrementally higher on his legs. Yup, definitely no brain cells left. Nothing left, except her kneeling before him. Smiling. And any thoughts of love or her parents or her heart were completely gone.

CHAPTER TWENTY-ONE

"You want me to tell you my detailed sexual fantasies of you in that dress while your parents are in the next room?"

"I hate to break it to you, but my parents have been all but in the next room every single time we've had sex."

"Right."

He looked so flustered and cute, she couldn't stop smiling. Which was good, because when he'd told her he loved her, she couldn't imagine smiling. Or breathing. Or, most of all, responding. It just kind of froze her brain, her mouth.

Not doing well with emotional crap was an understatement, and no one she didn't share genetic material with had ever told her they loved her before. What was she supposed to say?

Well, probably "I love you" back, but…mainly all her brain could work out was…*grahhhh*. So, sex, much better option. And maybe some part of her brain that couldn't express it verbally could express that love-ish feeling she had this way.

Anything was better than the jittery, heart-bursting

feeling constricting her chest. Arousal and release would take care of that.

Surely.

She pressed her palms firmly into his thighs. "Still with me?"

His lips curved into a smile, losing some of that flustered bafflement. "I do not appear to be going anywhere."

One of the many amazing things about him was that he could...do this. Make things lighter, easier. She wanted to do that, too. "So, about that desk..." She stopped her hands at the upper part of his thigh, enjoying the rough denim under her palms, the heat from his body, the fact that she could see the outline of his erection against his pants.

She would focus on those feelings, the ones she knew what to do with that had a clear-cut path. Get naked. Have sex. Release.

Maybe then she could muddle through love.

He cleared his throat. "Right. My...desk. And... you, in the red dress."

"Mmm."

"Bent over the desk, so I could, uh...you know, do things." He let out a disgusted breath. "Holy shit am I bad at this."

The giggle escaped before she could manipulate it into something a little less emasculating. She rested her forehead on his leg, trying to swallow down more laughter.

"Oh, go ahead, laugh it up."

"I'm sorry. I am." She tried to bite her lip, think about anything that might stop it. But another laugh slipped out. And then another. "Oh, I am sorry. It's not funny. It's just..." When she dared to look up at him he was staring at the ceiling. Though his mouth was curved in amusement, she couldn't help wondering if there wasn't something else under it, not nearly so pleasant.

"You don't have to be perfect, you know?"

His gaze dropped to her. "Was I trying to be?"

"Sometimes I think..." She inched her hands up to his waist, tugging at his sweater, so he bent forward and she pulled it off along with the T-shirt he wore underneath. She sighed. He might not be smooth with the dirty talk, but who needed to be when you looked like that?

She leaned forward and pressed a kiss to the center of his chest. "Sometimes I do think you try to be perfect. To be what everyone else wants. And I always seem to like you the best when you fail at that."

"That's somehow both warped and flattering at the same time."

"Leah Santino, warped and flattering. I'll add that to my business cards." He chuckled but stopped abruptly when she kissed him again, lower, somewhere around second level of ab. She slid her hands back over his thighs, not stopping until her fingers were at his waistband.

The rest of his chuckle was more of a hissed breath. "I apologize for laughing, though. I'll make it up to you." She flipped the button of his fly and when he made a strangled grunt in the back of his throat she quirked an eyebrow at him. "Did you have something to say?"

"Uh. No. No. Carry on. Be my guest, et cetera, et cetera."

She grinned, pulling the zipper down. "Take off your pants."

"You know, in my fantasies, I tend to call the shots."

"Then be my guest, et cetera, et cetera."

"All right." He brushed his fingertips across her temple, the falling-out tendrils of hair from her braid. One fingertip traced the curve of her ear. A move so sweet, so loving...

Guh.

"Take off your shirt. Slowly."

She didn't remove her hands from the waistband of his jeans. "You know, even in this scenario, I really hate taking orders."

He chuckled. "How about this. We both agree to get naked, no orders necessary."

"A compromise."

"I have a feeling we will be negotiating many over the course of this." Then his other finger traced her other ear and she felt like melting into the floor. She couldn't think of a time anyone had touched her like this. It wasn't a careful touch, as though she was fragile and might break. It wasn't a desperate touch as if she'd die tomorrow. It was sweet and appreciative, but it asked for nothing in return.

She opened her mouth to tell him that she loved him, but he leaned forward and kissed her before she could. Cupping her face, drawing her close, and she let herself go to…everything. Not just passion or attraction, but the depth of what she felt for him. And that really, truly was a first.

His fingers slipped under the fabric of her shirt, gently pulled up until they had to break the kiss to remove it completely. She was still kneeling, and he was still sitting on the edge of her bed. He skimmed his palms down her arms and grasped her elbows as though he meant to pull her onto the bed, but she wasn't quite ready for that.

She moved her arms out of his grasp, moving her hands to his jeans. "I'm going to finish what I started. Or start what I started. Or something because apparently I, too, am not good at the sexy, sexy talk." She shook her head, not feeling self-conscious so much as a desperate need to forget about words of all kinds. "So, please remove your pants."

"Impossible to say no to 'please,'" he said a little breathlessly, moving to his feet and shoving his pants and underwear down and kicking out of them.

She rocked back to her heels and just took him in. "It is really not fair how good you look naked."

"You're right. You should probably be naked, too."

She smiled, couldn't help it. Had she ever smiled so much during foreplay? She couldn't remember that ever being a thing, but she liked it. How…comfortable it made everything. She unhooked her bra and let it fall, but instead of taking off her pants, she got back on her knees and grasped his erection.

Hard and hot and smooth as she traveled the length of him. "This would be easier if you sat back down."

He was back on the bed before she even had the entire sentence out, and her smile never once died. She inched forward on her knees until she was close enough to lower her mouth to the tip of his penis.

When she touched her tongue to him he groaned loud enough she had to shush him. She ran her tongue down the thick length of him, the undercurrent of power heating in her veins, centering at her core.

When she looked up at him, his head was thrown back, the tendons of his neck taut as he made a much quieter, low guttural noise in his throat. So, she took him in her mouth, getting a kind of perverse glee that he had to be quiet, that she was making him not want to be.

She used her mouth until his fingers came to her shoulders, then tangled in her hair. Breathing harsh, he pulled her head away. "Leah, I need you…"

He pulled her onto the bed before she could do anything about it. She was under him in a flash, though he leveraged enough on his arms that she could wiggle out of her pants and underwear.

He needed something from her. He'd said it. Desperately. No one ever needed her. Aside from always being the one needing, she tended to shy away from someone depending on her. She knew how fragile that dependence would be.

But she couldn't find that normal fear of connection, of a future that would end a little soon. She couldn't be afraid of anything with Jacob lowering his mouth to hers, with his "I love you" still echoing in her head.

For the first time in a long time, she didn't have a thing to be afraid of.

JACOB GRABBED THE condom from the dresser and they both fumbled to put it on, breathing heavily, laughing a little when it was the wrong way and they had to flip it over.

He was desperate to be inside her, to lose himself and all these damn feelings in the pleasure of release. But if he did, he wasn't sure he could keep his dignity long enough to give that to her, as well.

So he slid his palm down her abdomen, carefully ignoring the scar right above. Her words from earlier popped into his head—*you don't have to be perfect*—but he shoved them away. He wasn't perfect at all, but he could give her what she wanted.

He slid a finger across her, wet and hot. He explored until she was arching against his hand, biting her lip, fingers digging into his shoulders.

Only then did he slide inside, holding her still while he ruthlessly held on to his control. He had to believe he could control some part of this, because everything else seemed so far out of his grasp.

The thought annoyed him, undercut the buzz of

arousal, so he withdrew almost completely and then plunged deep.

She had been in the driver's seat on her knees, but now he was. He was in control and he would drive her as crazy as she'd driven him. He'd give her what she wanted, everything that she wanted, and then... things would somehow be right.

Even in his hazy state he knew that didn't make sense, but he didn't care. He didn't care about anything except bringing her to orgasm. Maybe then she'd love him back.

He squeezed his eyes shut. *Screw you, brain.*

Luckily, Leah took that moment to pull him close and whisper "Harder" in his ear. Yes, they needed hard and fast and crazed or he would keep thinking and that was wrong.

So, he plunged deeper, thrust faster, holding tight on to her hips to keep the bed from making too much noise. His heart thundered in his ears and he could barely feel anything but her tight warmth around him and the breath staggering in and out of his lungs.

She said his name, her hands sliding off his sweat-slicked shoulders, but then she grasped his hips, pulling him even deeper, arching to meet each thrust until she whimpered in release.

He slowed his pace, wanting to draw out the last few minutes, slowly withdrawing, moving deep again, relishing in the feel of her smooth skin under his rough palms. Relishing the feel of everything about her.

She was his. If she didn't love him yet, she would.

This was everything he'd been looking for and failing at finding.

She grasped his hand, linking her fingers with his, her gaze meeting his. He leaned forward, touched his mouth to hers and was lost.

Her fingers traced up and down his spine until he worked up the strength to pull out and move off her. He kissed her cheek, then got out of bed and headed for the bathroom.

He disposed of the condom and washed his hands, looking at himself in the mirror.

As sure as he was of his own feelings, of her returning them at some point, as sure as he was of *them* as a couple, something about her not saying it back made him feel off.

But he plastered a smile on his face and walked back to the bed. *You don't have to be perfect.* He pushed that thought away. Of course he did. That was how a person got what they wanted. Being good and making the right choices.

He got back into bed, sliding his arm under her neck, full of all sorts of fake cheer. "All right, tell me one place."

"One place?" she asked sleepily, nuzzling into his shoulder.

He wondered if that feeling would ever get old. Her cozied up to him, sleepy and satisfied. Tough-as-nails, hard-ass Leah content and cozy against him. "One place you've fantasized about us having sex. You have to have at least one."

She chuckled, but went silent for a while. He thought she wasn't going to answer, but then she gave him a little poke in the side. "Your truck."

"My truck?" He grinned, some of the cheer becoming less fake. "Like, while it was moving? Going to or leaving a job? What are you wear—"

"Shut up, Jacob." She blew out a breath, linking her hand with his. She'd tensed a little, though he couldn't tell why. So he kissed her forehead and let the conversation go.

"For the record," she said in a very quiet voice, "the love thing... Well, I think—" She swallowed, but then she buried her head in the curve of his shoulder. "I love you, too," she mumbled.

He closed his eyes, and every last muscle in his body relaxed. He'd known it. Or hoped it or something, but the words were still a relief. He hadn't made a mistake. He hadn't miscalculated. She loved him, too, so this thing they were doing was right.

And nothing could change that.

CHAPTER TWENTY-TWO

LEAH WAS IN HELL. Shopping-with-Mom hell. But it was Mom's last full day, and Leah had agreed to do whatever she wanted. She just hadn't expected it to be shopping.

"You don't wear any jewelry," Mom tsked as Leah longingly thought of Marc and Dad ice fishing at the state park. She didn't love fishing, but she did love not shopping. In fact, she'd rather be at work.

With Jacob.

She wasn't sure that was a happy thought or an uncomfortable one or what. This whole *love* thing was beyond new. It was something she hadn't allowed herself to believe she'd have.

"How about these?" Mom held some giant dangly blue earrings against Leah's face.

"Mom, where would I ever wear those?"

"A date?"

A date. With Jacob. Crazy, but not crazy enough to wear those earrings. "I'm not huge into big and dangly. Can we go a little understated?"

Mom shook her head. "My only daughter and no

sparkles. No pink. She wants black and understated. Where did I go wrong?"

"I wouldn't blame yourself."

"You're right. All your father's fault, always letting you tinker with the cars. Humph." Mom picked up another pair of earrings. They were black and sparkly and still a little big for Leah, but when Mom looked at her hopefully, she forced a smile.

"Those are great."

Mom grinned. "That's my girl."

Leah's phone dinged, and she totally did not get a little gooey at the fact it was Jacob texting her. She was so above gooey.

Keep telling yourself that, Santino.

She brought the message up, suppressing a smile as she read. Jasmine Street house accepted my offer. Get ready for some overtime, baby. She wanted to be mad at him for getting another project, especially one this difficult and with no client involved.

But it would be the most challenging work of her career, and just the thought of it had her palms itching to start planning.

"That's from Jacob, I assume."

Leah looked up from her phone to see Mom with the earrings clutched to her chest, dreamy smile on her face.

"Yes, but it's about work."

"That smile is not about work."

"We just got a really exciting project."

Mom shook her head, wandering over to the next jewelry display case. "No one gets a smile like that over work."

Leah wasn't so sure about that, but she couldn't deny it might be at least a little about Jacob. Of course, the warm and squishy feelings disappeared when she realized what Mom was looking at. Rings.

"You should start dropping hints, honey. Nothing worse than a hideous engagement ring. Now, some girls do the ring shopping with the boys these days, but that seems tacky to me. A few hints and a smart man like Jacob should get it right."

"Mom…" Leah found her eyes trapped on the rings. She wasn't a jewelry girl. She wasn't an engagement-ring girl, but she also had to accept that if things went right with her and Jacob, this might be where it led. And as much as that scared her, she'd already taken that step. Jacob had crawled under all her defenses and excuses, and if they ended up here, could she really say no now?

"You're thinking about it, aren't you?" Mom made a girlie squealing sound. "You're opening up to the idea of getting married, aren't you? See? You need me here. If I hadn't been poking you about it, you'd still be all determined to say no to marriage."

The anxiety in Leah's stomach twisted harder. She didn't know how to deal with all of this. It was all so…soon. She needed time and…a plan. Which was funny since she was always making fun of Jacob and his plans.

Leah turned away from the display. She couldn't deal with that right now. Mom thought they'd been together for a year, not a few days. This part, if it even ever happened, which was a big *if*, was far away.

Mom being around all the time…that seemed a lot more imminent. "There's…no way I can convince you that you don't need to move here? That I'm okay. Better than okay. The life I've built for myself here isn't just what I want, but what I need."

Mom blinked at her, perplexed, maybe, damn it, even a little hurt. "But don't you want us here?"

Leah swallowed. She kept trying to be honest and getting kicked in the head by Mom's logic, but at the same time, honesty was giving her something with Jacob. Maybe if she kept trying. "Have you considered things might go back to the way they were? The fighting? The misunderstanding?"

"Believe it or not, I have." Mom pressed her lips together, grasping Leah's shoulders, the plastic of the earring package digging into her sweater. "And I hope we both learned something from that time. From the time apart. Maybe a little bit on how to bend and compromise. I will always—" she made air quotes as she spoke the next words "—'overworry,' as your father calls it, and I'm sure you do, too. And I'll never pretend I won't, but I can try to give you more space. I will. Because I won't want you to shut me out again."

Leah wasn't sure it made her feel any better.

Words like *try* and *overworry* didn't exactly instill a lot of confidence in her that things would change. But she had grown up and she had learned some lessons, too, so maybe it wouldn't be all bad.

"Can you try to be at least a little happy about it?"

The words twisted in her heart. "Mom, it's not that I'm unhappy. I'm just…worried. I want us to be like this, not like then."

Mom released her shoulders. "I do, too."

And Leah needed to remember that. As much as Mom's worry and seeming lack of trust was hurtful, she wanted them to be a family. She wanted them to get along. It wasn't mean or vicious; it just was, and maybe with some closer proximity they actually could work through some of that "overworry."

So, she smiled, and she actually meant it, at least partially. "I'm starving. Are we ready for lunch?"

"Oh, can we go somewhere a little fancy? I can barely drag your father to Wendy's these days."

"Your pick, Mom. It's your day." And it wouldn't kill Leah to do this on occasion. Like Mom said, bend. It didn't make her less of herself or set her on a path to being that miserable teenager. It wasn't breaking; it was balancing. If she could do it with her health, surely she could do it with her life.

JACOB PULLED UP to Leah's house, whistling as plans for the Jasmine Street house whirled in his head. Timelines and how to fit it into everyone's schedule. Kyle had been less than enthused, but once he'd heard Jacob's plans to sell the main house next year, he'd changed his tune a little bit. Jacob might take risks from time to time, but he wasn't fiscally irresponsible. Not with so many people depending on him for a paycheck.

He stepped out of his truck, checking his phone again. Mom and Dad hadn't returned his morning call, which was unusual. For the first time today, his mood dampened. It might be silly to worry, but his parents were usually as dependable as clockwork. And with Mom's flu lingering...

"Everything okay?"

He looked up to see Leah sitting on the stairs. She was wearing her oversize coat and a black stocking cap.

He grinned. "That excited to see me, had to meet me at the door?"

"Something like that." She pulled a little white box out of her pocket. "Got you something. A congratulations present of sorts."

He took a seat next to her on the cold steps. "And I just realized I haven't given you a Christmas present."

"I wasn't your secret Santa, and you weren't mine. Why would you give me a Christmas gift?"

He shrugged. "I should have gotten you one anyway. Unless the sex counts."

She gave his shoulder a shove. "I think we're okay. You can make it up to me next year."

He grinned, dropping his phone back in his pocket "Next year, huh? Is that a promise?"

She rolled her eyes. "Would you just open the damn thing?"

He took the box from her outstretched hand. Baffled by the tiny size, he lifted the lid. Inside was a tiny brass trumpet figurine. He pulled it out, turned it over in his hand. "I... Thank you."

"You don't get it, do you?"

"Not even a little bit."

She laughed, nudging him. "Remember the first night you spent here and you made that crack about the Walls of Jericho? Well, consider this your Clark Gable trumpet."

"Hey, you said you'd never seen that movie."

"I lied."

"Why?"

She sighed and looked out at her yard. "When I was a kid and home sick all the time, I used to watch every kind of movie that was on TV. And Mom loved the old ones, so I got to watch those even if I'd already used up my TV allotment for the day. So, I've seen *It Happened One Night* many times, but I... It's not really a fun, pleasant memory being sick and in pain. So I pretended like I'd never seen any of them, instead of...remembering."

She killed him sometimes. He couldn't imagine how hard that childhood would have been. To know, before you were even thirteen, how easy it would be to die. His heart constricted and he slung his arm around her shoulders, drawing her close.

"Thank you," he murmured into her ear, kissing her temple. She tensed, presumably because she knew where his mind was going, so he focused on making a joke. "I'll keep it on my desk and think of sex with you constantly."

She snorted and the tenseness in her shoulders dissipated, as he'd hoped.

"Anyway, congratulations on your terrible investment."

He kissed behind her ear, lingering until she shivered. "You can't wait to work on it. Admit it."

"Please. I told you it was a money pit."

"And you've already thought about how you'll rewire everything, the materials you'll need. You probably have a list." He moved his mouth to her neck, tugging at the collar of her jacket so he could press his lips to her collarbone.

"Don't know what you're talking about."

"Liar," he said, grasping her chin and turning her to face him. Her lips were pressed together in that I-don't-want-to-smile smile, so he kissed her until she leaned into him.

"I love you," he murmured against her mouth, because the feeling slammed into him a million different ways. That she would buy him a gift, that she was just as excited as he was about the project and didn't want to admit it, that she was here, hands clutching his coat.

She pulled back just a hair, smiled. "I love you, too."

"Look at that—no stuttering, no adding 'I think.' Why, we might just be grown-ups after all."

"Don't get carried away now."

His phone rang and he held up a finger. "Hold that thought. I've been trying to get ahold of Mom and Dad all day."

It was Grace's name on the caller ID, but maybe she was with them. "Hey, Grace, what's up?"

"Jacob."

The grave note in her voice immediately made his stomach sink. "What's going on? Are you with Mom and Dad?"

"Y-yes."

Her stutter did nothing to ease the pit of dread. He pushed to his feet. "Where are you? Home?"

"No. I… Jacob, I need you to be calm, okay?"

"Grace, tell me."

He barely noticed that Leah had stood with him, and her gloved hand twining with his did nothing to ease the fear at Grace's silence.

"I'm at the hospital. Mom… Apparently Mom had some surgery."

"What? Surgery? What?"

"I'm sorry. I'm trying to spit it out. There was a…c-cancerous tumor, and she's getting it removed. She didn't want to worry us beforehand. But Dad was getting worried and called me and asked me to call you."

"Bluff City General?"

"Yes. You're coming?"

"Of course I'm fucking coming. Text me where to go." He hit End so forcefully it was a wonder his screen didn't break. He was already striding to his car.

"Jacob, what's going on?"

"I have to go to the hospital."

"Is it Grace? Is everything ok—"

"It's my mother. She's having a tumor removed. I have to go." He reached for his truck door, barely registering that his arm was shaking until Leah's hand covered his.

"Let me drive you."

He couldn't bear to look at her, to look at anything beyond the handle of his truck door. If he did, he might lose what little control he had on the emotions raging through him.

"It's your last night with your parents. Go on inside. I'll call you later."

"Jacob." She pried his hand from the door. "I'm going to drive you. I'm going to walk you in. I'm going to see if you or Grace need anything, and then I will come back and spend the rest of the evening with my family. Got it?"

He was afraid if he argued, he'd blow. Completely. All the anger and frustration raging inside of him, right next to fear. Absolute bone-shaking fear. So he nodded curtly and followed her to her truck.

He was grateful she didn't try to talk. She just started her truck, tapped something on her phone—

he assumed a message to her family about what she was doing—and then backed out of the driveway. Once she was on the main road, without looking at him, without saying anything, she took his hand.

The gesture was…nice. Just nice, not asking for anything. Comfort. She was offering him comfort, and it made him want to curl up in her lap or something equally childish.

Instead, he cleared his throat and drew his hand away. He stared hard at the yellow lines in the center of the road. "Grace was upset."

"The hospital is an upsetting place."

For the first time since he'd answered his phone, he looked at her. Her face was blank, if a little tense. Her knuckles white on the steering wheel. "Hospitals bother you."

"I'll deal."

She said it so forcefully he had no doubt she would. What he wondered was how well *he'd* deal. "Why didn't they tell me?"

"I don't know, honey."

She didn't throw around endearments often. Whether it was a direct retaliation for him calling her *baby* all the time or something she said naturally, he didn't know. But it helped his jaw relax, just a little.

He looked back at the road. "What if…?"

"Don't what-if it. We're going to focus on getting there, on finding out what's going on. That's all. Not much farther now."

Beauty of living in a smallish city, he guessed.

"She hadn't been feeling well. I knew that, but she said it was the flu."

Leah was silent for a few ticking seconds. "I guess that's her way of coping."

"I guess you would know."

She flicked a glance at him. "Yup."

"I really instill a lot of trust in the women I love." Because what were the chances two women in his life were hiding their life-threatening issues from him? He had to be the common denominator, didn't he? Someone had said that somewhere along the way.

"Jacob, the way we handle things isn't about you."

For some reason that put him back to when Barry was loose and threatening Grace. How often she'd told him, *This isn't about you.*

Maybe that was what he needed to realize. Not a damn thing was about him. Not good. Not bad. He was in control of nothing. Ever.

He could barely breathe through the lump in his throat. How was this happening again?

Leah approached the hospital and Jacob read the text from Grace so they could park in the appropriate place.

He had the door open before she'd even pushed the gearshift into Park. Somewhere in the recesses of his brain he thought he should probably wait for Leah to catch up, but he couldn't make himself slow down.

He followed Grace's directions through the maze of the hospital, frustration mounting after he realized he'd taken a wrong turn. Finally, he found the right waiting room, Dad and Grace huddled together on a little bench.

Both looked as if they'd been crying and Jacob felt shaky and unsure. He felt like an outsider, as if he didn't belong here. He almost turned around, but Leah stepped next to him.

Jacob swallowed all the emotions he felt and stepped into the room. Dad and Grace stood and he walked over and stiffly hugged both of them. "Tell me what's going on."

Grace and Dad exchanged a look, and when Dad nodded, Grace took a deep breath. She tried to smile, but it was more of a shaky grimace. "Apparently, they found a lump at one of Mom's checkups a few weeks ago."

"Where?" He winced at the own demand in his voice. It wasn't fair to be angry with Grace. She hadn't kept this from him, and he couldn't even be angry at Dad or Mom for keeping him in the dark.

But that was what he felt. Anger. Burning and bubbling. And no matter how many times he tried to swallow it down, it kept growing.

"Her...breast. It's...breast cancer, but..." Grace took a shaky breath and looked at Dad. "It's going to be okay. We know she can beat it because..."

Dad stepped in, put a hand on Jacob's shoulder. "I know this may come as a shock, but when you were in high school, Mom had—"

"You don't think I fucking knew?" Jacob could

feel tears burning his eyes, but he fought them with everything he had.

"You…knew…"

"The weight she lost. The wig. The…everything. You really, really thought I didn't put two and two together?" *Stop yelling. Stop yelling.* But he couldn't. "You think so little of me? Both of you? I knew. I damn well knew the mother I loved was going through chemo and hell, and no one wanted me to know, so I had to pretend."

Grace sat down in a chair and covered her face with her hands, sobs obviously racking her body. Dad didn't move, but tears streamed down his cheeks.

He'd never seen his father cry. Never…even back then. He sank into his own chair and, screw it, let his own tears fall. And when someone put their arm around him, he knew it was Leah. So he leaned into it.

What the hell else was there to do?

CHAPTER TWENTY-THREE

LEAH DIDN'T EVEN begin to know how to navigate this situation. Three people crying. Sickness and death hanging in the air around them. And a past she wasn't a part of.

She'd never been on this side of the coin before. And she didn't know what she was supposed to do. At all.

Except hurt. She rested her head against Jacob's shoulder, only holding on to her own tears because it wasn't her place. It wasn't her mother, though she did know and like Mrs. McKnight.

Mr. McKnight cleared his throat, and Jacob looked up. Though she knew Jacob had shed some tears, only his red-rimmed eyes gave any indication.

"She was supposed to be out an hour ago," Mr. McKnight said unevenly.

"Why didn't she tell me? I'm not a kid anymore. This…"

"We were going to. We wanted to get through Christmas, and then with Grace's announcement…"

Grace let out a little choked noise and Leah had to close her eyes. It was a role reversal she hadn't at all expected or prepared for. To be waiting for news on someone else's prognosis.

"This is such bullshit."

Leah winced at the hurt and pain in Jacob's voice. "Jacob…"

"What? It is. An hour ago? What if something's wrong and we didn't know? And for what? So we didn't spend Christmas doing what we could together? So Grace could have a moment? Was that really worth this?"

"Not now, Jacob," Grace said wearily.

"Then when?" he demanded, pushing to his feet and raking fingers through his hair. "When? When it's too damn late to matter?"

Mr. McKnight stood, some of the anguish on his face tightening. "Don't you dare say that to me right now."

"You're mad? *You're* mad? I should have been here! I should have known then. Things should be a million ways different than they are, so you do not get to be mad."

"My wife is in there with a malignant tumor. I damn well get to be whatever I want. Now, you sit down and be quiet, young man, or you are welcome to go."

Leah's breath caught. Jesus, this could not be going any worse. She didn't know if it was her place, but as the only one with any kind of distance from the situation, maybe she should get involved.

Not at all certain of what she was doing, Leah

stepped between the two seething, hurting men. "Jacob, walk with me."

She tugged on his arm, but he didn't move. She braced herself for another accusation, more angry words, but after another moment he turned to her and let her lead him away.

"Let's just step outside for a few minutes, huh?" There was a door right next to the waiting room that led outside. Maybe some fresh air would...calm him. Everything.

"Yes, that'll fix every damn thing, won't it?"

Leah bit her lip against the snippy comment that was her instinctual response. Not what he needed right now. He needed to calm down. Get some perspective. Work through his anger before he stepped back into that waiting room.

This is what he'll be like when it's you...

The thought was selfish and came out of nowhere, but it made her stomach roll over. She took a deep breath of the frigid air, hoping that the nausea faded.

It didn't. She wanted to blame part of it on the hospital. The lights, the linoleum, the people, the smell that all hospitals seemed to have. It brought her back to a lot of unpleasant days.

But it all had to do with the reality that someday she'd be in his mother's place, and this was how he'd be. They could talk about her condition ad nauseam. They could prepare and discuss, but if something happened out of the blue, Jacob would be the angry, lashing-out guy in the waiting room while everyone else tried to keep it together.

She'd already lived through that. She didn't want to do it again.

She squeezed her eyes shut and pressed a hand to her stomach, trying to will away that thought. Not what the here and now was about. She'd have to deal with that thought later. Much, much later.

"I can't believe…" He looked off at some distant point in the dark night beyond the parking lot, jaw working, eyes filled with tears he seemed unwilling to shed.

"I know you're upset. And angry." She swallowed against the squeakiness in her voice. "Scared, and you have a right to all those feelings."

"Gee, thank you for your permission," he muttered, turning away from her, jamming his hands in his pockets.

It was hard to swallow the retort. So damn hard she curled her hands into fists. "I would very much appreciate it if you didn't talk to me that way."

"And I would appreciate you not trying to tell me how to feel."

"I'm not doing that."

"Yes, you are. I'm not scared. I'm not upset. I'm *livid*. I'm fucking terrified. And I'm so damn furious I could hit my own father."

"Don't you think he's all those things, too?"

"Of course he is. But he got to prepare for this. To understand what was happening. He got to take her here and hug her and kiss her before..." Jacob's voice broke. "You want to comfort me, Leah? Here's a tip. Don't be on their fucking side. Don't treat me like a child."

"I'm not doing that. I'm not trying to do that." Her words were choked because she didn't know what to do, didn't know how to help him. And she desperately wanted to. To take away his pain or ease it. At least undercut the anger inside of him that was overshadowing everything.

"Well, try a little harder. I don't need this shit from you."

"I know you're angry, but I don't plan on being your punching bag." She said it as evenly as she could, as stoically as possible because he was walking on dangerous ground. They both were.

"Good to know. And what do you plan on being? Unhelpful? Condescending? On their side?"

She wanted to cry. She wanted to hit *him* and knock some sense into his fear and grief that he was wielding like anger. "There aren't sides. This isn't a war. Your mother—"

"Could be dead," he said flatly. "That's what could be happening right now. Do you have any idea what it's like to be kept in the dark like this? To find out just when things seem...right and balanced? To have it not be the first damn time?"

"No, but I know what it's like to be in your mother's shoes, and she shouldn't wake up to find the people who need to take care of her at each other's throats.

Because she isn't dead. She didn't die the first time, and the likelihood of her dying in surgery to remove a tumor from her breast is slim."

His gaze met hers for the first time, the range of emotions reflected in his gaze so raw it hurt her heart.

"You're a cancer expert now? Heart transplant equals you know all about every damn procedure?"

She ignored it. Let the snotty comment roll right off her back. Grief made her do shitty things, too, right? "When I was in the hospital, my parents were constantly at each other's throats. They tried to hide it, but I knew. And the minute we got home, they wouldn't hide it. The disagreements on how to handle me right there in front of my face. It's shit to be sick and hurting and know you're causing everyone's anger and stress. Do not do that to your mother."

"I appreciate the perspective, but don't tell me what to do."

"Then stop being a dick so I don't have to."

"Go home, Leah. I don't want you here anymore. You'd think someone with your experience wouldn't be so terrible at this."

She swallowed down the hurt and squared her shoulders. "I'm not going anywhere. Maybe you don't want me, but Grace will."

"Fine."

"Fine." She stomped back inside knowing she'd somehow screwed this all up. She should have comforted him and made him feel better, not worse. Not add on to his plate. Not think about herself. About their future.

But he was wrong. So damn wrong, and she'd been on the receiving end of that wrong too many times to let it slide. If that made her a horrible person, well, it wouldn't be the first time.

JACOB STOOD APART from Leah and Grace. Dad had been taken back to Mom only a few minutes after he and Leah had returned.

Surgery had gone as well as could be expected. Her heart rate had dropped a little bit at a crucial point, causing the delay, but otherwise, the tumor had been removed.

And now the road to cancer recovery would begin. Again.

The fear. The pretending, because even though he knew this time around, there would be fake smiles and "you look greats" that nobody would believe. He tried to swallow, but the fizzling lump that had taken up residence in his throat made it impossible.

He pushed off the wall. "I'm going in there."

"They said only Dad."

"I don't give a crap."

Before he could get anywhere, Kyle stepped into the waiting room, holding a duffel bag and groceries.

"I think I got everything you asked for," he said, taking a seat next to Grace. He placed the bags on the floor and slid an arm around Grace's shoulders, kissing her on the forehead. "Your dad's in there?"

Grace nodded and Jacob flicked a glance at Leah, but she was staring at her feet. Why couldn't he be like Grace? Upset but calm. Leaning on the people she loved instead of treating them like shit.

He sank into a chair, his determination to do something gone. Because every time he opened his mouth, ugliness spewed out. Because...well, it was all he had. All he felt. How could he just take this in stride? They were good people. They made good choices. Worked hard. Paid their taxes. They weren't perfect, but damn it, they were on the right side of the line.

Why did they keep getting punished for it?

Leah crossed over to him, though she stopped well out of his reach. "I guess...I'll go."

"Good." He didn't exactly use a snippy tone of voice, but "good" was a definite jerk move. He couldn't seem to find a way to control his words.

"Why are you acting like this?" she asked, not so much sounding exasperated as hurt.

Why did he keep hurting her? Apparently he wasn't on the right side of anything at the moment. Apparently he did make wrong choices. He was not a good person or he'd be able to handle this, be able to lean on Leah instead of pushing her away.

He took a shaky breath. "I don't know." And he didn't know how to unclench, how to lean, how to... let go of the anger. But anger was something under his control. Anger was his. If he lost it, and only grief and fear took its place, he didn't know who he'd be.

"It's not helping anyone."

"I know." But it wasn't about anyone else. It was about surviving all the emotions raging inside him.

"Let me stay. Let me help."

"No. Thank you." He didn't know why he was angry at her or if he even was. He only knew when he saw sympathy on her face, his anger fell away, and all the hurt made him incapable of doing anything. And he had to be able to do something. He had to fix this somehow. Maybe she just needed to leave him alone so he could figure it out.

So he could stop thinking about how no one gave him credit, not even her, for being capable of handling something like this.

So he could stop thinking they were right.

"Jacob..."

"Say goodbye to your parents for me."

She sighed. "All right." Then she trailed her fingers across his hand. "You can call me if you need something."

He nodded, staring at the place where her fingers had brushed. He wouldn't. He couldn't. Asking for help, leaning, letting go would mean he couldn't make things right or better. Maybe yelling didn't accomplish that, either, but at least it felt like motion.

The gaping hole of pain in his gut seemed to open wider, grow deeper, but he couldn't make himself move to ask her to come back.

He should have said "I love you." He should have given her a hug. He should have...not yelled at his dad. He should have done everything differently.

But Mom shouldn't be dealing with cancer again, so…there.

The silent seconds ticked by, occasionally punctuated by the sound of someone else in the waiting room taking a call or getting news.

He hated all of them. Their tired faces and worried low chatter. He wished they'd all disappear.

He wished *he* could disappear.

Grace's phone chimed. "They're moving Mom to her room. We can see her."

Jacob got stiffly to his feet. Though he wasn't good for much of anything apparently, he did help Kyle gather the provisions he'd brought at Grace's request. In silence, they followed Grace down linoleum-lined halls, into an elevator.

When they stepped out of the elevator, they were greeted by Dad and a small room with a couch and a fridge and a coffeemaker.

"A few days here," Dad said, attempting a smile but only managing not to frown. "Luckily, there aren't specific visiting hours—we can come and stay whenever we like—but probably only one of us can sleep here comfortably."

"We should take turns," Grace said, taking Dad's hand.

He nodded. "We'll see how it goes. I know she'd like to see you two. She's worried and still a little groggy. I think we should do it one at a time, just until the anesthesia's fully worn off. Gracie?"

She glanced back at him. "Maybe Jacob should go first."

Dad turned to him, jaw tight. "I don't want you upsetting her."

What was happening? How was he screwing it all up so badly? "I won't," he managed to choke out, but he probably would. Because he couldn't get it together. No matter how hard he squeezed, everything trickled out like sand.

But he took a deep breath and followed Dad to Mom's room. Dad opened the door, but he didn't step inside, just gestured Jacob in.

Jacob didn't trust himself to speak, but he did squeeze Dad's shoulder as he passed. He wasn't going to upset Mom. He'd done a great job hurting everyone else, but he could handle this. He *would* handle this.

Mom lay in her hospital bed, eyes closed, her complexion ashen. Everything inside him seized, making moving almost impossible. He could barely breathe. What was he supposed to do?

Because he had the sickening realization that back when he'd been in high school and pretended not to know what had been going on, it had been partially because it was what Mom wanted, but also because…because…

The tears trickled down his cheeks. He couldn't keep them in check. All those years ago and he'd pretended because he hadn't wanted to see this. The hard stuff. Pretending was easier and he was a coward.

Mom's eyes fluttered open, and when her gaze landed on him, her mouth curved into a kind of sympathetic smile. Her guidance counselor, you-poor-thing smile.

Which just proved what an asshole he was.

"Hey, honey."

"Hey." He swallowed against the thick lump in his throat, but it didn't dislodge. Stiffly, he moved to the chair next to her bed. He wiped his face with his sleeve and then took her non-IV hand in his.

Then, because he couldn't hold on to it, the pain, the fear, the self-disgust, he leaned his forehead against her hand and cried.

"It's going to be okay."

"That's my line for you," he said in a creaky voice, trying to breathe, center himself, find that control he needed to make things right. To be perfect for her.

"I'm your mother, so it will always be my line to you."

"Not today." He sat up, swallowed down the rest of the emotion. He had to get ahold of himself, of this, because she deserved a son who could handle everything. So he looked her in the eye and, even though he didn't know if it was true, said the words he desperately wanted to believe. "Everything is going to be okay."

Her eyes filled with tears, but she offered a wobbly smile. "It is. I beat it once. I'll beat it again." She tugged her hand out of his, rested her palm against his cheek. "You knew and you didn't tell anyone all those years ago?"

"You didn't want me to know."

"The cooking classes, and you started helping your grandparents out more. You spent less time with friends. I should have known."

"I didn't want you to. I wanted you to get better, and you did."

She let out a shaky breath. "I did. Oh, Jake." She closed her eyes and sank deeper into the pillows. "I'm not going to lie to you. This sucks so hard."

Jacob choked out something resembling a laugh.

"And it's going to keep sucking for a while, but I am alive, and there is that."

"There is."

She frowned over at him, looking sleepy but determined. "It's not a scorecard, you know. You don't get what you deserve. Didn't what happened with Grace teach us all that?"

"But—"

"You can't control the bad, and until you accept that...it's a hell of a lot harder to deal. I used to worry we'd sheltered you too much, that you just didn't know what kind of blows life could deliver, but I don't think that's it. In a weird way, we taught you to respect doing the right thing too much, to help others too much, because you seem to think you can fix everything. Honey, you can't."

"I know that."

Mom snorted. "Don't try to B.S. me while I'm lying

in a hospital, young man. I don't have the energy to smack your head."

"Mom…"

"Be sad. Be scared. It's okay. Better than trying to make sense of the nonsensical crap life throws our way." She yawned. "Oh, I'm getting all fuzzy again."

She kind of drifted out, whether on purpose so he couldn't argue or more likely from the exhaustion that smudged under her eyes.

Every instinct he had wanted to fight her words, argue with them. Of course he could fix this. If he made sure she got the best care, rested. If he helped out… If he…

But everything sounded desperate and childish in his head with Mom's words bouncing around in there, too.

But the weird part was, for the first time since he'd gotten the call, he managed a real, full breath.

CHAPTER TWENTY-FOUR

LEAH PULLED HER truck into her garage, pushed the gearshift into Park and then stared at the windshield.

She didn't understand what had happened. She didn't know what to do. Actually, she was most afraid she did know what to do.

You can't be with someone like that...

She squeezed her eyes shut against the thought, because now was not the time. There were more important things to deal with. For her, getting her parents sent back to Minnesota tomorrow morning. For him, a lot harder tasks. Emotionally draining. She could not be thinking about herself right now.

She leaned her forehead against the steering wheel, desperately fighting tears. Why wouldn't he let her help? Why wouldn't he lean on her? Maybe he had every right to be a dick under the circumstances. Maybe she should just ignore it.

But she couldn't, because she saw her future with him, and it was uglier than the one she'd already been afraid of. Guilt was one thing, having to worry about whether someone was flying off the handle... calling her stupid...yelling at family...

On a sigh, she forced herself out of the truck and into the house through the mudroom. She could hear the strains of the TV, Dad's low rumbly laugh. Which for some reason made her think of Mr. McKnight crying.

God, life was cruel, and she didn't know what to do about that when the man she loved wouldn't let her in. Walk away, apparently.

Guilt twisted with the sadness. Maybe she should have stayed. Comforted him against his will. But every nasty word, every snap… It just made her think about her future and knowing he couldn't handle it.

Would he blame her for making bad choices like he had after the Martin job? Would he treat Grace or Mom the way he'd treated her and his dad today?

She stepped into the living room, trying to smile as her mom swerved in her seat, looking sympathetic and hopeful. "Is everything okay?"

"Jacob's mom got out of surgery and is doing as well as can be expected."

"You could have stayed, honey. We're okay, really. And Jacob probably needs you."

"No, he made it very clear he doesn't." That made her chest ache, so she turned away. "I'm just going to take a shower and get all these hospital germs off me." And maybe the pain and hurt and confusion.

He's going to be this way with you.

She desperately needed to get rid of that horrible

repeating thought, because what had happened tonight wasn't about her at all.

But someday it will be.

She slammed into the bathroom, flipping the water as hot as she could stand and shedding her clothes in angry jerky movements. Once she stepped into the scalding spray she let herself cry. She wasn't sure how long it lasted, but she went until she was completely spent. Until the only thing she could think about was crawling into bed and sleeping all night long.

And she would not think about how she'd shared that bed with Jacob the past few nights. She would not think about telling him she loved him and somehow jinxing every damn thing.

"Oh, you idiot," she muttered to herself, drying off and pulling on sweats.

When she stepped out of the bathroom, Mom was very primly sitting on the little armchair, wrinkling her nose at Leah's bookshelf.

"There are almost-naked men on these books."

"There are indeed." Leah wanted to smile or feel something other than emotional exhaustion, but no such luck. She sank into her bed, first in a sitting position, and then she went ahead and crawled under the covers. Even when Mom was sitting there, she didn't have the energy to do anything but lie in bed.

"Tell me what happened. Why you aren't still there?" Mom rested her arm on Leah's shoulder.

"He didn't want me there."

"Why on earth not?"

Leah shrugged, wishing Mom's comforting hand would leave, but it didn't. "I don't know. He was being…terrible. And maybe he has a right to be. It was a shock, and he was angry and upset, but…I don't like the way he treated me or his family. I don't like the way he dealt with it at all. And he pushed me away, so what else was I supposed to do?"

"I'm sorry, honey."

Leah buried her face in the pillow. She thought she'd gotten ahold of her emotions in the shower, but they were already bubbling back to the surface. Mom stroking her hair as though she was five years old again didn't help.

She wanted to cry and be told it was going to be all right, but more, she wanted to be able to believe it. Unfortunately, that had become impossible many years ago.

Leah sniffled, moving her head back into a sideways position so she could breathe. "I don't think I can do it, Mom, knowing that's how he'd be," she whispered. The words were…not okay. Not now, but maybe if she said them aloud to someone separate from the situation, they'd stop poking at her brain, haunting her.

"How he'd… You mean, if you were the one in the hospital?"

"*When* I'm the one in the hospital."

"You don't know…. You can't predict what will happen."

"The odds of me being in a hospital bed in the next twenty-some years, for whatever reason, serious or not, are pretty high."

"Okay," Mom conceded, still brushing her hands over Leah's hair. "Yes, chances are high."

"I used to think I'd feel guilty, if someone married me and had to go through that, and I would. I still would. I was willing to maybe…try anyway, but knowing he'd…blame me or hurt everyone in the process? Maybe it's too much to ask. Maybe it doesn't exist to find someone who can just… handle it. But I can't…I can't add that on, Mom. It's hard enough being sick—worse knowing the people who love you are arguing themselves to death over it."

Mom's hands paused and then she drew them into her lap. "Your father and I did quite the number on you, huh?"

"It's not your fault. I just… I'm not sure there's a way to handle it that makes it any easier on the patient. I'm not sure it's fair to ask the people who love the patient to act a certain way. I don't know. I only know I can't handle it if I'm sick. It's bad enough watching it as a bystander."

"So…what are you going to do?"

"I can't do anything, because what kind of woman tells the man she loves she can't be with him when his mother has cancer? It's…wrong."

"I can't believe I'm going to disagree with you…"

Leah sat up. "Jesus, I can't, either."

Mom smiled, took her hand and patted it. "Sweetie, I know it bothers you that I want you to have someone to watch after you. And I even understand why, but the bottom line is, someday I won't be here to take care of you when you can't take care of yourself."

Mom swallowed, shook her head. "I'll admit, maneuvering Marc into moving here is a bit of a concession that you might not have a husband to do it. And perhaps it's because he's agreed that I can say... if you can see right now that Jacob isn't going to be able to handle the health challenges you'll likely face, why, I hardly think it's wrong to express that to him. Sure, not today, but maybe once his mother's back at home and settled."

"Mom..." Leah couldn't even begin to believe her mother was agreeing with her, siding with her. "I—I do love him, though."

"Sometimes...oh, honey, sometimes love just isn't enough." Mom's expression went tight. "I love your father. You know I do. And we've managed to repair a lot of the rifts we had there for a while, but...if we hadn't worked very hard to understand each other's side, love wouldn't have been enough to overcome seeing a very serious subject very differently."

"And it helped your subject disappeared."

"It wasn't you, honey."

At Leah's raised eyebrow, Mom sighed. "It was... the situation. An uncontrollable, nobody-at-fault situation."

"That happened to beat inside my chest."

"Oh, hush. The point is, we were too stubborn to let that…difference of opinion be the end, but it was a lot more than love that brought us back together. So, regardless if you love him or if he loves you, if he can't give you what you're going to need, then it isn't right to stand by him."

"You think I should…break up with him? Now?"

"I think you have to do what's right for you, and leading him on just because he's going through a rough time isn't the answer. Wait maybe a few days, but find the right moment and tell him. He's not being what you need him to be."

Leah pressed her hand to her chest. The pain there was excruciating. But neither answer, neither choice, eased the pain.

"And…" Mom cleared her throat. "I regret what I said a few days ago, about not trusting you to take care of yourself. Maybe I didn't want to see it because it makes me feel so…disposable after spending so much of my life with you at the center." Mom shook her head. "You're very…capable. And strong. I envy your strength, actually. And I'm sorry it took this long."

"You're not disposable. I…I've missed you. Even knowing how hard things were, I so badly wanted you back in my life."

"I see that, too. Maybe that's why I can admit it now. Coming here…seeing your life. It mattered, my beautiful girl. And I like to think it'll make things better."

Leah swallowed, heart aching in a whole new way. "I think so, too."

JACOB WATCHED SNOW flutter down onto the parking lot below. The window to Mom's hospital room gave quite a view of Bluff City, gray and snowy. He could see the river in the distance, wished he was on that damn bridge driving the hell away from all of this.

"Knock, knock."

At Leah's voice he popped to his feet. He should do something, say something, just blurt out an apology and screw the fact Dad, Mom and Grace were watching. But no words came out. He was paralyzed by the avalanche of feeling that would pour out after it.

"I was going to leave this at the nurses' station, but your door was open." Leah didn't glance at him, didn't once look his way. The stabbing pain in his chest felt all too real.

"Come in, sweetheart." Mom shifted a little higher in her elevated bed.

"Um, all us MC people put together a little care package." Leah placed a gift bag on the movable table next to Mom's bedside. "Just in case you're bored or need some sweets." Her smile was tense, pained.

"Aren't you all so sweet." Mom smiled broadly.

"You shouldn't have, but thank you for thinking of me, and thank everyone else, too."

"I will. And I thought I'd offer to get some lunch, if you guys were tired of hospital food."

"Kyle loaded us up with all sorts of things before he headed to work," Grace said, walking over and linking arms with Leah. "But thank you."

"Anytime."

"Your parents got off all right?" Jacob's voice was hoarse from not saying much of anything today. Yes, that was what he'd blame it on. He hadn't showered since he'd insisted on staying with Mom last night. Where else would he have gone? Obviously not Leah's, and an empty MC had zero appeal.

He'd barely slept, and he felt like shit run over, but it was still better than those options would have been.

You could have gone to Leah's and apologized.

"They got off just fine. Left bright and early. Should be back to Minnesota in time for dinner. Um, Marc stayed, though. He has an interview at Bluff City P.D. on Friday." She unhooked her arm from Grace's and looked around the room once more. "Well, I should head to work and catch up. If I can help out at all, you guys know how to get ahold of me."

For the first time in too long he managed to get his limbs to work properly when it came to her. He reached out for her wrist. "Leah." The way she withdrew her hand made his gut tighten. "Um, you have a few minutes?"

She looked around the room and then nodded. Stiffly, he followed her into the hall. Which wasn't much in the way of privacy, what with the open door and nurses' station not far off.

"Hi," he offered lamely.

"Hi," she returned with a pained smile. She looked…uncomfortable. As if she'd rather be anywhere else.

He'd done that, and he didn't have the words to fix it. Every time he tried to get apologies out of his mouth, everything seized up. Excessive emotion behind it, the words the only dam to keep them inside.

"Um, Kyle and Susan have gotten almost everything for the New Year's party canceled, but I should get over there and help tie up any loose ends."

"Leah, just, um, give me a few days to…deal."

He didn't know why that would make tears fill her eyes. "Yeah," she said, barely audible.

"I know I was a jerk, but…" If he said the rest, he'd lose whatever grip on sanity he had. She just had to know…. He tried to take her hand, but she stepped away. "What's going on?"

"Nothing. I just have to go. We'll talk later. When you're… Later."

"Talk about what, exactly?" Because he had the sinking suspicion this wasn't just about him being an ass. This was deeper. Bigger.

"Don't do this now." She shook her head, the last word coming out desperate and broken. "Please."

"What am I doing?"

"Talking about this isn't a good idea right now."

Yeah, definitely not just about him treating her poorly. "What exactly is this?"

"Jacob—"

"I love you." At least he could get that out. Sure, it was tight and nearly indecipherable, but he'd said it.

"I..." Her eyes darted to the room and back to him. "I have to go."

His stomach did a slow roll. Things were definitely...not right. "Tell me. Straight-out. Don't tiptoe around it because of what's going on. I want to know."

She shook her head and for a moment he thought she wouldn't say anything, but then she squared her shoulders and looked him in the eye. "Last night...I saw a glimpse into our future, and I can't live with it." Her voice broke, but the tears in her eyes didn't fall. "I'm sorry. I can't do this with you."

"That's...it?"

"Look, we can talk more later. When things are more calm and it isn't so..." She made useless hand gestures.

"But it's over. What's there to talk about?"

"I just meant if you needed more explanation."

"You're breaking up with me." For the first time he felt...nothing. Blissfully blank and numb. "I'm pretty sure I knew this would happen, so no explanation necessary."

She looked down, a tear trickling down her cheek. Christ, why were they always crying so damn much?

She cleared her throat. "I tried, but..."

"It's my fault. Yes, I get it. I have been here before." Again and again. Not what anyone needed, no matter how hard he tried.

"Don't..." She looked back into the room, but he didn't. He stood perfectly still looking at a poster about how to cover your mouth correctly while coughing.

Something inside him had snapped. All he felt was a kind of numbness that made it rather easy to stand here and understand. This was his fault. Because when push came to shove, when things came right down to it, he couldn't control himself; he couldn't be perfect; he couldn't make the right choices.

When shit hit the fan, so did he. So there wasn't any point in arguing, in being mad or hurt. This was just...it. A thing he'd chosen, more or less. He'd known what she needed from him, and he'd thought he'd given it to her.

But then it hadn't been about her, and he'd lost.

"It's not your fault. I just...can't. But I'm still your friend. If you need—"

He stepped away from her and her outstretched hand. "No. Not that. Not now."

"I still care. I still lo—"

"Go away, Leah. That's the last damn thing I want

to hear." He turned away, walking back into the hospital room.

His family was silent and still, but he didn't dare look at them or out in the hall to see if Leah had left. He just walked stiffly to his spot at the window from earlier and went back to watching the snow fall.

Honestly, he didn't know what the hell else to do.

CHAPTER TWENTY-FIVE

LEAH SHOULDN'T BE HERE. It wasn't as though she'd never poked around Jacob's office before. There had been times he'd been out of town or had the day off and she'd needed paperwork he kept in his meticulously organized desk.

But everything was different now. There'd been talk of fantasies and terrible moments in hospital hallways and...everything associated with Jacob seemed wrong.

And it hurts. It damn well hurts.

Yes, that, too. She couldn't seem to stop hurting. But Susan had asked her to get the Abesso's Lighting file, and since it was something Leah needed to actually do her job today, here she was.

Her hands weren't steady as she flipped through the top drawer of Jacob's files. When the door creaked she all but jumped a foot.

"What are you doing in here?" a gruff voice demanded.

Jacob stood in the doorway to his office looking like...hell. Absolute hell. He was pale and his dark hair a mess, the short beard on his face looking grizzly and unmanaged. So not Jacob.

His eyes were red-rimmed, his lips chapped, and the urge to cross the room and hug him was so great she kept the drawer open to have a physical barrier between them.

"I needed a file," she said in a squeaky, guilty-sounding voice. "What are you...? We thought you'd..."

"They kicked me out." He took one step into the office, hands jammed into his pockets. "Not in a bad way, I mean. Mom settled in at home yesterday, and this afternoon they were all taking naps, and they wanted me to...breathe."

"So you came to work?"

"That's what I do best."

Leah nodded because she didn't know what to say. She didn't know...what he wanted from her or if she was even in a place to give it to him. She was tied up in so many knots, she didn't know where to pull to loosen any of them.

"I'll...get out of your hair."

His eyebrows drew together, and because he was still standing right next to the door, and she'd all but barricaded herself behind the open filing-cabinet drawer, there was no way to accomplish that.

"Can you tell me...how to fix this?"

She didn't trust herself to speak, so she only shook her head.

"I know I should apologize for how I treated you that night. And I want to. I do, but every time I try..." His voice was tight with pain, his expression drawn together in anguish. "I haven't apologized because I can't without falling apart."

"It's okay to fall apart."

"No, it isn't, because when I do, people don't want to be with me."

"Jacob, I..." She didn't know what to say to that. It broke her heart more than it already felt like it was broken, but she couldn't deny that him falling apart was exactly what had sent her packing. "It's not you."

The sound he expelled from his throat was probably supposed to be a laugh, but it didn't sound like one. "'It's not you. It's me.' You're seriously using that line on me?"

"It's true."

"It's bullshit. You not wanting to be with me is a direct result of me losing my crap that night. Seeing your future in it. So, it's me, Leah. It's all me."

"You're not wrong. You weren't wrong to get upset. Maybe taking it out on people was kind of crappy, but you had a right. You'd been lied to, multiple times, about something that was important. I don't deny you your anger, Jacob. I'm angry for you."

She clutched the file to her chest, trying to find some center of calm and honesty that would somehow make this okay.

How could this ever be okay?

She swallowed the words and the lump that went with them. "However, someday I'll probably be in similar shoes as your mother. Maybe even directly because of something I did. Maybe you'll blame me and call me stupid. Maybe you'll just lose it in the hospital room. Maybe you'll get that blank look on your face that's supposed to fool me into thinking you aren't torn up inside."

With each *maybe* she felt a little stronger. A little more right. "I don't like any of those things. I've already been there, when I know the people in the waiting room are at each other's throats. I've already had to listen to people tell me I'm not strong enough to deal with my own issues.

"So, it's me, Jacob. Because of who I am and what I've been through, I need to know the person…who chooses to get roped into anything with me is going to treat my family, the people we love, the staff and doctors and nurses who are there to take care of me… I need to know those people will be treated with kindness and gentleness. And I'll be given the benefit of the doubt, not just…pretended at."

"Is that supposed to change my mind about whose fault this is? Because that still sounds like I'm the problem."

"What I'm trying to say is that I do love you, but—"

"Maybe you could not be in my office."

God, that hurt, but he had every right. Who broke up with a guy and kept telling him she loved him? That was a serious jerk move, even if it was the truth. So she nodded once, pushing the drawer closed and skirting around him, putting as much space between them as possible.

"Wait. Here." He jammed a hand into his coat pocket and found a bag of animal crackers. "Not that," he grumbled, tossing it on his desk. He rummaged in his pocket again and pulled something out in a clenched fist. When he uncurled his fist, the little gold trumpet glimmered on his palm.

She stepped away from him, horrified that he'd even think to give that back to her. Horrified that she was so close to tears yet again. "No. No, I don't want that."

"Well, I don't want it, either."

When his gaze went to the trash can, a sound escaped her lips. Not quite a sob, but something idiotically close.

"Here." He shoved the little figurine at her, but she couldn't make herself take it.

"I'm very sorry I hurt you." There were more words she wanted to say, but they weren't nearly as nice. So she just walked out of the office, leaving him standing there with an outstretched arm.

Anger slammed into her chest so hard, she stopped. She tried to talk herself out of the furious words building, the inappropriate comebacks just dying to come out, but in the end her frustration and hurt won.

She whirled around and stomped back to his door. "If you throw that away, I will..." She looked at the filing cabinet. "I will take out every other file and throw them out the window, contents first. So… don't."

And then, because she was *ridiculous,* she turned on a heel and left. She stormed into Susan's office. "Here's the stupid file."

"Whoa. Wait. Where are you going?"

"To my damn work shed to cry."

"Give me ten. I'll bring the soy ice cream."

Leah gave Susan a curt nod. She'd really prefer to be alone, but, well, she might as well cry all over her friends. It wasn't as if things were going to get better anytime soon.

JACOB SAT AT his desk, staring unseeing at the glossy surface. After a while he opened his clenched fist. The trumpet had dug little grooves into his palm.

He glanced at the trash can, thought of Leah angrily telling him not to throw it away. Thought of that moment on the porch when he'd thought everything was aligning.

He dropped it into the bin, where it fell with a satisfying clank. The satisfaction was brief, quickly followed by sadness and pain and, damn it, guilt.

He was just about to go fish it out when Kyle stepped into his office.

"Oh, Jacob…I didn't know you were here."

"Who knew my office was Grand Central station when I was gone," he muttered.

"I was actually looking for Leah. Or Susan. They seem to have disappeared. Are you…working?"

"I was told to leave home, so here I am."

"I believe you were told to get some sleep."

"I'm not in the mood for family crap from you." Jacob curled his hands into fists. He was tired of people being careful around him. Trying to find some way to switch him off. Didn't they think if he knew how, he'd do it?

"Of course."

"I really hate it when you use the butler tone."

"I'll leave you to it, then." Kyle gave a tight smile and turned to leave.

But the whole exchange reminded him of how Kyle used to be—closed off. How things had changed for him once Grace had come into the picture. "How did you change?" Jacob demanded.

Kyle turned, eyebrows up. "Come again?"

"How did you change yourself? You used to be so closed off and cold and Grace came along and you changed and I want to know how. How do you change yourself?" There had to be some…answer he was missing. Some piece to the puzzle so he could fix it.

Kyle had changed. For Grace. Maybe there was some way he could change for Leah. Love was supposed to conquer all, right?

Well, except for death.

Yeah, well, no one was currently dying.

"I…I'm not sure I have an answer for that."

"Find one." He needed an answer, some hope, something.

"If this is about Leah, I'm not sure my experience—"

"Christ, screw off, then." Jacob pushed away from his desk, not sure what he was going to do. In the end, he just stood there glaring at the little flash of gold in his trash can.

"Change wasn't…isn't easy." Kyle cleared his throat. "It wasn't even really a change. It was…being who I was without the shell on top of it. Which was rather…scary. Hard, definitely. Still a bit difficult at times."

Kyle blew out a breath, stepping a little bit farther into the room. "With everything that happened, I suppose I learned a few things I hadn't believed before. I thought I could ignore the parts of myself I didn't particularly like, but it ended up being impossible. You can't really be with someone only partially. You can't hide the bad parts. And either they accept those bad parts or they don't."

That wasn't the answer Jacob wanted. Because… he wasn't hiding any bad parts. Leah had seen it, and that was why she was walking away. So, that wasn't an answer. It was a condemnation.

"The thing is, you and Leah are different from Grace and me. Different people…different obstacles. I thought… There was a time I thought the things that stood between Grace and me were insurmountable, if you'll recall. But, obviously, that was not the case, and you had a hand in making me realize that."

Kyle did possibly the most un-Kyle-like thing he'd ever done and patted Jacob on the shoulder. "Everyone has obstacles. It's about being truthful about them and determining if they are something that can be dealt with…or not."

"And if not?"

"I don't know, Jacob. I suppose you let it go or walk away. Plenty of people do."

"I don't want to do that."

"Well, then…your only option is dealing with the obstacles."

That was his strong suit in business. Troubleshooting problems. Working through intricate building codes, historical details, clientele. He did it all so easily there because it *was* easy. Something he could write out on paper and weigh the aesthetics against legalities and practicalities.

Life had no codes, no rights or wrongs. And when problems arose he…ignored, walked away, exploded, but he didn't deal. He didn't think rationally about obstacles, because there was never a right answer or an end result to measure his success. There was only Mom not dying or Grace surviving her ex-boyfriend's attack all those years ago.

"For what it's worth, being as honest as possible, even when it makes you look weak or like a fool… I could be wrong, but it seems to be the only thing that works."

Jacob swallowed. Weak. Fool. Yes, he was very afraid of being all of those things. Of not being what someone wanted. Of not helping because someone might think less of him.

And then losing all of that in the face of his family when times got tough.

Something wasn't right about that, and he had a bad feeling that Kyle was dead on the money. The pretending, the mask, the ignoring tactics he'd used most of his life—they weren't working here because he couldn't keep any of them in place, and then he lashed out lest his sensitive underbelly show too much.

Christ, he was a mess.

He'd told Leah he couldn't apologize because what came out after would just be falling apart, and he still believed that. But if that falling apart happened more truthfully and less out of fear, maybe she could see past this obstacle.

Jacob blinked, trying to get ahold of the emotions working through him. But it didn't work, and maybe that was the point. He bent over and reached into the trash can.

"Um…are you all right?" Kyle asked, clearly concerned he was rummaging around in the trash.

Jacob grabbed the trumpet and shoved it in his pocket. His first instinct was to say he was fine, but he wasn't. So he shook his head. "Nope. Not even a little bit."

"Jacob…"

"I'm heading out. If Grace needs anything, have her call me."

It was…insane. The words *wrong* and *failure* bounced around in his head, but they felt powerless. In his heart, he knew it was the fear that was a lie.

And it was time to face it.

CHAPTER TWENTY-SIX

LEAH TRUDGED INTO her house, dropping her work bag and then wrinkling her nose at the smell emanating from somewhere inside.

"Marc?"

"Hey."

Her brother stood in her cramped kitchen, stirring a pot of something that smelled like home. "You've cooked every night."

He shrugged, which was about the extent of their conversations. A few sentences, a few shrugs. It had become easy, really, even if they weren't on the best terms. Someone was here, had dinner waiting when she got home, exchanged fake pleasantries. Somehow in the span of a week she'd gotten used to her house being packed to the gills, gotten used to sharing a bed, a room, a shower.

The sharp pang she couldn't seem to eradicate poked deeper. Jacob had pissed her off this afternoon and she still missed him. How long was it going to take for that crap to recede?

Leah settled herself at the table. She couldn't exactly be cheerful, but she wasn't going to pout and wallow. "Man, after you and Mom being here, my usual turkey sandwich is going to seem pretty lame."

"I'm sure Mom will send you meals like one of those diet programs."

"How was your interview?" Anything to change the subject off Mom, which was a subject she wasn't comfortable with him about. Because while she felt that Mom's visit had put them on the path to healing, she still knew that between her and Marc, parents were a tricky thing.

"Well, I…"

Leah looked up as he handed her a bowl and spoon. "They offered you a job, didn't they?"

Marc nodded, his normal stoic reserve completely unreadable as he took the seat opposite her. "I'll have to take some qualifications, finish up my notice in Minnesota, and then it'd only be on a probationary term the first three months through field training, but I could be starting and moving as early as March."

"That's great."

"You actually sound sincere."

"I actually am. I think. For now." Leah chuckled. "I reserve the right to change my opinion, but I think I'm getting used to the idea."

"Well, anyway, maybe it'll be a good place to start fresh for all of us."

"I hope so. I think so, actually. I could use some… fresh starts."

"You're really done with the guy?"

It was the first time Marc brought it up, which had been one of the positives to him staying behind. Company without having to talk about Jacob, since all Kelly and Susan wanted to do was talk, talk, talk the whole relationship to death. Try to find a way they could help work it out. The ones who hadn't believed it *would* work out were trying to work it out for her.

That was friendship, she supposed, and as much as she hated the talking, she loved their concern and their attempts to help.

Leah shrugged, hoping to come off nonchalant. "It just wasn't going to work. I was hoping we could be friends, but…" She took a bite of soup she didn't really taste. "Well, anyway."

"You cannot be friends with an ex."

"Of course you can."

"No way. Why on earth, if you couldn't be romantically involved, would you go back to friendship?"

"Because you were friends to begin with. Because the reason it ended is just… No one did anything wrong. There's just this thing in the way."

"Why?"

"What do you mean 'why'? It just is. It's in the way. The way he'd be when I was sick. I can't just ignore that."

"Why not? You'll be sick. You'll hardly know."

"I knew Mom and Dad were fighting constantly, thank you very much." She stirred her soup too aggressively and some dripped over the side. She poked at the lines of red liquid on the edge of her bowl.

"They—" Marc cleared his throat. "I know, the other day, I made it seem as though everything boiled down to your sickness. I was irritated with my own…stuff. Mom and Dad always fight. After they got back together. After you left, even knowing you were fine. They fight. It's who they are."

Leah frowned, trying to make sense of that. "Well, okay, but me being sick certainly didn't help."

"No."

"So I'm not sure what point you're trying to make."

Marc shrugged. "I guess I don't really have one."

They ate their soup in silence, Leah occasionally staring at Marc and trying to figure him out. What he was trying to say. What…

Ugh, she was so tired of thinking so hard.

"Look, I know it's way beyond my place as the brother you barely tolerate, but, I don't know, the guy seemed to make you happy or whatever. The crappy future seems a lame excuse to end that."

"You're getting a little too comfortable here, buddy." Which earned her a very rare Marc smile. Which was nice. Really nice. After this afternoon's altercation with Jacob, she had a feeling her inclusion in some of the less business-related activities at MC might not be that fun anymore. So having some family around that could occasionally take a joke and smile might be nice.

She got up to put her bowl in the sink and on the way gave him an awkward one-armed hug. "Thanks."

"Anytime."

Before she could rinse out her bowl, a knock sounded on the door. "Ugh, I hope it's not one of those guys trying to sell me a freaking deck."

"You really shouldn't answer it. Sometimes those guys are scammers. There have been cases where they push the door—"

"Lalalalala," Leah said, putting her hands over her ears. "I'm not listening to your scare tactics."

"It's not a scare tactic. It's something that happens," Marc replied, following her to the door.

"Whatever. I do own a gun."

"Do you have the appropriate licenses? Where do you keep it? Is—"

"Sweet Jesus, if this is what having you around is going to be like, I'm taking back what I said about being happy you're moving here." She wrenched open the door, ready to give the salesman a piece of her mind.

But her heart stopped instead. "Jacob."

"Hi. I know I'm probably not who you want to see."

"I…" She swallowed, because of course she wanted to see him. She just wanted all the circumstances to be different.

"I'm going to go…read," Marc said, though Leah barely heard him.

"I guess you two have made amends."

"Something like that." She fidgeted with the door. "Um, why are you here?"

"I don't want to press my luck, but it's kind of freezing. Could I...?" He gestured inside.

Leah swallowed and stepped out of the way. When she closed the door behind him, she just leaned against it. Whatever he was here for, looking all penitent...she was in for...something hard.

"How's your mom?"

"You asked me that this afternoon. Not much has changed."

"Right."

"I'm not here to talk about my mother."

Oh, crap.

"Work?" she asked hopefully.

The edges of his mouth quirked just a hint up. "No, Leah, I'd like to talk about us. You said we could."

"I did?"

He took a step toward her and she wished she had somewhere to go. Somewhere to run. But she was pressed up against her door as far as she could go, and he was close, looking at her with those intense brown eyes.

"When you told me you had heart surgery, I could barely breathe. To think I'd worked side by side with you and had no clue that you'd gone through something so huge."

"What…what are you talking about?" Where had this come from? What was he doing?

"The truth. I'm telling you the truth."

"But—"

"When you showed me your scar, it took everything in me not to look, to ask questions, to know everything."

She didn't want to know this. It…changed things. Or did it? Maybe it didn't change anything at all.

"Then you told me about the transplant, and…" He took another step toward her, and as much as she wanted to look away, tell him to stop, she couldn't. She was stuck, and he was close, and what she really wanted to do was wrap her arms around him.

Not allowed, lady.

"I knew you didn't want me to make a big deal out of it, so I tried not to and sometimes I did okay and sometimes I failed. But it was a big deal. It *is* a big deal. Because it…it's scary. It scared the hell out of me. And I'm not supposed to be scared. I'm not supposed to be angry. I'm supposed to be supportive and calm, and I tried. I really tried."

He took a deep shaky breath. "I lost it after the Martins and then much worse at the hospital because I was scared. Scared that…well, scared of what I didn't know about your conditions. Then with Mom, scared I'd lose her now, that I wouldn't have had a chance to…I don't know, be the perfect son. And you're right to make a parallel, because I would feel the same about you. I would be scared and afraid

I hadn't been perfect for you and I would probably screw everything up."

Leah tried to form words to stop him. Tried to do anything that could...change all this or erase it. She didn't want his truth. It made her all...vulnerable.

"I suck at dealing with bad stuff. I'll try to get better, and I actually think maybe if I'm not so damn afraid of being afraid, it could work. If I could be honest with not just everyone else, but with myself. I could get better, but I won't be perfect. I might yell at the wrong person or be rude to a nurse."

"It's not just about that."

"Then what's it about?"

"I don't..." She couldn't think with him standing so close, with him saying this stuff.

"I was a jackass, but my family still loves me. My father and I had made up by the next morning. Grace has been fussing over me like a mother hen. We love each other and we care, and in that caring comes forgiveness for our mistakes. Like Mom and Dad hiding things and me losing my temper."

"But...they're your family. They...have to forgive you."

His expression lost some of that grim determination. "Don't you want to forgive me?"

"It's not about forgiveness. There's nothing to forgive. This is just the way we are."

"I want to tell you I'll be better. I'll be perfect and give you everything you want. I want to be able to do that, but I'm not perfect. I'm not…even when I try so hard to be. I wish I could be."

"Why are you saying this?"

"The thing is, you told me I didn't have to be perfect. You told me I could fall apart. So here I am, failing, falling apart. Because…I love you, and maybe I could love someone else, too, but it wouldn't be like this. It wouldn't be me. But more than that, it wouldn't be you. You see me. You get me. You even call me on my B.S. So I don't want my shortcomings to be the end. I can't let it be the end."

"Can't let it?"

"I'm prepared to beg. Say please. I don't think being apart does anything except ignore the problem. Did leaving home really solve your problems, or did it only put them off until you were more capable of handling the situation?"

She couldn't think straight enough to figure out if he was really making sense or if she was just desperate for him to be. Desperate for him. But he just kept *going,* his words hacking away all the things she was so sure about.

"I could lie. I could probably even sweep you off your feet. I could hide it all under the fake guy you see through anyway. I'm scared. Your health struggles will always scare me, but it's because I love you. We could walk away right now, and I'll probably still be the asshole yelling in the waiting room."

"Is that supposed to make me feel better?"

"No, it's supposed to be the truth. This is our

obstacle. But it's…weird because it might not happen. Maybe it pops up tomorrow, maybe in a few years. Maybe I get sick and die first. We don't know where this obstacle lands and jams tight, but I think we have time. I think we have time to learn how to crawl over it."

"Maybe *I* don't know how."

"Then we should figure it out together."

Her heart hammered in her chest because…that sounded so good she could cry, but could she really just…believe? Believe they'd figure it out? Hope her future health problems wouldn't be too terrible? Hope if she went a little too far at work he wouldn't explode?

That seemed awfully…optimistic, but was that really the end of the world?

JACOB DIDN'T KNOW what else to say as Leah looked at him with wide, watery eyes. He'd laid it all out. Every last ugly piece of himself, and he felt as if he had some kind of gaping wound and his guts were flopping around on the floor.

But she didn't say anything and he didn't know how else to make her see. He just had to stand here and wait and hope the words mattered enough. Were honest enough to win.

"I… What…" She looked up at the ceiling. "Jacob. I'd hate to see us just keep hurting each other over and over."

"Why?" She made a little outraged sound and he pushed forward. "Life does plenty of hurting. I am an expert at running away from it, but all it seems to do is catch up with me. So maybe it's time to take the good even if bad comes along with it."

She pressed a hand to her chest, right where her scar was. The heart that wasn't hers, that might give out too soon. Might. But for now... He put his hand over hers.

Her shoulders slumped. "You shouldn't be scared all the time. I shouldn't put that on you."

"You're not. I am." He turned her palm so it touched his, linking fingers. "We could walk away, see other people, but you're still my electrician. You're still my friend. And, no matter what happened, you'll always be someone I love. So, here's the deal—I'd be scared. Together or not. It's inevitable, unchangeable. You sealed that deal when you agreed to take a job with me."

"So it's my fault?"

"Absolutely. I blame it all on you." He took the last step so they were toe to toe, his mouth not too far from hers. He'd only have to nod, but it wasn't time for that yet.

Her throat moved as she swallowed, her eyes not leaving his. "I do...love you."

"I know."

"B-but sometimes love isn't enough or the only thing."

"I know that, too. It won't be perfect. But Kyle said something that made me think..."

"Kyle?"

Jacob managed his first smile of the evening. "Believe it or not. He is quite wise in the ways of love."

Leah wrinkled her nose, which made him laugh for the first time in a few days. It felt rusty and good—damn good. "The point is, I asked him how he changed for Grace. Because I thought that's what I had to do for you."

"I don't want you to—"

"Hush," he interrupted, gratified when she scowled at him. "But he said it wasn't so much change as being honest. Honest about the obstacles and deciding if you wanted to beat them. I want to. Anything that comes up, I want to find a way to get around it with you."

She was quiet. The entire house was quiet. He could hear a clock ticking from the living room and someone rev their engine outside. He could hear his breathing and hers, but she didn't speak or move.

"I need to know one thing first," she finally said on little more than a whisper.

"Anything."

"What did you do with the trumpet?"

He grinned, dropping her hand and pulling the little figurine out of his pocket. "Right here, baby."

"Damn it." She blinked a few times, eyes intent on the trumpet before she lifted her gaze to him. "I...don't know. I don't know what the right thing to do is."

"Maybe there isn't really a right thing. No blueprint. No right answer. Maybe it's just a risk you have to take. *We* have to take because we're more interested in being together than being right."

"Jacob McKnight telling me there's no blueprint. Is this an alternate dimension?"

"Leah."

"I…" She closed her eyes briefly, then focused in on him. "Okay, this is about telling the truth? The truth is you scare me because sometimes I do get to thinking you're perfect, even though I know you're not. And…I'm not perfect. I don't try to be. I don't want to be. And I don't want to be defined by my health, but I can't ignore that it's a part of me or factors into my decisions."

Hesitantly, her hands rested on his chest. "But I love you. And that is kind of, well, like you said, not something that's going away any more than my health problems."

"Are you calling me a health problem?"

She didn't laugh, but she almost smiled. "I'm saying…you're right, Jacob. Possibly two of my most hated words in the English language. You're right— my feelings won't go away. You're right—you don't have to be perfect and you're right that being with you is more important to me than being right."

"Even when I act like an asshole?"

"Don't think I won't kick your ass to the curb if you're too much of one." Her hands traveled up his chest, to his shoulders, then his neck. "But you're not. You're a good man. And I love you. And I was wrong to walk away. I was wrong to back down."

"Not totally."

"No, it was wrong, because I told you you didn't have to be perfect, and I meant it." Her hands moved to his face. "Now I think we're done talking."

"We a—"

She cut him off with a kiss. One he gladly sank into, sliding his hands into her hair, pressing her against the front door.

All the tension inside him released, and even as foolish as it was, he really did feel as if he could face anything as long as he had her. To yell at him when he was being an ass, to give him a hard time, but most of all to love him even when he wasn't perfect.

"You know, I did have a few more things to say," he murmured when she broke the kiss.

"Jeez, you're talkative tonight."

"I know I said no blueprints, but…" She groaned as he pulled an actual blueprint out of his back pocket.

"You want to talk about work now?"

He smiled. "No. Not exactly, anyway. This is the blueprint to the Jasmine Street house."

"I'm really failing to see how this is not work related." But she was looking over the paper as he unfolded it, eyes eager and assessing.

"I was thinking…this could be our project."

She looked from the blueprint to him. "Ours?"

The nerves that had washed away with her acceptance of his apology resurfaced, but he powered on. "Like, we could plan it together. And…live in it together when it was done. I'm selling the big house. This'll be the office. And, well, if you plan it with me, it would be ours. A blueprint we make together."

She just stared at him for the longest time, not saying anything. He wanted to prompt her into saying something, anything, but he forced himself to wait.

"So, like, I could say, I want that wall torn down and a door put in the back. You'd just...do it?"

"Um, no. You will suggest that, and we will discuss it and determine if it's feasible and reasonable. Together."

Her mouth quirked into a smile. "Together, huh?"

"Compromises and all that."

She nodded and wrapped her arms around his neck. "A blueprint we make together."

"Exactly."

He could see her swallow, eyes all shiny, but no tears. He hoped they could be done with tears for a while.

"I think that sounds...perfect."

He grinned. "Probably not perfect. But good. Really good."

And she pressed her lips to his and it was good, and maybe even a little perfect.

EPILOGUE

"THIS BETTER BE GOOD," Leah yelled into the Jasmine house. Jacob had texted her to meet him here and now she couldn't find him despite his truck out front. She'd been in this itchy floral-print dress all day for Grace's bridal shower and she was so over it.

The bridal shower had been nice. Fun, even. Good to see Mrs. McKnight really looking stronger every day now that she'd finished her chemo treatment. Great to see Grace all giddy and happy.

But that didn't make this ridiculously girlie dress she'd been forced to wear any more comfortable.

"Jacob?" Oh, where the hell was he? Demanding she come over without changing and now he was nowhere to be seen. The house was dark except for the kitchen in the back. She stood there and pulled out her phone, but before she could bring up the window to text him she noticed lights outside.

She stepped into the backyard. The trees were just beginning to tinge with the colors of fall. The setting sun cast an orangish glow to the yard, which had been a mess of overgrown grass and bushes the last time she'd seen it.

There were a lot of new additions to the backyard as well, but the one that stopped her short was her work shed being right there in the corner of the yard, a string of twinkling lights around the roof.

She stepped toward it, hugging her arms around herself. The early fall evening was cooling off rapidly.

When she stepped inside, Jacob was sitting at her workbench. Everything was irritatingly organized and clean looking, but she supposed she'd give him a pass since he had moved her work shed across town.

"Hi," he greeted her with a smile, as if this was a normal everyday thing.

"What in the hell are you doing?"

He grinned. "You know, somehow I knew you wouldn't greet me with 'Hello, darling, I've missed you all day.'"

"You're in my workshop. Which is not…where it's supposed to be."

He pushed to his feet. He was wearing his nice jeans, the dark green button-down shirt that made his eyes look so pretty. When she'd told him that, he'd vowed to never wear it again out of protest at being called "pretty."

What was going on here?

"We got an offer on the big house," he said, crossing the small space to her. "For the asking price."

"Whoa." The asking price was nothing to sneeze at.

"I know. A little soon, but…" He shrugged. "We've got enough done here to make it work."

"You mean move in. Together."

"Don't pretend you're freaked out. I can't remember the last time I didn't spend the night at your house, and this has been the plan since—"

"Not that, you idiot." She shoved him out of the way and pointed accusingly at the empty wall in the back.

"What?"

"Where's Joe?" She wagged her finger at the conspicuous empty spot. "He was right there yesterday."

"Come on, now."

"Put Joe back and nobody gets hurt."

"I was hoping you'd want to put something else up there. Like, I don't know, pictures of people you actually know. Maybe pictures from Grace's wedding…our wedding…"

"From—" She blinked at him, but he just stood there as if he'd stopped talking after "Grace's wedding." "Um."

And then he grinned, picking a velvet box up off her workbench. She hadn't noticed that when she'd walked in.

"Um."

"You can't be surprised."

"Of course I am!" She backed away from him. Velvet box. Wedding. Um. She wasn't surprised he was asking. She was just surprised he was asking at *this* moment. In her work shed. In the yard at the Jasmine house.

Their house.

She thought there'd be buildup. Warning. Bu she'd been so wrapped up in work and bridesmai duties...

"I need to sit down." She found a spot on her bench But then he knelt on one knee in front of her. "Oh shit, don't do *that*."

He chuckled, but he didn't get up. Instead, he too her hand. "Leah."

"No. No. Don't be all romantic. I'll cry."

"You'll survive, baby."

"Jacob—"

"Will you please be quiet so I can do this prop erly? And please note I said 'please.'"

Leah bit her lip. Okay. She could do this. Be pro posed to. She just had to sit there and possibly sto swearing at him.

"Leah, pain in my ass, love of my life—"

"Hey!"

"I love you. Being with you makes me happy, ever when you *are* a pain in the ass. Because I admir your strength, I am in awe of you on a daily basis It won't always be easy, it won't always be perfect but for the rest of our lives I want to climb over an obstacles with you. As husband and wife."

She didn't cry. Probably because she was deter mined not to. But if she talked, she might. And wha was more, she didn't have his way with words, and it was pointless to try to match that. So she kissec him instead. As earnestly as he'd spoken, with a much love as she could muster.

She pulled back, running her palms over his beard. 'Jacob, I know we've talked about it, but the no-kids thing…"

He raised an eyebrow, because they *had* talked about it. A lot, actually, because for her that had been a big sticking point before he'd even started thinking about an engagement. She wanted to make sure they were on the same page. That no kids was really something he could live with.

And he'd convinced her. That his life could be just as rich and fulfilled without a child of his own. He'd probably be an uncle. He could get involved with kids' organizations. He had promised that she—that they—were enough. And she believed him.

"Okay, I won't bring it up again. But if you ever feel—"

"Are you going to answer my question before you bring up everything else we've already decided on?"

"It's important."

"It is, but I also weighed it against other important things. You're important. We're important. I'm good, and I'm asking to build a life with you knowing full well what that entails."

Her heart ached, but in that good way he made her feel. As though she was so damn lucky to have found him and this.

"All right, let's see it."

Jacob tsked. "You really need to work on your romance tolerance." But he flipped open the lid to a slim band. It didn't have just one diamond, but a

ring of them encrusted against the silver. Something
simple and wearable for work.

She had no doubt he'd done that on purpose. And
that he would take that kind of care was something
that would never fail to make her swoony.

"I love you," she said, framing his face in her
hands.

"And I love you. Always." He lifted her hand to
his lips, pressed a kiss to her palm before sliding the
ring onto her finger. Then he glanced back at the
empty wall. "Now, about that Joe Mauer poster…"

"Joe stays." She leaned her head onto his shoulder. "And so will you." Of that, she had no doubt.

* * * * *

LARGER-PRINT BOOKS!

GET 2 FREE LARGER-PRINT NOVELS PLUS

2 FREE GIFTS!

♦HARLEQUIN®

Romance

From the Heart, For the Heart

YES! Please send me 2 FREE LARGER-PRINT Harlequin® Romance novels and my 2 FREE gifts (gifts are worth about $10). After receiving them, if I don't wish to receive any more books, I can return the shipping statement marked "cancel." If I don't cancel, I will receive 4 brand-new novels every month and be billed just $4.84 per book in the U.S. or $5.24 per book in Canada. That's a savings of at least 19% off the cover price! It's quite a bargain! Shipping and handling is just 50¢ per book in the U.S. and 75¢ per book in Canada.* I understand that accepting the 2 free books and gifts places me under no obligation to buy anything. I can always return a shipment and cancel at any time. Even if I never buy another book, the two free books and gifts are mine to keep forever.

119/319 HDN F43Y

Name	(PLEASE PRINT)

Address	Apt. #

City	State/Prov.	Zip/Postal Code

Signature (if under 18, a parent or guardian must sign)

Mail to the **Harlequin® Reader Service:**
IN U.S.A.: P.O. Box 1867, Buffalo, NY 14240-1867
IN CANADA: P.O. Box 609, Fort Erie, Ontario L2A 5X3

Want to try two free books from another line?
Call 1-800-873-8635 or visit www.ReaderService.com.

* Terms and prices subject to change without notice. Prices do not include applicable taxes. Sales tax applicable in N.Y. Canadian residents will be charged applicable taxes. Offer not valid in Quebec. This offer is limited to one order per household. Not valid for current subscribers to Harlequin Romance Larger-Print books. All orders subject to credit approval. Credit or debit balances in a customer's account(s) may be offset by any other outstanding balance owed by or to the customer. Please allow 4 to 6 weeks for delivery. Offer available while quantities last.

Your Privacy—The Harlequin® Reader Service is committed to protecting your privacy. Our Privacy Policy is available online at www.ReaderService.com or upon request from the Harlequin Reader Service.

We make a portion of our mailing list available to reputable third parties that offer products we believe may interest you. If you prefer that we not exchange your name with third parties, or if you wish to clarify or modify your communication preferences, please visit us at www.ReaderService.com/consumerchoice or write to us at Harlequin Reader Service Preference Service, P.O. Box 9062, Buffalo, NY 14269. Include your complete name and address.

HRLP13R